EVERYTHING IS TEMPORARY

By Jon Cohn

Paperback ISBN: 979-8-9880619-3-9

Ebook ISBN: 979-8-9880619-4-6

Cover Artists: Covers by Christian www.coversbychristian.com

Delaney Cohn

Editor: Lyndsey Smith, Horrorsmith Editing www.horrorsmithediting.com

For Luna.
You were the best friend anyone could ask for. Even though your time on
this earth was temporary, you will always be a part of our family.

1

MAYA

"Can I have another Christmas cookie?" Maya asked when Mom and Dad tucked her into bed.

They gave each other a look, one that carried the weight of a whole conversation. It was the same nonverbal talk they'd had each time she asked for something since being diagnosed with Leukemia nearly a year ago. Mom's eyebrows curled like a puppy's, and Dad squeezed his puffy lips together, only breaking from their eye contact to look at eleven-year-old Maya as if she were a porcelain doll—capable of breaking at any moment.

"No" had been the answer whenever she tried to push her luck, asking for things that would have been normal a year ago. She held hope they might give in this time, especially considering Maya's appetite had been practically nonexistent for the last few months.

But somehow, they always figured out their answer without a single word passing between them. Mom shook her head, looking a little disappointed as she scrunched Maya's sheets under the sides of her mattress, making her bed tight and snuggly, like a burrito.

"You've had a lot of excitement already today and enough sugar to keep you awake for a week."

"But it's not even eight!" Maya complained, pointing to the Mickey Mouse clock next to her bed.

"It's time to rest. We'll have more cookies tomorrow, okay?"

Mom loved to finish giving orders with a question, as if Maya had any say in it. Though, to be fair, it *had* been a big day, and she was feeling exhausted.

Maya nodded, a yawn pushing itself through her aching lungs. "Fine. Then we'll have cookies for breakfast," she said with a confident grin.

Mom snorted out a laugh, which lately was quickly followed by her eyes going glassy. "Lunch," she replied. "You can have cookies with lunch. You want Luna on?" Mom turned away from Maya, walking to the little black and white doggie night-light across the room.

Maya nodded. "Yes, please."

Mom spent longer than necessary switching the light on, and when she turned around, Maya searched for wetness around Mom's eyes. Nothing but the faintest trace of moisture cupped along her dark bottom lids.

"Love you, sweetheart. Sleep well." Mom stroked Maya's short black hair—it had slowly started coming back in since Maya finished chemotherapy—and kissed her forehead.

"See you in the morning," Dad said, kissing her as well.

They shut the door behind them, and exhaustion quickly overcame Maya. She thought about the celebration they'd had today, how grateful she was to have had her best friend, Emma, with her during their outing.

It didn't take long for her to drift into sleep.

Shriiiik. Thud.

Maya opened her eyes, feeling incredibly groggy. She glanced over at her clock, her eyes blurry with sleep. Luna's light had gone out, and without it, the darkness made it impossible to tell where Mickey's hands were pointing.

A chill ran through her, almost making her teeth chatter. Maya tried to rub her eyes, but her bed was tucked in so tightly, she couldn't even bring her hands up to her face. Through her sleep-encrusted vision, she was able to squint at the wall across the room.

The window was open.

Mom and Dad must have forgotten to close it at bedtime, even though she could have sworn they had. Maya's whole body shuddered, a combination of cold and fear running its way from the top of her head down to the tips of her toes. Even with the extra blankets, the night air pouring in made it way too cold for Maya to be able to get back to sleep. She would simply have to muster the strength to get up and shut it.

Yet she couldn't move.

Maya had experienced days where it took all the energy she had just to get up and walk to the bathroom, but that had been mostly during treatment. Lately, she had started to feel a little better. Her parents began allowing Emma over to the house more, and today, Maya even got to go somewhere other than the doctor's office; they went out to celebrate Christmas.

No matter how hard she tried, she couldn't force her body into action this time.

Her arms shook, and the chilling breeze of the night tickled her mostly bald scalp. Ninety percent of body heat escaped through the head—that's what the doctor said when he gave her a cozy pink beanie she'd worn almost all the time until recently, when her hair finally started growing back in.

She had to get to that window.

It was only when she shoved herself up onto her elbows that another shudder passed through her, but this time, it was not brought on by the cold.

There was a presence in the room.

Darkness hiding in darkness.

Her eyes were still bleary, and without Luna's illumination, every corner of the room seemed like it could have contained an entire circus without her noticing. But somehow, she knew something was there, and it was watching her.

Maya almost called out to the shadows, but she couldn't get her lips moving. Cancer had already robbed her of the last year of her life, but she had never felt more helpless than in this moment. From the corner of her eye, she thought she saw something move across the floor. She turned her head but only found a scattering of some dolls that she and Emma had played with earlier in the evening.

They all remained perfectly still, as they were supposed to.

It took every ounce of her minuscule strength reserves to keep herself sitting up. As she stared at her dolls, waiting to see if any of them would move, she felt—but didn't see—something much larger. It crossed the room from the opposite side of the dolls, quickly but silently.

Maya's eyes watered, her arms giving out and dropping her flat onto her back. The springs of her bed groaned beneath her, and a heavy weight pressed on her chest. She'd had plenty of breathing issues in the last year. Catching her breath sometimes felt like a nearly impossible task. But this was different.

Like something was sitting on her.

Something heavy.

Maya tried to open her mouth to scream, but her throat tightened. Panic shot through her, but even with the adrenaline and fear, she still couldn't bring her arms out of the bedsheets Mom had tucked so tightly around her frail body. Incoherent thoughts ran through Maya's mind, and all she wanted was to call out for Mom and Dad, but they were in their bedroom down the hall—a million miles away.

She was just a mouse quietly choking on her own throat while the grim reaper bore its weight onto her.

Her heart raced, and fireworks exploded in the corners of her eyes.

The rest of her vision went dark.

Only, the fireworks weren't white...

They twinkled red and green.

2

SARAH

Mondays had become a hectic affair in the Barnes household. I had just started my own marketing firm after nearly fifteen years of working my way up from intern to management. It was late April, and even though sixth grade was nearing an end for my daughter, Emma, every new week felt like the beginning of a new year for me.

I was in the midst of multitasking—preparing breakfast for my family and reviewing the mental checklist of what jobs lay ahead of me for today—when my husband, Tom, shuffled into the kitchen and grabbed me around the waist from behind.

"Good morning, Sarah." He kissed my neck, reigniting the passion we'd indulged in yesterday while our daughter spent the day with her friend. Between raising an eleven-year-old and me starting a company, we didn't have a lot of opportunities for intimacy, so we took every chance we got. Tom was an artist who worked from home, so he could afford to still revel in a slow morning, but I had to shift gears to prepare for the work week.

I decided that a few minutes of playful fun couldn't hurt. Emma wouldn't get up until she was basically dragged downstairs, and I still had some time before I needed to be out the door. I wriggled my hips backward into his body and felt his hand slide from my waist up my torso.

He brought his mouth close to my ear, and I felt his warm breath against me as he whispered, "Is that fresh coffee?"

Just before reaching my chest, his hand diverted, reaching out toward the counter and poaching a steaming cup of dark roast I had just poured for myself.

"You son of a bitch." I smirked and spun around to face him. "Is that all you want to press me for? A fresh cup of coffee?"

"What else would I press you for?" he said with a wink and a goofy grin. He took a sip, then quickly pulled his head back, fluttering his hand over the lip in an ineffective method of cooling the drink. "Oh! Too hot!"

"That's what you get for toying with my emotions." I kissed him on the cheek and grabbed a spatula to mix around the scrambled eggs I was cooking on the stove.

Tom was building up a retort for our playful banter when the cordless phone on the far side of the counter rang. The caller ID read: "Johnson." I picked up the phone and pressed the button to accept the call.

"Tamika, how's—"

"Sarah, I don't know how to say this." There was a long pause on the line. Just from the tone of her voice, my heart began to pound. "Maya passed last night, in her sleep." Her words were shaky—she had been crying.

I felt like I knew what I was supposed to say, but in the moment, it didn't feel good enough. "Oh my God, Tamika, I'm so—"

"Our daughter is dead. My little girl is gone!" Tamika shrieked in heaving sobs.

It felt like a dagger had been run through my heart. Maya and Emma had been practically sisters, and the Johnsons had been close family friends for years. I wanted to reach through the phone and hug Tamika as she wailed into the receiver. It felt wrong for me to be a disembodied voice on the other end of a line instead of standing there, holding her through her grief.

I slid to the floor, mirroring what I imagined Tamika was doing at her house a mile away. Tom didn't need to hear her end to know what was happening. He joined me on the tile floor, holding me in the way I thought Tamika should've been, pain etched on his face. My blood froze as I watched him glance at the ceiling, clearly moving on to the looming situation about to erupt in our house.

We would have to tell our daughter that her best friend was dead.

For five minutes, I listened to Tamika, offering my support wherever able and choking back tears of my own. I needed to hold strong, not only for her, but for Emma. Tom only climbed to his feet when the foul smell of burning eggs started to smoke throughout our small kitchen. He turned off the stove and dumped the charred mess into the sink, letting the pan hiss violently when it met with the water inside.

Our conversation ended when Tamika managed to pull herself together long enough to tell me she had other calls to make. I promised I would come over as soon as I could to help her with the arrangements.

My legs were shaking. It felt like I was losing a piece of my own family as well. Emma and Maya had been inseparable since they were three years old. The two had met at a block party one summer, when they were both getting their faces painted as tigers. They called themselves the Tiger Sisters, a name that stuck with them long past the point where it became embarrassing for them and endearing for us.

I almost broke down, realizing I'd never hear our own daughter bemoaning me telling the story of the Tiger Sisters again.

No. It wasn't the time. I could break down all I wanted later, but Tom and I both needed to be strong for what was sure to be one of the hardest things we'd ever had to do.

"Come here," Tom said, his arms ready to receive me.

A minute ago, things had been playful, perfect. Now, he was a rock of emotional support.

I shoved a few breaths out of me and held him as tightly as I could, gritting my teeth against a dam of tears.

"We have to figure out how to tell her." I squeezed my eyes shut.

I was the planner of the family, the organizer. Compartmentalization and setting goals were how I managed to push through the hard times. Tom was the perfect counterpart to my logic-focused mind. He understood emotion and embraced the world with compassion and maturity. Tom was warmer and always knew the right thing to say in difficult moments.

"I think we need to do it softly but honestly and keep focused on our support for her. Remember what Doctor Backer said—we need to let her feel her feelings and be ready for any sort of reaction."

I nodded, recalling the counseling sessions we had done with a child psychologist, preparing both ourselves and our daughter for the possibility this day might come. "He also said that we should share any stories or memories that might help her. That includes our own." I hesitated to bring it up but felt like I needed to prompt him. "Do you think you could talk about your mom, if it helps?"

Tom's face blanched. He was a pro when it came to being an emotional sponge for me and Emma, but when it came to talking about his past, he was a steel vault. His eyes cast down, staring a thousand miles beneath the earth. Finally, he nodded. "If it comes to that, yeah. But let's try to keep things focused on her."

We climbed the stairs hand in hand and stood for nearly a minute outside her door before either of us could work up the courage to knock and gently let ourselves in.

"Five more minutes," Emma moaned, her head buried in her pillow. She then sat up, and without opening her eyes, her face scrunched up like she'd just sucked on a lemon. "What *is* that? Smells like burnt eggs." She rubbed her eyes, and in the span of two seconds, she went from a sleepy pre-teen to a terrified child. "What's wrong? Why are you both in here?"

I wanted to turn and run from the room, but Tom gripped my hand, as if he could read my thoughts and was sending me a lifeline of emotional strength. We both sat on the corner of her bed, and Tom began to speak.

"Listen, honey, we have some bad news we have to tell you. Last night, Maya passed away."

Emma made a sound that was almost a giggle. "What? No, that's not right. I just saw her yesterday."

"I know you did, and she was so lucky to get to get to spend her last day with you. The doctors say she went peacefully in her sleep. She didn't feel any pain." None of what Tom just said had been mentioned by Tamika, but Tom was doing his best to break the news as gently as possible.

"No, you're wrong." Emma's eyebrows turned dark and angry. "Why would you say that?"

"It's true," I said. "I just got off the phone with Mrs. Johnson. I'm so sorry." I tried to say the words to comfort her, but I felt like they sounded hollow coming from me.

"No!" she shouted. "She was getting better! Yesterday was the first day that we were able to spend the whole day together in forever. We even got to go out with her parents!" Tears rolled down her face.

Tom gave my hand one more squeeze, again reading my mind and handling two emotional crises at once.

"No one can ever take that memory from you. Just because she's not here anymore doesn't mean she isn't an important part of your life. The memories you keep of her will always be with you."

"But she's my best friend. What am I supposed to do without Maya?"

"We will always be here for you, no matter what." I tried again to bring comfort to my little girl, whose world was crumbling before my eyes.

Emma suddenly shot up straight, her breath shuddering in her lungs, her eyes wide. "Oh God, it's my fault."

"Don't say that—" I said, but Tom gave my hand a quick pulse, this time cutting me off from potentially making things worse.

"I know it feels that way," he jumped in before Emma could process my fumble. Tom took a deep breath, released himself from me, and slid further toward our little girl. "I never told you this, but when I was a little younger than you, my mother died suddenly."

"She did?" Emma's breath pumped so quickly, I worried she was about to hyperventilate.

Tom nodded. "I thought the exact same thing. I had this feeling, deep inside, like I was to blame."

"What happened?" Emma mewed.

"I'd spent the whole day begging her to play with me, to do this, do that, and then suddenly, she was gone. Deep down, I knew it wasn't really my fault, but I had this hurt inside of me that I didn't know what to do with. It was just too much to bear."

"Did it ever get better?" Emma hiccuped through sobs.

"It took a long time, and it never fully goes away, but yeah, each day got a little easier. What's important is that I had to *feel* my feelings, whatever they were. Some days, I felt like it was my fault; other days, I felt mad at the world for taking her away from me. Mostly, I just felt sad, like there was this huge emptiness in my life where part of me used to be. However you're feeling, it's okay; it's normal. Just know that no one is going to blame you for experiencing your emotions, whatever they are. We both love you more than anything, and nothing is ever going to change that."

Emma threw herself into her father's arms, and he held her tight, repeating in a soft coo that everything was going to be okay.

"Do I have to go to school today?" Emma finally said.

"No," Tom replied with a breathy laugh.

3

SIX MONTHS LATER

A muscle-clad model almost half my age walked up to me, wearing nothing but a pair of blue briefs covered in lightning bolts.

"What do you think?" he asked.

"It's about time," I said, just loud enough for my assistant, Jen, to hear.

Toward the back of my modest-sized office sat my client, Jarrett, a late-twenties CEO of an underwear start-up. Despite showing up over two hours late, he seemed more interested in flirting with Becky—my only other employee—than actually working on the commercial he'd hired me to shoot. The spot we were working on today was for a pair of high-end, "fun" themed underpants. Though I had urged CEO Jarrett to let my team come up with the full marketing plan, he had insisted we build a script around their logline: *Thunderwear—It's fun to wear!*

I signaled over to the film crew that it was finally time to get this show on the road. They were a group of community college students using equipment I had rented from a local film supplier.

Once I finally had everyone in position and ready to start shooting, I felt a buzz in my blazer pocket. I pulled out my phone. Tom was calling.

I stepped away from what was becoming a very expensive hangout session and moved over to my personal office, shutting the door behind me.

"Okay, Sarah, don't freak out," Tom began.

"What happened?" I asked with all the urgency he was trying to preface against.

"Everything's all right. We just need to go down to the Mission Valley Mall and straighten out a couple things. Emma called. She's fine, but I guess she got in trouble for something, and we have to talk to security or a manager."

"What did she do? Are they calling the police?"

"They didn't say anything about cops. She sounded pretty upset. I mostly wanted to keep her calm until we could get there."

Emma's behavioral issues had been slowly escalating since Maya's death, but this was the first time she had actually gotten into trouble outside of our family unit. It came as no surprise that she'd called Tom over me; he had an almost infinite level of patience when dealing with her frequent outbursts. I knew he only meant to help by trying to keep me from getting upset, but his seeming lack of urgency only served to stress me out even further.

I looked over to the clock on my office wall. It was just about eleven, and if I left now, it would be an uphill battle for my team to make sure the amateur film crew did their job to Jarett's satisfaction.

It could wait. Family was more important.

"Are you at the house? I'll pick you up on the way."

After ending the call, I pulled Jen aside and told her I had a pressing matter but would be back as soon as I could.

"Absolutely, Sarah, I can handle it," she said, doing her best to reassure me. A minute later, Jen was setting up the first shot, and I was in my car on the way home to pick up Tom.

When we first moved in together, we each had a car. But after seeing how close we were to restaurants, grocery stores, and the galleries of the bustling bohemian North Park District of San Diego, Tom had decided to sell his vehicle and ride his bicycle everywhere.

To his credit, it made parking a hell of a lot easier, and he never had to deal with road rage.

I pulled into our driveway, hoping to see Tom waiting for me at the curb but knowing him well enough not to expect it. After honking the horn, I then waited while worrying about our daughter. My tall, lanky husband bustled out the door of a detached garage he used as his art studio. His hands were wet, and he was wiping them off on a gray hoodie with red stripes running diagonally across it.

"Sorry, I had to finish painting an eye. I couldn't leave it crooked," he panted, taking his seat in the car.

I forced myself to loosen up a little. It wasn't Tom's fault he had a tendency to get hyper-fixated on painting. In some ways, his whole-hearted passion for his work was one of his best qualities. It's what initially attracted me to him in the first place.

"How did Emma sound? Was she scared?" I asked, beginning the ten-minute drive to the mall.

"I would say more irritated than anything. That's how I knew she was okay—she still sounded like she wanted nothing to do with us." He gave me a forced laugh, and from my periphery, I could feel him searching for a hint of a smile. In the end, he found one, even if I had to force it a little too. "Whatever it is, we shouldn't go too hard on her. She's still adjusting to things."

While it was *technically* possible Tom was referring to Emma's first two months of being a seventh grader at a brand new middle school, it was clear he was instead talking about Maya.

In the wake of Maya's passing last April, Emma only showed up to her old school a handful of times. Her teachers were very under-standing and aware of their bond. They made huge allowances for Emma, giving her mostly As and Bs, despite her barely showing up for the remainder of the year. In the summer months, she had glued herself to Tom and me.

Emma had spent the majority of her days watching her father paint in his studio. Tom tried to help in his own way, guiding her to pour her energies into a form of art therapy he'd adapted from an old technique he used to practice in college. Each day, they would pick an emotion and would paint whatever subject matter they felt matched that emotion until they were both satisfied. At that point, they would move their pieces to a designated space on our living room wall, in view of both the dinner table and family room couch, so we could appreciate their art all evening.

The first thing they would do the next morning was take those canvases down and begin by painting a layer of black over the previous day's work. Tom explained that everything they had painted before still existed, whether we could see it or not. He then recited his mantra I'd been hearing ever since the day I met him, back when we were in college: "Everything is temporary."

It was a therapeutic exercise, and Emma seemed to respond really well to the symbolism of it. Unfortunately, it did nothing to prepare her for dealing with grief in any real or practical way. That was left to me, to try and get her to follow the other instructions Doctor Backer had suggested. He had made it clear that getting Emma back into a normal routine would be paramount, explaining consistency would help her find stability while working her way through this extremely challenging time.

Much like Tom, I'd dealt with loss at an early age, though it wasn't quite the same as what he or Emma had been through. I was born in Beirut, and my family moved to America when I was four to escape the growing dangers of the Lebanese Civil War. My aunt and uncle died shortly after, along with a few of my parents' friends, but I was too young to truly understand it at the time and didn't know them well enough to have the kind of bond Emma and Maya had forged. I have no memory of trying to form a routine. All my memories from that time were just clips and phrases, most of which I remembered without any sort of context.

When summer ended—and Emma started her first day at a new school—it was as if a switch had been flipped. The more we tried to spend time with her, the more we seemed to drive her away. Tom and I went from being her entire world to distant enemies in a span of barely a week.

In the two months since seventh grade had started, she'd chopped up her beautiful long hair, started wearing heavy black eyeliner, and had become obsessed with a TV show and book series called *The Sandman*. I'd read the books when I was her age, but even my attempts to connect with her over those stories just seemed to disgust her even more.

The only person she ever talked about was a friend she had made at school named Janice, who she flat-out refused to bring by the house. In one of the few full conversations she allowed us to have, Emma explained that Janice had a sister who died, and now Janice was the only person who truly understood her. The two had become bound at the hip, with Emma spending almost every afternoon and weekend at Janice's house.

"Did you hear if Janice was with Emma?" I asked Tom. They were supposed to be at the mall together today, and I wondered if this might finally be my chance to meet the new best friend.

Tom shook his head. "She didn't mention it. She just said she's being held by security."

I tried to push my worries down, speeding up onto the freeway. Tom could sense me starting to spiral with anxiety. I was a worrier by nature, and this incident couldn't have come at a worse time for me professionally. He gently grabbed my shoulder, and I felt an IV of calm drip from him to me.

"All that matters is that we know she's fine. Whatever this is, we can figure it out and focus on trying to find a way to help her."

Tom managed to help me release some tension while also gently reminding me we should be taking Emma's behavioral outbursts as a continued way of her expressing grief. His philosophy was, we should always approach her misbehavior with compassion and love instead of punishment or anger.

"Things will get better. Remember, everything is temporary."

4

SARAH

We parked underground near the movie theater, then made our way toward the nearest escalator. The smell of freshly baked cookies above made my stomach grumble, reminding me lunchtime was just around the corner.

"Where's security in this place?" I pulled my phone from my pocket, needing something to focus on.

Tom stopped me, rubbing small circles around my back. I looked him in the eyes, which were softened by his dark expressive brows.

"Hey, it's okay. I'm sure someone at the theater can tell us—" Tom stopped mid-sentence as his eyes moved past me.

"What is it?" I asked, but he remained silent, turning his head slightly, continuing to stare at something. I pivoted to look at what had distracted him. "Tom, what's the matter?"

His eyes flicked back to me in a sudden panic—totally uncharacteristic for him. His soothing hand turned into a claw against my back. His head was craned behind us, tracing something, or someone, that must have ridden past us on the escalator heading down.

I searched wildly to see what was putting him on edge. A group of teenage girls, all talking amongst themselves with shopping bags on their arms...A couple in their twenties, lambasting some movie they'd just seen...An overweight balding man in a red sweatshirt, checking his watch...I tried to think back a few seconds when I first scanned the escalator but couldn't pinpoint anything odd or familiar about any of the people riding down.

"Did you just recognize someone?" I asked quietly.

Tom's eyes narrowed, honing in on the man in red. "Maybe. I don't know. I just got a weird vibe."

Tom was a bit of a space cadet. It came with the territory of being a professional artist, but usually he was at least a bit more articulate than this.

"What kind of vibe?" I asked.

He shook his head. "I don't know. Something just seemed creepy about him."

I felt Tom relax a little when we made it off the escalator, but now I was almost as concerned for him as I was about Emma. He was usually the one to say "excuse me" to people who bumped into him on the street, and yet simply riding an escalator past someone had put him on high alert.

We walked to the movie theater and got directions to security. I led the way from there, with Tom continually turning around to check behind us as if we were being followed. He still seemed unfocused by the time we reached the security room.

I grabbed his hoodie by the collar and pulled it forward so it didn't sag down his back. "Hey, where are you right now? Talk to me."

Tom nodded while looking me in the eyes, making an active effort to focus on the task at hand. "I'm here. Sorry."

"Do you need a minute?" I asked, knowing he would be the one primarily responsible for taking care of Emma, while I sorted out whatever trouble she was in with mall security.

"I'm fine," Tom insisted. "Let's go get our daughter."

I opened the door to a stark, cold office that smelled of stale coffee. In it were white-painted stone walls, a line of green lockers, a desk with a bunch of security monitors in front of it, a guard, and our daughter. She was sitting in an uncomfortable-looking plastic chair with her arms crossed. Even though she tried her best to keep appearing sullen, she couldn't hide the expression of relief when she saw us enter.

Tom rushed to her side, putting an arm around her. "Emma, are you okay?"

"I'm fine," she said, half-heartedly pulling away from her father's touch.

"What happened?" I asked either Emma or the guard, whichever would answer me first.

"Are you Sarah and Tom Barnes?" a mustached man who looked to be in his early fifties asked. "I'm Officer Riley, mall security. The reason I've called you down here today is that your daughter was caught destroying mall property. It doesn't seem to me like it was done out of malicious intent, which is why we will not be contacting the police at this time. However, based on mall security guidelines, there is a mandatory fine that must be paid. And in the case of a minor, we had to detain her until a parent or legal guardian could collect her."

"So, she's not in trouble?" Tom asked.

The guard teeter-tottered his head side to side. "Not legally. I talked to her about respecting mall property and, like I said, had to detain her. But after that, it's up to you how you punish her."

Emma let out a loud huff from the other side of the room.

"What did she destroy?" I asked the guard.

"One of the kiddie rides next to Target. You know, the ones for children that you drop a coin in and it goes up and down? I have the footage queued up."

He pointed to a video on one of his dozen security monitors. It displayed a set of three stationary rides in front of the big-box store. Emma was standing on one shaped like Santa's sleigh, with one foot on the bench and another on the gold-painted front rim of the sled. She was hunched forward, holding onto a pair of oversized plastic reins leading to Rudolph the Red Nosed Reindeer in front.

One moment, the ride was bouncing up and down, tilting back and forth, and the next, the reins seemed to disconnect from the sleigh entirely. As a result, Emma lost her balance, sliding forward and accidentally kicking Rudolph's antler off the side of his head. Luckily, she managed to recover her balance before she could injure herself.

Emma was obviously too old for this kind of behavior. It was immature and unsafe, and I'd had to leave work in the middle of a busy day to watch this. On the other hand, it was the most animated I'd seen her in the last six months. In the moments leading up to the slip, she had looked like she was actually having fun, and for that, I didn't have it in me to be mad. In fact, I had to tamp down a slight giggle when turning around to face her.

Just like Tom had predicted, it was no big deal, at least not in the grand scheme of things. In a flash, I imagined us getting a copy of the tape and showing it to her on her twenty-first birthday for a laugh.

"Where's Janice?" I asked, remembering her elusive new friend.

"I didn't see any other girl in the video," Officer Riley said.

"She was at Target, getting a snack. She probably thinks I ditched her," Emma replied.

"I'm sorry on my daughter's behalf." I dug around my purse and pulled out a business card, handing it to the guard. "Please send an invoice as soon as you know what it will cost to repair, and we'll pay for it."

Officer Riley nodded. "Thanks, ma'am. You know, some folks aren't as ready to take responsibility for—"

"That's him!" Tom shouted from nowhere, running up to the screen in sudden excitement.

"What are you talking about?" I asked, confused and a little embarrassed by his outburst.

"That's the guy from the escalator!" Tom pointed to a grainy still frame of a man in the background of Emma's video.

I couldn't make out the face, but the red sweatshirt seemed like it could belong to the same person.

"Play the video again."

The guard pressed the spacebar on a keyboard, and the video started over. Rudolph's antler reattached itself as Emma rode high on Santa's sleigh, but the bald man was nowhere to be seen. It wasn't until she fell that he came into view in the bottom right corner of the monitor.

"Was he watching her?" Tom turned to face his daughter. "Do you know him?"

Emma looked insulted. "What? Ew. No."

"Can you give me a different angle?" Tom asked the guard.

"Sorry. The cameras are only in high-traffic spots, like outside the entrance to Target."

Tom tapped the spacebar and replayed the video. To him, it seemed to confirm whatever suspicions he was harboring. In what I would admit was a bizarre reversal of roles, I couldn't see what he was so anxious about. Whatever relief I'd felt from seeing our daughter safe quickly evaporated as I redoubled my concern for Tom. Something about this man was clearly bothering him, and it worried me that I couldn't understand why.

"What happened next?" he asked. "Can you show us more?"

"Tom, what are you doing?" My voice was quiet and stern. I grabbed him by the arm to get him to face me and was shocked when he pulled away, focusing his attention back on the screen.

The guard clicked a few buttons, then resumed the video. Emma tumbled out of the sleigh, and the man in red glanced over to her as he walked toward Target.

"Look at that. He looked right at her." Tom pressed a paint-crusted finger against the screen. "Who is he? What are you doing with this man?"

The whole situation felt upside down. *I* was supposed to be the anxious one, Tom the voice of reason. I grabbed him again, this time digging my nails into his arm to make sure he paid attention to me.

"Tom, you need to calm down, right now."

He chewed his lip, clearly frustrated, his eyes darting between me and the screen.

"Look at me. What's going on?"

Tom winced several times, like he was about to say something, before finally blowing out a hard puff of breath. "I don't know. That guy, he just feels...wrong."

Whatever he was seeing, I was missing. But his behavior was starting to truly worry me.

Just to be sure, I checked with Officer Riley to see if he recognized the man. He said he wasn't aware of any complaints or issues regarding anyone matching his description, but he would do a little more digging and get back to us if there were any red flags.

With that, we were told to expect an invoice for the broken reindeer in the next few weeks and were free to take Emma home. All in all, things could have been worse. Emma wasn't in any legal trouble, and it was clear from the video that she wasn't trying to harm herself or anyone else.

The three of us walked back to the car in silence. I had no expectations of hearing a word from Emma's mouth until Tom or I initiated, and even then, I didn't anticipate much. Instead, I kept an eye on Tom. He had seemed to cool off after we left the office, but I'd been with him long enough to know everything was not all right.

I used the moments of quiet as an opportunity to begin building the conversation we would have tonight. Despite Tom's bizarre outburst, we would need to find a way to get on the same page and have a talk with Emma. Tom would start out by explaining we weren't upset, emphasizing how much she was loved. Then I would explain how her actions could have been dangerous and she needed to be more careful and respectful of public property.

After that, I would need to have a much more serious talk with my husband.

5

SARAH

By the time we pulled up to our home, I had rehearsed a few key phrases in my head enough times that, no matter where the conversation went with Emma, I wouldn't lose focus on the important details. Preparation and mental repetition of target points were the cornerstones of how I approached work and parenting, which seemed to overlap more and more as Emma got older.

Tom was the "good cop," and normally, I trusted him to follow my lead. Whenever there were punishments or stern talking-to's to be had, his role was to remind her we cared. If things got heated, he would help bring the temperature down—something I admittedly had trouble doing sometimes.

Meanwhile, I had no idea how to broach the conversation with Tom about his erratic behavior today. Emma had acted out enough times due to her grief that we sort of had a playbook in place. It maintained structure for her and also helped us deal with our own grief from losing Maya. However, whatever Tom was going through was totally alien to me, and I had no idea how to even begin *that* talk.

As if to prove the point I was ruminating about, Tom skipped our unspoken planning session and opened his mouth as soon as we walked through the door. "Sit down, young lady," he commanded in an unusually stern tone, pointing to the couch.

Emma huffed her way across our carpeted living room and sank into the brown faux-leather couch with her arms crossed. Outside, the sun had been obscured by an overcast haze that had taken over the day. It cast a gloom over our house, making things seem even more dour.

Tom paced anxiously back and forth. I tried to pull him upstairs so we could have a few minutes to calm down and get on the same page regarding the Emma situation.

Instead, Tom blurted out of nowhere, "Why did you choose to ride the Santa sleigh?"

Emma and I both looked at him, baffled by his question. I was just beginning to wrap my head around his new obsession with the guy at the mall, and he'd immediately thrown me a curveball.

"I don't know." Emma shrugged, her voice brimming with petulance. "I didn't want anything from Target, so I was just messing around until Janice came back."

Tom shook his head. "No. There was a helicopter and a race car right next to them. Why would you choose to ride Santa's sleigh over those?"

"Tom, can I have a word upstairs?" I interrupted, now worried he might be in the midst of a crisis greater than I was comprehending.

There was a tense silence in the room, and he finally stopped pacing. It felt like all of us were holding our breaths, waiting to see what he would do next.

Finally, he exhaled and nodded. "You stay there," he pointed to Emma.

Our daughter outwardly shrugged, but her eyes flicked over to me for a second. I could almost hear her pleading with me to talk some sense into him, and I hoped I could find a way to do just that.

I followed Tom upstairs, though instead of heading to our bedroom, he took a detour into Emma's room. "Tom, do you mind telling me what the hell this has been about today? You're scaring her." What I really meant was, *you're scaring me.*

"There's something she's not telling us," he said, shutting the door. "I can feel it."

"As opposed to when there *is* something she's telling us?"

He shook his head, his skinny frame nearly vibrating with nervous energy. Tom began pacing again, but this time with manic purpose. He opened her drawers, dug through her clothes, then went through her closet, searching for something.

"What are you doing now?" My breath climbed up into my throat. He was becoming more unstable by the minute, and I had no idea how to help him. I wanted to grab him, to shake some sense into him, but he was tearing the room apart like a hurricane, and I was nervous about getting too close.

Tom doubled down on his search, clearly looking for something specific, though what it was, I had no idea. "I just have this bad feeling, and it keeps getting worse. Have you ever just felt like something terrible is going to happen? And you just know all the pieces are there, but by the time you put them all together, it'll be too late?"

I didn't. The things he was saying reminded me of interviews with schizophrenics and severe OCD patients I'd seen in documentaries.

"I'm trying to understand you, but you're not making a lot of sense here. Is this really all about Emma?" I asked, trying to follow whatever shaky logic he was presenting. "Why did you make such a big deal about the Santa sleigh? Could this be more about your mom than what happened today?"

"No. Maybe." Tom had mentioned to Emma about his mother's sudden passing, but what he had omitted was, she had died on Christmas Day when he was ten years old. For as long as I'd known him, he had actively avoided all things related to the holiday. He never even talked to me about it, beyond the most basic facts. Tom had spent most of his youth living with his father, who also had grown to resent anything related to Christmas. "I just have this feeling. This undeniable, sinking feeling that keeps growing. I can't stop it, and I feel like the answer is here."

At that, he resumed his search, dropping to his hands and knees to look under the bed. He pulled out a backpack and gasped when he looked inside. "Aha!" he shouted in some combination of disgust and triumph.

"What is it?" By the time I finished asking, he had already crossed the room and thrown the door open. "Will you wait a minute?" I begged.

Tom stormed down the stairs, stopping right in front of our daughter and dropping her bag on the ground. He held out a red and green pointed hat with a round brass bell at the end.

"Do you mind telling me what you're doing with this?" Tom demanded, as if he were holding out a bong. He shook the hat in front of our daughter's face for emphasis, causing the bell to jingle around.

"What?" Emma said with a sneer.

"Tom, what is that?" I asked.

"It's an elf hat!" he shouted, as if it were the explanation to everything.

"So what?" Emma asked.

"Where did you get it?"

"From school."

Tom shook his head. "It's October." He was breathing heavily. Suddenly, his eyes went wide, as if he had made another connection. "Did Janice give this to you?"

"Why would Janice have anything to do with a stupid hat?" Emma tried to sound sullen but was clearly starting to look afraid. "She's just a friend from school."

"Tom, you're losing it. You need to calm down." I tried once more to placate him, but the situation had spun out of control a long time ago, and I had absolutely no idea how to handle his constant and wild shifts in topic.

Deep in my bones, I knew he would never do anything to hurt either of us. But short of that, I had no idea what he might do. He had bounced from an odd man in a sweater to a kiddie ride, to a hat, and now had shifted his focus onto Emma's friend, all in the span of an hour.

"Show me a picture of Janice." He held out his hand expectantly. "I want to see what she looks like."

"What? No." Emma tucked her elbow against her hoodie pocket where she kept her phone.

I considered jumping in between them as my husband and daughter stared each other down. Before I could get there, Tom nodded, taking a step back.

"All right, then. How about we call Janice's house? See what she has to say about this?"

"No!" Emma screamed with sudden urgency. "You can't call her!"

It was too late. Tom was already stalking into the kitchen. He pulled out drawers until he found the school directory. Something twisted inside of me—a switch had flipped. There was something in the way Emma reacted to Tom announcing he was calling Janice that showed more than just embarrassment of an irate father calling a friend's mom. I felt that fear strike through me again, like there was some critical piece of information I was missing.

But this time, it came from Emma.

"You said her last name was Beck, right?" Tom asked, flipping through the booklet.

I hurried to Emma on the couch while Tom used the phone in the kitchen. "Emma, do you know what your father's talking about?"

"No! I just don't want Dad to ruin the only friend I've made at school. Everyone else calls me a freak. She's the only one who understands me. Please, I'm begging you, don't let him do this!"

I could already hear him talking on the line. The one saving grace was that at least he had the faculties to not sound belligerent while on the phone. The conversation was alarmingly brief, and as I heard his footsteps cross the tile floor of the kitchen and reenter the carpeted area, I watched Emma's face shift from the fidgeting terror of embarrassment to the stillness of horror from being caught.

I turned to face my husband, and I could swear his face was as red as the stripes on his hoodie.

"Emma. Are you ready to tell us what's really been going on?"

Emma's face also turned bright red. She offered no explanation, so Tom resumed.

"I just spoke to Mrs. Beck. Janice wasn't at the mall today. In fact, she says you've never even been over to their house and that Janice has never even mentioned your name before. What do you have to say for yourself?"

Emma's face shifted on a dime from panic to a resentful smirk. "I just thought I'd be able to get you off my back if it sounded like I had a friend."

I was taken aback by this admission. Every day, every weekend since school started, Emma had claimed to be with Janice. Now I was angry too and couldn't hide it from my voice.

"Then where have you been all this time?"

"I don't know. Anywhere but here."

"That's not a good enough answer. You're twelve years old, and we have the right to know where you are going after school."

"I mostly just hang out at the library until it closes. On the weekend, I ride my bike to Balboa Park."

"And the mall?"

"Yeah, I ride there sometimes too."

I didn't know how to react to this new information. It's a short bike ride from our house to Balboa Park, but to ride all the way to the mall on a bicycle would take close to an hour. Without getting on the freeway, she would need to leave the safety of our artistic village and ride through an industrial park in a rougher part of town.

"I don't understand," I said, hearing my own voice crack as I sank to my knees to level my face with hers. "You'd rather spend all this time alone than be with your family? This summer, we were all so close…"

"Yeah, and then you kicked me out to make me go to this shithole of a school full of assholes that hate me. Everything sucks, and I hate it. Everyone abandons me."

"We didn't abandon you," I said, trying to sound sympathetic. "You had to go to school some time. Why didn't you come to us about this? If you were having trouble, we could have helped…"

"How, Mom? How is sitting me down and telling me that every-thing I'm feeling is normal going to actually help me? What does it matter that my grieving is 'normal' when everyone at school won't stop calling me 'dead girl'?"

"I don't know, habibeh," I replied, using the Arabic pet name for her my mom used to call me when I was a girl. "We can talk to the school counselor or go back to the therapist. If the kids won't stop bullying you, we can look into another school, maybe give you another fresh start."

Emma let out an anxious sigh, showing that, while she hated the idea, there was at least a little comfort to be had in knowing she had options. It was my hope I was making it clear to her we were here to do anything to help.

"Okay, now be honest about the other thing," Tom said, tensing up the room again. "What about the hat?"

Whatever ground I had gained was immediately lost. Emma wailed in frustration at her father. "For the last time, it's just part of a costume from school! I don't know why you're making such a big deal about this!"

"That excuse isn't going to fly, young lady. It's not even December. Why would they be giving you a Christmas hat in October?"

"Because it's not from *this* school! I got it last year, at Scotch Elementary, you fucking asshole!" Emma threw herself to her feet and started to storm upstairs.

"Don't you use that language with me! Tell me why you used the name 'Janice'!" Tom started to follow her upstairs, but this time, I grabbed him hard by the wrist, holding his scarecrow of a frame back.

"I hate you!" Emma screamed before slamming the door to her bedroom.

"What the fuck is wrong with you?" I let my anger reignite toward Tom. "Have you totally lost your mind?"

"She said her friend's name was Janice!" he reiterated, as if that meant something.

"Who cares what name she used?"

For a second, he just stared at me, stuck somewhere between anger and fear. Inside my hand, I felt his bony wrist start to shiver. I watched as his shoulders tightened up and the color drained from his face.

"I don't know. I can't explain it. I felt fine all day, even after I got the call about her being in trouble. It wasn't until I saw that guy... There was something about him. It brought me to this place, this horrible place that just kept building until I felt like I couldn't breathe. And that name...Janice. I can't...I can't..."

Tom finally broke down in sobs, his anger melting. In a matter of hours, I'd watched him turn from a zen master, to a paranoid lunatic, and finally, a scared little boy.

"I can't do this," he gasped, throwing his arms around me.

For as many transformations as he'd undergone, I'd been put through the ringer for every insane step of the way. Whatever he was dealing with, we would figure it out, for better or worse.

6

SARAH

We left Emma alone for the rest of the night and had a long talk about what had happened during the day. Tom and I had both been so stressed in the last six months, trying to keep Emma together, part of us hadn't allowed ourselves to mourn the loss of what was essentially a member of our family.

Stress like that can manifest in any number of ways. In my mind, the combination of our repressed feelings, dealing with Emma's grief, and everything I had carried home from my new business brought us to a point where Tom just finally snapped. The Christmas connection, no matter how tangential it seemed to be, had been the tipping point that sent him into a full-on breakdown. More tears were shed, on both our parts, after which came the heavy exhaustion that follows a big fight, and we passed out in each other's arms.

I woke up at 3 a.m. and rolled over to find comfort in Tom.

He wasn't there.

Sitting up, I checked the bathroom, which was dark. From the corner of my eye, I saw a light emanating from our bedroom window facing our backyard, so I peeled back the curtain. The lights to Tom's art studio were on. For as much as I hoped we could return to normalcy after our tumultuous Sunday, something told me Tom wasn't even close to getting to the bottom of whatever had shifted his world upside down. Whatever it was, I decided confronting him in the middle of the night was probably not the best way to go about it.

The paintings Tom made were always highly metaphorical and usually served as a way for him to process whatever problems he was dealing with. While it was rare, it wasn't completely uncommon to see him working in the middle of the night, trying to paint his way through his feelings. I only hoped he could find a way to work through this enough that it would keep him from any more incidents with our daughter. We were a team, and I needed Tom to help hold us together just as badly as Emma did.

Come morning, he was still cloistered away. I'd hoped his absence would give me a chance to patch things up with Emma before she left for school. She was despondent in the kitchen when I offered to make her homemade waffles. Even though it was only a ten-minute walk through a safe neighborhood, she grudgingly accepted my offer to drive her to school, remembering her bike was still parked at the mall.

After dropping her off nearly two blocks from Friars Middle—her one condition of letting me drive—I had to try and shift my focus to an entirely different set of problems. I had a nagging feeling my day was only going to get worse once I got into the office.

I hate it when I'm right.

At least my team had managed to finish shooting the *Thunderwear* ad yesterday without me, and as we went through the unedited footage, I marked off all but two shots on my checklist. Close enough. It wasn't until I asked for the photo proofs that Jen's face turned.

"I thought we were just shooting the video spot." She gestured to the clipboard I'd given her. "I went through and hit everything that was on the list."

I ignored the fact she missed the two shots and instead peeled the paper back over the clipboard. "Did you look at any of the other pages?"

"Oh my God, I'm so sorry," Jen said.

"And let me guess, the client took the product back with him at the end of the day? Not that it matters without us re-hiring the model."

It took another two hours for Jarett, the Thunderwear CEO, to find the time to return with the product.

"I don't believe this." Jarrett gritted his teeth in condescension.

"I'm so sorry we missed this yesterday," I said, doing my best to appease the little weasel. "I'll make sure the photo shoot and processing are taken off your bill."

He snickered, clearly feeling vindicated. "It better be."

Because our original model had booked another job for today, Becky called her boyfriend as a stand-in, who she promised was "super ripped" and, more importantly, available right now.

What walked through our door fifteen minutes later was anything but. His eyes were small and red, hair mussed. He looked stoned and like he hadn't showered. When he took his shirt off, there was almost no muscle to be seen.

"Just don't take any shots of his face," I told Becky, who was to act as our makeshift photographer for the day.

We had just started with our photo shoot when I felt my phone buzz.

"Hello?"

"This is a call from the inmate telephone system at San Diego County Jail," a robotic woman's voice said.

Oh God, what did Emma do now? I wondered, feeling an immediate pang of worry for my daughter's safety. Yesterday, it was mall security; today, it was jail? The robot gave me a long preamble about the call being recorded and then prompted me to press a button to accept charges.

"It's me. I need your help."

Tom.

He sounded even worse than last night.

"I've been arrested."

"What?" My shocked voice echoed through the office, and the photo shoot stopped dead in its tracks. Waving my hand at Becky to keep going, I rushed over to my office, slamming the door behind me. "What did you do?"

"Attempted Murder. At least that's what they told me during booking."

My legs nearly gave out. My body was somehow processing the words faster than my brain. I struggled to wrap my head around what he was telling me. "You murdered someone?"

"No, of course not," he said with frighteningly little conviction. "I can explain everything, just not now. The police said I'm on a recorded line, and anything I say to you can be used against me."

"Who did you try to kill?" I asked, still trying to understand the words *attempted murder.*

"I didn't...She wasn't what I...Look, I really don't think I should say much while on the line. I need your help. First, you have to find a criminal defense lawyer. Maybe someone who specializes in arson cases?"

"Arson? You tried to burn someone to death?" My anxiety hit a crescendo, then melted back into an odd sense of numbness running down me. "Where do I even find a lawyer?" I asked, suddenly forgetting basic concepts, like the internet.

"I don't know. I just...I'm sorry."

"It's okay. You'll be okay. I'll figure it out," I said, speaking on autopilot as if I were reassuring Emma. Meanwhile, my brain was distantly echoing the words he'd said to me, and I was vaguely hoping they would sink in soon.

"This is going to sound weird, but I remembered something extremely important. In the upper rafters of my studio, there's a box with the words 'Tom's Junk' written on it. I need you to take it down very carefully and open it up. Inside, there's a book." He paused as if it were getting harder for him to speak by the word.

I almost thought he'd disconnected, except I could hear him breathing heavily through the receiver.

"What book? What do I do with it?"

"I...Um...," he stammered, sounding like he already regretted bringing it up. Finally, he forced himself to finish his thought. "I think it's probably important that you read it. It might explain some of what's been going on with me."

"What's it called?" I asked, barely keeping track of the conversation.

"There's only one book in there, and it should be near the top. You'll know it when you see it. I have to go now. Find a lawyer. They should be able to help with everything else. I love you."

"I love you."

Then he was gone.

I tried to replay the conversation in my head as I packed up my things. The whole world felt off-balance, and I was having trouble remembering details from just a minute ago. I charged out of my office, explaining in as few words as possible that an emergency had come up and I had to go.

"Again?" Jarett said with palpable disdain in his voice. "This is totally unacceptable."

"I'm sorry, but I have to leave now. It's a family emergency."

"That's what you said yesterday. What do you have that's so much more important than Thunderwear?"

"My husband's been arrested for trying to murder someone, and now I have to figure out how to find a lawyer to defend him. Is that good enough for you?" I couldn't help but shout.

The man shrunk back, nodding meekly. He suddenly looked about as old as my daughter.

I'd made it about halfway to my car when Jen came running out to meet me.

"Jen, I'm sorry for that outburst. It was unprofessional. Can you—"

"Absolutely, I can handle the rest of today. I actually wanted to give you this." She pulled out one of her business cards, flipped it over, then started scribbling a name and phone number on it with a pen.

"My uncle is a criminal defense attorney. I heard you needed a lawyer and thought you might want to give him a call."

I didn't realize how much I needed a hug until my arms were already around her.

As I rushed home, I fed numbers from the card into my phone until a car horn pulled my eyes to the road. I'd blown through a stop sign and was maybe two feet away from smashing headfirst into another vehicle. They slammed on their brakes while I swerved the wheel, feeling my phone fly from my lap. I narrowly dodged a disaster.

The driver screamed obscenities at me and slowly resumed his path across the intersection. I could barely hear it through my own heartbeat banging in my ears. When I pulled over to catch my breath, my hands were shaking.

I ran through the mental checklist to gather my bearings—a trick that sometimes served to help me calm down. Manage the Thunderwear campaign...Devote my attention toward Emma's ongoing emotional crisis...Hire a lawyer to help with Tom's breakdown leading to a sudden attempt at murder...Deal with my own grief at losing Maya...Read a book that somehow was supposed to explain everything...Avoid front-ending strangers while going thirty miles an hour...I fished my hands around by my feet, retrieved my lost phone, then called the number Jen had sent me.

The phone rang six or seven times. I was ready for it to go to voicemail, when a man's voice came through in a hushed tone.

"This is Eric Walsh."

It caught me by surprise, even though I had been the one calling him. "My name is Sarah Barnes. My husband's been arrested." I didn't know what else I was supposed to say, so I just got straight to the point.

"I'm sorry, who gave you this number?" He said it as if it were an accusation.

"My coworker, Jen Walsh. She recommended you."

"Hang on a second," he said—muffled sounds, then silence for a few seconds. "Sorry about that. I don't give my personal cell number out to many people. Normally, all my prospective clients go through my office manager first. Your name's Sarah, correct? Can you tell me a little more about what happened?" He still spoke quietly, though his demeanor had shifted dramatically to show sympathy.

"I don't know. He just said that he had been charged with attempted murder...and something about arson."

"That's all right. I'll have my team gather all the information before I meet with him and keep you up-to-date. Can you give me his full name?"

"Tom Barnes. Sorry, Thomas."

"I'm going to contact the police and get back to you soon. In the meantime, I want you to just stay home, sit tight, and—this is important—I need you to not talk to anyone until I call again."

I nodded my head on reflex, wishing I were home already. "Okay."

"Now I have just one more question for you, Sarah. Do you, at this time, feel threatened? Do you have cause to believe you or other family members are in danger from anyone, including the police?"

"No."

The lawyer said a couple of more things about finishing with a client before hanging up, but I was too distracted to hear him. He'd made me realize I had absolutely no idea who Tom would be driven to kill. Confrontational is one of the last words I would have used to describe him. He never held grudges or got aggressive. If anything, he worked hard to ignore conflict as much as possible. Who would he hate so much that he would try to murder them?

My mind went back to the guy he saw at the mall yesterday who triggered this whole breakdown, but it seemed impossible Tom could have somehow tracked down a total stranger over the course of one night and then made the decision to try and end their life, with fire of all things.

I drove the rest of the way home, doing my best to observe all traffic laws. When I pulled into the driveway, I put the car in park and just stared through the windshield. Part of me knew I should be doing something, but instead, I just sat there, completely immobilized, staring blankly at the green wood-paneled studio. It felt like my head was full of glue, and it took a significant amount of mental effort to even remember the things on the checklist I had run through only minutes ago. My mind wandered, distracted by whatever I could see in front of me. I noticed, for the first time, how shabby the patching green paint on the front of our house looked compared to the studio, which had been remodeled only a few years ago.

The lights were still on inside of Tom's studio. It made me wonder if he had been in there when I woke up this morning, or even in the middle of the night.

The book.

It had sounded so important on the phone. In the back of my mind, there were a million things I should be worrying about, things I should be doing, but Tom had been so emphatic about me finding this book, I couldn't help but feel like I needed to look for that first.

Tom had turned the garage door into a wall with large opaque windows for light exposure, so getting in and out was easy through a side door. When I stepped inside, I felt a pang of loss hit me that I didn't expect. The detached building had a concentrated aroma of the paint supply smells that always hung on Tom, that I called his "artist's cologne." The aroma hit me like a punch to the gut. It was a dose of reality starting to pierce through my brain fog and get me to understand the things I took for granted, that I might be about to lose.

On an easel sat a canvas with a half-painted picture of a tiger standing in a field of sunflowers. Most of it was still just a sketch. The only things he had finished painting were her eyes, which looked exactly like our daughter's.

They were perfect.

I didn't know if Tom would ever come home again. Even if he did, would he finish the painting, or would things be too different by then? Did the Tom I knew even exist anymore, or would this experience change him, change our family, into something else? All these thoughts had me tiptoeing dangerously close to a full breakdown myself, so I did my best to put it out of my mind and get the box I'd come for.

Roughly a third of the ceiling was a large storage space left over from when the building had been a garage. Using a stepstool, I climbed up to sift through the items. It was mostly filled with Halloween decorations and art supplies. I had to move a number of boxes to the floor before I was able to find the one labeled "Tom's Junk," which was tucked into the back right corner.

As I pulled it from the ceiling to place on the floor, something inside let out a familiar jingle. The box was old and looked like it hadn't been opened in decades. I unfolded the cardboard flaps, squinting my eyes and holding my breath against dust. When I peered inside, it took me a second to figure out what I was looking at.

There was a lot of green fabric with red and white trim and a number of ball-shaped bells attached. It appeared to be some sort of costume. On top of it sat a square-shaped red ornament box. I found what I was looking for pressed against the side—a thin paperback book called *Everything Is Temporary*. At the bottom of the cover was the author's name, Tom Barnes.

I opened the book and began to read.

EXHIBIT 1A: AN EXCERPT FROM EVERYTHING IS TEMPORARY, BY TOM BARNES

"Rebel training!" Larry Enholm shouted just before throwing a handful of push pins into the overhead fan of Mrs. Callahan's six-grade classroom. It was a new game he'd invented to torture his class-mates any time the teacher left the room. After his announcement, everyone would have mere seconds to find cover under their desks before he hurled a dozen little daggers into the spinning blades of chaos.

Unfortunately for Tim Barnett, he had been walking back along the red brick path from the drinking fountain when the rebel yell was called, and as he stepped through the door, he was stabbed in the cheek by a tiny projectile. Tim yowled in surprise, his eyes glaring down at the green plastic backing of the pin embedded in his face. The pain doubled when he reached up to try and pull it out. He flinched, and that's when he noticed Larry laughing at him.

"Pussy!" Larry said as the rest of the class stared in morbid fasci-nation. "You just failed Rebel training."

"I wasn't ready," Tim objected, making excuses as if it were his fault he was unprepared for Larry's homemade shrapnel bomb. "You could have shot my eye out!" he said, borrowing a line from *A Christmas Story*, his favorite movie.

He made another move to pull the pin from his face, but Larry rushed to his side. "Oh my gosh, I'm so sorry. Here, let me help you with that." Before Tim could object or pull away, Larry brought up his meaty hand and flicked the bottom of the push pin, sending a twitch of pain through Tim as the tack tore across his skin.

Tim's eye snapped shut on reflex moments before the sharp plastic edge of the pin smacked into his lid.

"What did you go and close your eye for? You messed it all up!"

Larry Enholm enjoyed hurting other people, but nothing seemed to bring him more joy than targeting Tim.

Tim even remembered the first words Larry had ever spoken to him. On the first day of kindergarten, every student at Dundie Elementary had been assigned to either the White Team or the Blue Team. At the end of each year, the team with the most exemplary students would win and get an embroidered patch added to an ever-growing banner. Tim had been assigned White Team; Larry was Blue. Larry had walked right up to Tim, said, "Looks like we're enemies," then slugged him in the stomach.

Things only got worse from there.

Tim brought his hand up to his cheek and smeared a large bead of blood across his face. He wanted to cry. More than that, he wanted to fight back. He couldn't explain why this, of all the hundreds of abuses he'd taken, was the straw that broke the camel's back. It just was.

"Fuck you, Larry!" Tim shouted, bringing up his spaghetti arm and swinging for the face of the kid who had eight inches on him and at least twenty pounds. He didn't expect it to do much, but it caught Larry off guard, connecting with his ear.

"Tim Barnett, what do you think you're doing?" Mrs. Callahan said from the doorway. Her doughy face was already starting to turn as red as one of the fresh dry-erase markers in her hand.

"He started it!" Tim replied on instinct, knowing it would do nothing to help his situation with either Mrs. Callahan or Larry.

"Both of you, to the principal's office. Now." She pointed her finger out of the room to make sure they knew she was serious.

Larry looked at Tim and grinned. As they walked along the brick path toward Mr. Evans's office, Larry leaned over and whispered, "After school, I'm going to destroy you."

It was the end of the day, and both boys had been let off with a stern warning by Mr. Evans. Unfortunately, administrative punishment was the least of Tim's worries. He stared at the clock, waiting for the moment when Mrs. Callahan would excuse class for the day. As far as he figured, Tim had two advantages over Larry. First, his desk was located closer to the door. Second, he was the fastest sprinter in school—aside from Julia Diaz, a girl he'd had a crush on since the third grade.

"All right, class," Mrs. Callahan said, signaling she was wrapping things up. She announced the homework for the evening.

Everyone else wrote down their assignments in their notebooks, but Tim had already zipped up his backpack and had it slung over one shoulder. Read a chapter, answer some questions—he could figure out homework if he actually made it home alive.

As soon as she said the words, "see you tomorrow," Tim was out of his seat and halfway to the door. "Oh, Tim. Would you mind staying behind for a minute?"

For a second, Tim considered pretending he didn't hear his teacher and letting his momentum build until he could run the eight blocks to his home. As much as his head wanted to run with this plan, his legs wouldn't let him. He'd already been in enough trouble today. If Mrs. Callahan called his old man and said he'd skipped out on an after-school talk, he could be in for even more hell at home. Tim let the wind go out of his sails, then trudged his way to her desk, catching a wink from Larry as he sauntered out of the classroom.

"Listen, Tim. I just thought it might be worth having a little check-in to see how everything is going."

It was going to be okay until about five seconds ago, Tim wanted to say. "It's fine."

"I know things haven't been easy for you," she said, stating the obvious. "I know you're a good kid, most of the time." She enunciated the last part like she was tempering Tim's expectations. It was true—he rarely made trouble, though occasionally on days like this, he found himself on the wrong side of it. From a teacher's perspective, it was just as bad as being the cause. "I also am well aware of the challenges of having to deal with someone like Larry Enholm on a daily basis."

That was the understatement of the century. What she knew of Larry's bullying only scratched the surface of the torture to which Tim had been subjected.

Tim's mother had died suddenly from an aneurysm on Christmas Day just over a year ago. When Tim returned from winter break, he had been given nothing but compassion and understanding from his teachers and fellow students. Even the love of his life, Julia Diaz, had started talking to him. She'd offered help wherever she could, with her perfect smile and kind, dark eyes.

Of course, the one exception to all of this had been Larry, who seemed to double-down on making Tim's already brittle life as miserable as possible. One of the more notable examples that stuck in Tim's mind was when Larry told the whole class Tim's mom had committed suicide as a Christmas gift to herself because she wanted to get away from her loser son.

"I didn't start it today," Tim said.

"I know you didn't, but it doesn't excuse that kind of behavior. You're going to come across people like Larry all your life who will push you around and try to get a rise out of you. Next year, you're going to be starting at a new school, and whether Larry is there or not, you will find people who will try to put you down."

If I even survive that long, Tim thought.

"You're a smart, creative kid who could have a bright future in front of you one day. Don't let the Larrys of the world mess that up for you. If you just don't engage, he will eventually either leave you alone, or you will graduate and never have to see him again."

Tim nodded, waiting for Mrs. Callahan to excuse him so he could practice not engaging with Larry's fist. When she finally released him, he took his first few steps cautiously out of the classroom. He doubted Larry would pounce on him while still on school property, but that didn't mean Tim was safe, by any means.

He scanned the PE field just outside the classroom. The coast was clear, at least for now. Tim crossed the brick walkway, turned right at the drinking fountain, then kept his eyes peeled, making his way past the red metal gates and leaving school grounds. The immediate driveway outside was full of parents in cars, picking up their children. Normally, Tim would make a left onto Oakmont, but instead, he attempted to blend in with a group of kids crossing the street, venturing an extra block over. Tim turned the corner around a tall series of hedges, feeling clever, and nearly walked straight into Larry.

"Time for your final test, rebel scum." Larry looked down at the scrawny kid. Even with Tim's extra efforts to evade the bully, it was as if Larry had a predator's senses. He couldn't do better than a D in math, but he was an ace tracker.

Larry was big for his age and had a face that reminded Tim of a pig. His nose was wide and upturned and his eyes too far apart, just like his front teeth. His hair was a messy bowl cut with little white flakes of eczema accumulating on his shoulders and arms.

"You got me sent to Mr. Evans's office today, you little shit." Larry grabbed Tim by the collar before he could react.

Tim considered fighting back—he'd already landed one hit against Larry today—but it hadn't even looked like it hurt him, even when caught by surprise. Larry looked around to make sure there were no adults around. A few kids saw the incoming pounding and crossed to the other side of the street.

Tim didn't blame them. He'd do the same in their situation.

Larry grinned, knowing he was safe to taunt Tim further. "Didn't your mom ever tell you it's not nice to hit people? Oh wait, she's dead." Larry followed up his insult with a sucker punch to Tim's stomach.

Tim's feet gave out, but there was nowhere to fall—Larry had him gripped tightly by the collar. His backpack slid down his arm, and

Tim caught one strap before it completely fell to the ground. In a moment of fantasy, Tim imagined himself swinging the bag up, using it as a weapon to smash Larry upside the head. In reality, the bag was heavy with books, and Tim could barely even maintain his grip on the strap in between gasps for breath.

"Now, I want to make something clear." Larry took a step forward, even though he already held Tim firmly in his hands. "I'm the one with the power here. If I say, 'Rebel training,' you take cover. If you get hit, that's your fault. If I'm hungry and decide to eat your lunch, it's because you left it out. Again, that would be your fault. Understand?"

Tim tried again to lift his backpack in one last futile attempt to escape but realized that, in stepping forward, Larry had actually placed his foot through the ring of the other backpack's strap. It prevented Tim from swinging the bag up, even if he wanted to.

But it did give him another idea.

Larry shook Tim and repeated himself. "I said, do you understand?"

Tim nodded. His next move would almost surely make things worse, but in the moment, all he cared about was survival. "I think so. What you're saying is, if you end up not beating the ever-loving shit out of me today, it's my fault for making you such an idiot?"

Larry's face shifted to confusion. It wouldn't last long before that became a fist driving straight into Tim's face. With his hand gripped tightly to the strap of his backpack, Tim brought his leg forward, then kicked the bag backward with as much force as his little pencil-leg could muster. The strap that was wrapped around Larry's leg slid up to the bend in his knee, and the sudden force caused it to buckle.

To someone as small as Tim, Larry might as well have been Gulliver crashing down onto the Lilliputians. Luckily, in his effort to brace for impact, Larry released Tim from his grasp. With one quick maneuver, Tim was free from the bully's grip and off running before he even saw Larry hit the ground.

He needed as much of a head start as he could get. If Larry caught him now, the beating Tim would receive would be ten times what he would've suffered before. Because Larry had been standing between Tim and his route home, Tim ran the other way instead, hoping to lose him by making random turns at the corner of each suburban block.

Based on the volume of his shouting and swearing, Tim figured Larry must have regained his composure quickly and couldn't be more than half a block behind him. Tim made a random left, then another down an unpaved alley. It was only a few seconds before he heard another set of feet tearing up the gravel in pursuit.

Tim made a right onto Jacaranda, only realizing too late the street came to a dead end. If Tim didn't think of something fast, he would be reaching his own dead end too.

That's when he saw it—a faint gleam of light at the other end of the black cave of doom.

About halfway down the block of cookie-cutter brown and white houses sat one painted entirely green. Even though it was late March, the gutters were still lined with colored string lights, and a large inflatable Santa Claus perched on the roof, peering down the chimney, next to a blow-up Rudolph, his nose glowing oh-so-bright. In a narrow gap between the side of the house and its fence stood a wooden sign attached to a candy-striped pole. It had a big red arrow pointing down the narrow path and a sign that read: "Christmas House, Come On In!"

Tim didn't hesitate and booked it down the path.

7

SARAH

I sat on the floor of Tom's studio for nearly an hour, reading the first few chapters of *Everything Is Temporary*. It was clear the Tim Barnett character in the book was meant to be a stand-in for Tom Barnes. The names were almost identical, and of course, there was the fact his mother had died on Christmas Day. It certainly didn't paint a glowing picture of his childhood, but so far, nothing explained why he had been behaving so erratically.

When I had met Tom in college, he was obsessed with staying in the present. He carried around a book on Buddhism called *Shambhala: The Sacred Path of the Warrior* that he'd read so many times the cover looked like it was about to fall off. Tom took it so seriously at the time, it was a major factor in us initially breaking up. I assumed he never talked about his past because it was part of his philosophy, but even when we reconnected four years later in San Diego, he still never mentioned anything about his past. Now, I was starting to think he had adopted that philosophy as a coping mechanism to escape having to think about the events of his childhood.

Mostly, it just made me feel sad he had bottled up so much of his youth and chosen not to share any of it with me. It made my heart ache, and I wanted nothing more than to wrap my arms around him and tell him everything would be okay.

It also raised some other questions, like why he despised Christmas so much. In the book, it seemed like he was obsessed with the holiday, despite the trauma that took place on that day. What had happened to give him such a radical shift in his perspective?

Growing up as a westernized-Muslim, Christmas was never something my family took part in. It's not because we were devout in our religion—far from it, especially after moving to California. We just never really *got* the holiday spirit. It never occurred to me there could have been something more complex regarding Tom's relationship with Christmas.

Two things happened next in rapid succession, though I couldn't pinpoint which came first. The front door of the house slammed shut with enough force for me to hear it from inside Tom's studio. Emma must have walked straight home from school, now that the jig with Janice was up. The second thing was, my phone rang, and the caller ID read: "Eric Walsh."

Panic rose in my throat. I had been waiting for this call to learn more about Tom's situation. But the last thing I wanted was for Emma to catch me, leaving me unprepared for how to explain something I didn't understand myself. I felt a twinge of guilt as I hid from my daughter, turning off the lights to Tom's studio and shutting the door.

"Hello?" I said quietly into the receiver.

"Sarah, Eric Walsh. I'm about to meet with your husband in lockup, but my team's gotten back to me about some preliminary details. I'd like to go over them with you now. As soon as you pay my initial fee, I will officially become the representation for your husband and will fight my hardest to get him an acquittal. Does that all sound good so far?"

"Mom!" Emma's voice dully rang from somewhere upstairs, sounding irritated, as always.

I put one finger in my ear. "Yes, that's fine." I had no idea what his fees would entail—I probably didn't want to know.

"Excellent. Then let me get to it. Your husband, Thomas Barnes, was arrested this morning at 10:42 a.m. He was spotted by a patrol car, riding a bicycle near a burning house located at—"

"Daaaaad!" Emma was now stomping around the house, actively searching for her parents and forcing me to miss the address given by the lawyer.

Upon hearing her call for his name, knowing there would be no response any time soon, I felt the knife of guilt twist inside of me.

"Are you still there, Sarah?" the voice said over the line.

"Yes, sorry, what did you say?"

"I asked if you were familiar with the home." He repeated the address to me.

"I know the street. It's not too far from our house. But no, I don't know anyone who lives there."

"It looks like the fire department was able to contain the fire fairly quickly, and no one was hurt. The house belongs to one Carl Owens. Does that name mean anything to you?"

I answered honestly. "I've never heard that name in my life."

"Well, according to this report, your husband was found with an empty can of lighter fluid, which was used in an attempt to burn down Mr. Owens's home while he was inside. The arson unit will test to see if it's a match to the accelerant used inside the house, but for argument's sake, we'll assume it comes back positive."

I swallowed hard, trying to digest the confirmation there was no mix-up, no wrongful arrest. For whatever reason, Tom *did* do this.

"So what does that mean, exactly? That he's guilty?"

"I can't say for certain, but right now, it's looking likely."

"Mom, where are you? I can see the car outside. I know you're home." Emma's shouting carried her all the way to the backyard.

The door behind me burst open. I swung my head around, eyes wide in surprise, surely looking like a kid who had just been caught with their hand in the cookie jar.

"Mom, what the heck are you doing in here?"

While regaining my composure as the figure of authority, I put out a hand and whispered, "In a minute," trying my best to placate her but also making it clear this call was important.

"Ugggghh," she moaned in frustration, pulling out her phone and leaning against the doorframe while I continued with Eric Walsh.

"So, what happens next?" I asked.

"Depending on his situation in the holding cell, you may or may not hear from him tonight. Most likely tomorrow, though I'd urge you not to discuss any details of the case."

"When can I see him?"

"Unless you have a hundred thousand dollars lying around, the earliest you will get to see him again is at his arraignment. Depending on the judge we're assigned, I'm between very and extremely confident that your husband will be back home with you that night on bail. Luckily, this happened on a Monday, so the latest the arraignment should be is Thursday."

"Thursday?"

"It'll likely be sooner than that. The courts want him arraigned just as fast as we do. Turning the wheel of justice and all that."

I glanced up at my daughter, terrified she might be learning this information in the worst way possible. Thankfully, she seemed completely disengaged from my conversation, tapping away at her phone.

"So, we're supposed to just sit and wait?" I was doing my best to keep my voice from matching my feelings—wanting to climb out of my own skin.

"Once we hang up, I'm going to have my office manager call you to process payment."

"Thank you."

"I won't lie and say this isn't going to be expensive. My services don't come cheap. But if Jen sent you to me, you probably already know you're in very capable hands. This is likely going to be one of the toughest things you're ever going to go through, but rest assured, Mrs. Barnes, I'm going to be with you every step of the way."

Those last words hit me like a jackhammer. In the past six months, we'd lost an eleven-year-old girl who was practically Emma's sister, I'd lost my best friend, Tamika, who told me it was just too hard for her to be around me anymore, my daughter's life was in shambles, and most recently, my husband had experienced a meltdown on a level I was still trying to process. Having been told the hardest part hadn't even started yet made it nearly impossible to breathe. It was as if I had just reached the peak of Mount Everest, only to discover I was barely at the base camp for a mountain ten times its size. I was already pushed to what I thought was the limit of how much I could handle, and now they're telling me this was just the beginning?

Somehow, I had to find a way to cram all these feelings back inside for the twelve-year-old standing two feet away from me.

"Are you done now?" Emma said after I'd hung up, as if she'd been waiting there for hours.

"Habibeh, we need to talk." I had no idea where to start, caught completely defenseless, with none of my coping mechanisms at hand. Emma had literally been standing in front of me as I heard the scarce details about what Tom had done. I was still trying to process it myself, never mind figuring out a way to explain it to an adolescent. Even if I could find a way to break the news to my daughter, I still had more questions than answers.

For a second, I thought about lying, telling Emma her father was called away for something. My mind went blank even trying to cook up any plausible excuse for why a man who worked at home and had no extended family would even be gone.

"Mom, are you okay?"

I took a deep breath, more to stall for time than anything. It had already been such a hard year for her. Learning about Tom's situation on top of Maya's death felt like too much for anyone to deal with, let alone a kid just trying to make it through middle school. Without any other way of framing it, I couldn't hold it in any longer.

"Your father's been arrested."

Emma's reaction was about as far from my expectations as possible. She laughed, for the first time since school started. "Come on, Mom. He wasn't *that* bad yesterday."

It made things even harder for me, watching her face shift from the smiling little girl I used to know to a familiar look of total heartbreak. It was no secret that, of the two of us, Tom was the favorite parent. I would have given anything for him to be here right now.

"I'm so sorry. I don't have all the details, but apparently, he tried to hurt someone, and the police took him into custody. We're already working hard to bring him home and—"

"That's not fair," she said, interrupting my explanation of what little facts I had. "Dad wouldn't hurt anyone."

"I know, and I wish I could tell you more right now, but I'm just learning this all too."

"It has to be a mistake, right? When's Dad coming home?" Her voice turned into a squeak. Tears ran down her face, causing her heavy black mascara to follow in darkened smudges.

"I don't know. We've got him the best lawyer, and together, we're all going to figure it out."

"Who would he try to hurt? Dad doesn't even speak up when restaurants screw up his order."

"Some man. I wish I knew. They said his name was Carl Owens." A shiver ran through me when Emma's eyes grew wide with recognition. "What is it? Do you know him?"

She shook her head, more in confusion than denial. "That doesn't make sense. Mr. Owens wouldn't hurt a fly. Why would Dad want to hurt him?"

"Who is Mr. Owens?" I demanded, finding a foothold in the conversation by sinking into the upsettingly natural role of disciplinarian. As if I needed another reason to feel horrible right now, I was forced to find comfort in knowing that being the villain of my daughter's life was the one thing putting me on steady ground.

"Mr. Owens is just, like, this lonely old guy. I help him out with chores and stuff after school."

"Oh my God." I put the pieces together in my head. "He's the man in the video at the mall. Tom was right—you *were* with him." Just when I thought things couldn't get any worse, I felt a stabbing pang of fear drive into me as I realized where my daughter had been spending all her time. "What did he do to you? Has he touched you?

Threatened you?" I grabbed Emma by the shoulders and squeezed, demanding answers and losing what little composure I had left.

"Ew, no. It's nothing like that." Emma tried to pull away from me, which only forced me to tighten my embrace—I wouldn't let her go this time. "Mom, he's not a pedophile or anything. He doesn't even like women."

I shook my head. Everything I understood about my family was slipping away. "Then what are you doing with him?"

"We're just, like, there for each other. He doesn't have any friends, and neither do I, so I help around the house with stuff, and in return, he's been helping me talk about Maya."

"Why are you talking to him about Maya?"

"Because he actually listens! You lecture; Dad gives me art lessons. Mr. Owens knows what it's like when best friends die. He's the only one who understands me." Her voice rose to a squeak as she made a realization. "And now Dad's gone and ruined the only good thing I had in my life."

The blows just kept coming. "How did you even meet him?"

"When Maya was sick, we heard about this program that helped kids get to experience Christmas at weird times of year. You know, just in case they weren't going to, like, make it? I found this house that was..."

EXHIBIT 1B: AN EXCERPT FROM EVERYTHING IS TEMPORARY, BY TOM BARNES

...the most beautiful place Tim had ever seen. After making his way through a side corridor leading to the backyard, Tim was so amazed, he forgot all about the bully trying to crack his skull. It was the first week of spring in Orange County, and yet somehow, Tim had walked into a winter wonderland.

The ground looked like it was covered in a fresh patch of snow, and all around was a model town seeming to stretch forever. Poinsettias and other winter flowers adorned the hedges lining the property. Everywhere he looked, there was the shimmer of tinsel and the twinkling of multi-colored lights. Tim climbed over the hump of a little wooden bridge rising above a babbling brook that didn't seem to have a clear start or end.

His heart swelled, images of his mother flooding his senses. It was almost as if he could feel her there with him. She had loved Christmas more than anything, and since her passing, his old man had outlawed all things festive.

"Hello, dear," a voice said.

Tim swung his head around, for a moment hearing his mom. Instead, he found an old woman with curly white hair and rosy cheeks. She stood at a sliding glass door in a red dress and white apron. From behind her came the smell of cookies, conjuring powerful memories of almost a dozen Christmas Eves when Mom would bake a fresh batch of chocolate chip cookies for Santa. Of course, most would be eaten before Tim would settle into bed for a restless night, waiting for the most magical day of the year.

"I saw the sign out front..." Tim suddenly realized it might be considered weird for a kid to randomly be wandering around some old lady's backyard. "It said to come in."

"And you're just in time." The old woman's words were filled with cheer. "I just made a fresh batch of cookies, and I have some hot chocolate on the stove. Would you like a snack?"

Tim's stomach rumbled. After his trip to the principal this morning, he had been too nervous to eat most of his lunch, worrying what Larry would do to him come 2:30. "I'd love some. My name's Tim."

"Well, Tim, it's an absolute pleasure to make your acquaintance. You can call me Mrs. Claus."

"Your backyard is beautiful," Tim said, carefully navigating the winding stone walkway leading to the house.

"That's very nice of you to say. In case you haven't noticed, Christmas holds a very special place in my heart."

"Mine too."

"Come on inside. I'll show you all the *real* decorations."

Tim knew better than to talk to strangers, never mind wander into their homes. But she was just an old lady. What was the worst she could do? Besides, this wasn't like some weirdo in a white van, offering candy.

This was an establishment.

There was a sign.

Surely, it wouldn't exist if the neighborhood didn't know it was safe.

If the backyard had been a winter wonderland, the inside of the house was something straight out of Higbee's Department Store window. In the corner of the living room sat a large green Christmas tree decorated with string lights and ornaments. The base was fully obscured by at least two dozen gold-wrapped presents. More tinsel and string lights glimmered across the room, leading up a banister to the second floor, and each door had a wreath hanging from it. A choo-choo sound forced Tim's eyes upward, where a train set chugged along a track suspended from the ceiling, running in a weaving pattern through the room. Each car of the train was loaded with red-coated nutcracker soldiers, all standing at perfect attention.

Pressed against the wall nearest the tree was a glass-covered cabinet hosting hundreds of ceramic Hummel figurines: nativity scenes; elves making toys; people dressed in winter clothes, exchanging gifts. Leading the pack was a cheery-looking Santa Claus with a sack slung over his back.

"I'll just be in the other room, preparing those cookies. Feel free to take a minute to look at all the decorations." Mrs. Claus wandered off into the kitchen.

Tim leaned in to get a better look at the figures, then jumped back in surprise when the ceramic Santa suddenly moved his hand up to his hat, adjusted it, then winked. Tim wanted to scream, but the best he could manage was a gasping cough. He leaped backward, but his feet tripped over themselves. Tim was falling, his head ready to meet the floor, when something bushy caught him in midair. It was a branch of the Christmas tree.

"Don't be afraid," a voice from inside the tree said. The branch lifted him back onto his trembling feet, then released him.

As soon as Tim looked at the tree in the corner, all the string lights went out, save for two acorn-shaped bulbs making up eyes and a pair of strings that looked like a scraggly-toothed mouth.

"Merry Christmas, Tim!" the tree said. As it spoke, the lights insinuating its lips lit up and went dark in perfect harmony so it mimicked movement.

Tim had no idea how it was able to produce its voice, but it spoke with a slight British accent and sounded like the Santa from *Miracle on 34th Street*.

"Merry Christmas?" Tim mumbled back, wondering if he'd suffered some sort of psychotic break. Maybe his escape from Larry had all been a hallucination, and he was currently lying on the pavement somewhere with a concussion, his bully pounding his head into submission.

"We didn't mean to scare you, Tim. My name is Evergreen." The tree's mouth-lights danced across his body as he spoke.

"What *are* you?" Tim asked defensively, doing his best to keep his voice from shaking in fear.

"Why, I'm an ambassador, of sorts. Have you ever heard of Christmas magic?"

Tim stammered something, though there was a disconnect between his brain and his mouth, stopping him from hearing his own words.

"Everything all right in there?" the old woman's voice called from the kitchen.

Tim swung his head around, eyes wide, searching for Mrs. Claus. She hadn't seemed to acknowledge the talking tree. She looked over him with a smile, though it got cut short when she saw the frightened confusion on Tim's face.

"Everything all right, Tim?" she asked.

"She can't see or hear us," Evergreen explained from behind. "Only children who understand the true meaning of Christmas. You're special, Tim."

Tim didn't want to come off as crazy to Mrs. Claus, even though what was happening was indeed quite insane. Rather than cause a fit in the moment, Tim swallowed his fear and put on a smile.

"I'm fine. Just a little overwhelmed," he said.

"There," Evergreen said, bringing Tim's attention back to him as Mrs. Claus returned to her work in the kitchen. "Now just the two of us can talk."

"Is this...Is this because of my mom?" Tim asked, trying to figure out if he was truly in the presence of the supernatural, or if he'd just lost his mind.

The lights on Evergreen's face rose and sank several times, insinuating a nod.

Ever since his mom's death, Tim had become obsessed with all things Christmas. Nearly every night before bed, after his old man had passed out drunk, Tim would fall asleep to his small collection of Christmas DVDs playing on his tiny bedroom TV.

Tim's fear began to subside faster than he expected and quickly turned into curiosity. "How are you able to move like this?"

"By Christmas magic, of course," Evergreen repeated, as if the explanation were obvious. "I'd like to meet some more of my friends. These are the Humble Hummels."

Tim looked to the cabinet. The shelves came to life, with dozens of Hummels moving on their own. The elves pounded their little hammers onto rocking horses, and the scarf-wearing citizens exchanged armfuls of gifts with each other. Santa waved with his large white mitten.

"And over here, we have the Candy Stripers..."

On a side table, nearly two dozen candy canes slithered to life like snakes, wriggling out of a glass cup and falling to the floor. They squiggled around in what looked like chaos until they all straightened themselves out and collectively used their bodies to form the words: "Hi Tim!"

From above, the train made another circle. The platoon of nutcrackers all gave him a "hut-hut" and saluted.

"Those are the Nutcracker Suite. Friendliest soldiers in town!" Evergreen said.

From the kitchen came the sound of a screeching kettle, making Tim jump.

"Cocoa's ready!" Mrs. Claus said, beckoning Tim to join her. She opened a cupboard above the kitchen counter and pulled out a red mug with Santa's face plastered across it. Mrs. Claus then put on a red fuzzy oven mitt and grabbed the handle of the kettle, pouring the dark brown contents into the mug.

As she bent down to open the oven, a rustling came from a clear plastic bag on one of the top shelves. A trio of marshmallows with tiny arms and legs climbed out of the package, then each dove one by one from the top shelf, straight into the cup. Tim stared in shock and amazement. Swirling inside were the three marshmallows. Their arms and legs had already dissolved, and now that he could see them up close, he noticed each one had a face. They smiled and winked at him, slowly melting into the hot drink.

"Should I feel bad eating these?" Tim asked.

Mrs. Claus laughed. "Oh, I see you found the marshmallows. Please, help yourself."

Tim slowly brought the mug to his lips and hesitantly took a sip. It was the perfect blend of sweetness, just hot enough to warm his tummy without burning the roof of his mouth.

"Have a cookie, while they're still fresh." Mrs. Claus gestured to the tray she had just placed on top of the stove.

It had been over a year since Tim had eaten homemade anything. He wasn't sure if his memories were tricking him, but the cookie tasted *exactly* like the ones his mom used to make. Mixed with the hot chocolate, the snacks wrapped him in a warm blanket of comfort he hadn't felt in as long as he could remember.

"How are they?" Mrs. Claus asked.

Tim had to fight back tears to give his response. "They're incredible." At risk of becoming overwhelmed with emotion, Tim felt the need to change the subject. "Do you keep your house decorated like this all year?"

Mrs. Claus beamed with pride. "I do. As you already know, Christmas is the most special time of year, when we all celebrate the love of our families, friends, and make that extra effort to do good for others. I wanted to be able to share that feeling with my community year-round, to remind us that there is always room in our hearts for Christmas cheer."

Tim nodded in agreement, wishing his old man could experience this but deep down knowing it probably would do little to change his hardened heart.

"So, tell me, Tim. What's your favorite Christmas movie?"

It was an easy answer. Ever since he had been a young boy, Tim and his mother both had a borderline unhealthy obsession with *A Christmas Story*. Starting on Thanksgiving and running all the way through December 25, rarely a day would go by that Tim wouldn't watch the film. His mother would have it on while cooking or doing chores around the house. She was able to drift in and out of screenings, but Tim always found himself sucked into the adventures of Ralphie Parker on his quest to get a Red Ryder 200-shot range model air rifle. He especially liked Ralphie's fantasy sequences, pretending he would be the star student in a class full of dunces or protecting his family from would-be robbers with his trusty rifle. And at the end of the film, Tim was always filled with joy when Ralphie got his perfect gift, despite everyone telling him he would shoot his eye out.

"Oh, I love that film!" Mrs. Claus said in response to Tim's answer. "You know, I was around during the forties, when the movie took place."

Tim was about to ask what *her* favorite movie was, when he noticed a thin hardback book next to the tray of cookies. The cover depicted two children on a sleigh in the middle of a dark snow-covered forest, riding over a bridge that looked like a larger version of the one in the backyard. On the other side of the bridge was a golden archway, with a sort of portal in the center leading to a bright world where two elderly people stood, waving. Across the top of the book was the title, *Over the River,* by Mrs. Claus.

"I see you've noticed my book," Mrs. Claus said with just a hint of trepidation.

"You wrote this?"

Mrs. Claus nodded and was silent for a minute. "Would you agree with me if I told you that Christmas was the most special time of year, especially for a child?"

Tim nodded, especially after what he had just experienced in the living room. But there was something about her tone that had taken on a sense of melancholy. Tim was unsure where she was going with this but felt a sense of unease slide over him.

"I opened the Christmas House so that people could experience the joy of the holiday all year, but sometimes, there are people who want to visit for special occasions. You see, I work with several children's hospitals around the county. There are so many wonderful kids out there who love Christmas just as much as you and I. But one of the most cruel and sad realities in life is that sometimes kids get sick.

I'm not talking about the kind of illness where you rest in bed for a few days and feel better. These are kids who will never recover. And even worse, they may not make it to experience another Christmas. For those children, I open my home, give them gifts and cookies, and then I like to read them this picture book I wrote that helps to explain the transition they're going to make to the next life. You see, everything is temporary. I try to help people celebrate the time they have, rather than feel sorrow over what they're missing."

Tim tried to think about what it would be like if he found out he would never see another Christmas and felt something small and fragile break inside of him. "So, you give them one last Christmas?"

She nodded, then looked curiously at Tim. "What do you think about that?"

Tim took a bite of a cookie to occupy his mouth while he thought about it. His old man had seen losing Mom on Christmas as a curse, some sort of cruel joke the world played on him. From Tim's perspective, he always felt grateful to have had at least part of one last Christmas together, and every time he saw anything Christmas-related, it made him feel just slightly closer to her. And now that he had seen Christmas magic firsthand, it renewed a sense of hope his mother was still out there somewhere, watching over him.

The idea there were not just people but children who would never get to have another Christmas seemed far more unfair than what had happened to his family.

"I think giving someone Christmas at any time of the year is one of the kindest things someone could do."

Mrs. Claus nodded. "Tim, please don't take this the wrong way, but is there someplace you're supposed to be right now?"

Tim shook his head. His old man wouldn't be back from work for at least another two hours. Normally, he would be at home by now, doing homework or watching *Home Alone*, alone.

"Can I tell you a secret?" Mrs. Claus asked. "Mr. Claus isn't around anymore. It's just been me on my own for the longest time. I could really use some more regular company around the house. I'm not as young as I used to be, and keeping everything clean takes all the energy I have. I can already tell you're a thoughtful young man who appreciates the Christmas House in the same special way that I do. How would you feel about helping me out a few days a week after school? I can pay you for your time. We can call it a part-time job, if you like."

Tim still wasn't sure if he was stuck in some sort of extended hallucination. If it was, it was a whole lot better than the hellscape he had been stuck in for the last year and a half. The idea of spending every afternoon with magic trees and fresh cookies seemed like a dream compared to the dreary two-bedroom apartment he'd moved into with his old man after Mom died. Most of the walls were still bare, the place always smelled like rotting food, and at night, they ate dinner on paper plates to avoid doing dishes.

"I'd love to."

Mrs. Claus clapped in excitement. "That's wonderful to hear. Let's get started on the right foot, then, shall we? I think there's a gift under the tree that would be perfect for you."

Tim furrowed his brow, wondering what she could possibly have under there that he could want. The two of them stepped back into the living room, where Evergreen's light-up eyes danced around the base of the tree, searching between packages.

Mrs. Claus didn't seem to notice the fantastic display of Evergreen's glowing face as she sorted through the golden wrapped boxes.

"Ah, here it is." She grabbed a box below where Evergreen had turned his lights into an arrow pointing directly at it.

"This is really for me?" Tim approached the wrapped box with caution.

The old woman nodded, and he tore into it without further hesitation. Inside was a matching green shirt and pair of pants, with red and white frills on the cuffs. It also came with a hat that had a jingle bell attached at the top. Tim checked the tag—the outfit was exactly his size.

"If you don't mind, I feel it helps get into the spirit of things, if you're dressed for the occasion. Wouldn't you agree, Little Elf?"

8

SARAH

By the time Emma finished describing Mr. Owens's house, there was a pit in my stomach. With the exception of magical living decorations, what she had described shared a good deal of similarity to the house mentioned in Tom's book. What concerned me even more was, I hadn't read far enough yet to know where the story went. It made me worry there might have been a much darker reason why Tom had never felt comfortable sharing his past with me.

Tom had always had a knack for magical realism in his paintings. While the descriptions of living ornaments were creative, it wasn't entirely shocking he would invent such fantastic elements to help him with his coping mechanisms. His paintings were all heavy with surreal metaphors his critics and clients seemed to understand and appreciate, even if I couldn't.

My phone rang again, this time from a number I didn't recognize. Emma's face lit up, suddenly full of hope.

"Is it Dad?"

"I don't know," I said, wishing I could have the time and space to figure out what was about to happen before potentially subjecting her to more bad news. If Tom were here, he'd know what to do.

The phone rang a second, then third time while I stood frozen, watching my little girl's eyes sparkle with hope.

"I want to hear." She moved toward me for the first time since learning of Tom's situation.

I thought about her outburst last night, Emma declaring we had abandoned her. For better or worse, she and I were a team now, more than ever. Whatever we went through, we would be there together.

"This is Sarah," I said, answering the phone.

A woman named Missy introduced herself as the lawyer's office manager. She was calling to go over payment and scheduling.

"Can you put it on speaker?" Emma asked.

I did as she requested, figuring nothing in this call could be too upsetting, at least to her. If Tom was going to be absent from our family for a while, I would need to find a way to build a more trusting emotional connection with Emma, and this seemed like as good a place as any to start.

Missy explained the details as if she'd had this conversation a thousand times before. "If your husband is granted bail, you can expect to spend up to ten thousand dollars on a bondsman, on top of a five-thousand-dollar retainer fee for Eric Walsh."

I had to chew on the inside of my cheeks to keep my eyes from bugging out of my head when I heard those numbers. Between Tom's art and my startup, we barely had enough on hand to pay those fees and still maintain our mortgage, my employees' salaries, Emma's tuition, and food for our family. Conversely, all Emma had gathered from the conversation were the words she was hoping for.

"So you think he's going to come home? Erm, granted bail?" she asked.

"Sorry, who is this?" Missy asked.

"That's my daughter," I explained. "We're all very anxious to see Tom."

"Uh-huh," she said, in a tone clearly indicating judgment of my parenting for letting a twelve-year-old listen in on this call.

Fuck her, I thought. *Just give the kid a little hope.*

"I can't say one way or another, but generally in cases like this, bail is the likely outcome. The good news is that your husband was processed relatively early, and it seems like it's been an otherwise slow day for the SDPD. Tom's arraignment has already been scheduled for early tomorrow afternoon."

"Dad's coming home!" Emma cheered, with almost as much excitement as if she had just learned we were going to Disneyland. "Yessssss."

Missy continued her explanation, while Emma collapsed to the floor of Tom's studio in relief. "If the case does go to trial, you can expect to spend up to one hundred and fifty thousand dollars on legal fees."

Doing my best to hide my sticker shock, I clenched my teeth down so hard on my cheek that I tasted blood. I couldn't even wrap my head around the idea of coming up with that kind of money, only for a *chance* at having my husband back.

"Is that all right?" Missy asked.

There's no way we had that kind of money, at least the way we were currently living. But if it meant there was a shot at bringing my family back together, I would have to find a way.

"Yes," I said.

Missy gave me a few more details of where to be and when, then assured me Eric Walsh would be in touch.

"Do you think he did it?" Emma asked after I ended the call.

"Of course not. This is all just a big misunderstanding. We'll get this cleared up in no time, and then we'll all be together again." I had to force myself to sound like I believed it for Emma. Inside, I felt like I was falling into a bottomless hole, with nothing to grab onto.

The rest of the night crawled by. As much as I wanted to continue reading Tom's book, Emma needed me more. Neither of us had much of an appetite, and after forcing down some plain buttered noodles, we settled into my bed and began another rewatch of *The Sandman*. It had quickly become Emma's comfort show, and we eventually drifted into an uneasy night of tossing and turning.

9

SARAH

The morning reignited emotions when—after spending half the sleepless night deliberating—I decided it was best if Emma went to school. I had a full day of misery ahead of me already, and I didn't feel confident that I could make it through without breaking down into tears. Witnessing that was the last thing Emma needed.

I almost crumbled twice in the car. As soon as we pulled up to her school, she gripped me tightly and begged me not to leave her, going as far as to call me "Mami," a name she hadn't used since she was seven.

I was finally able to convince her that, by the time she got out of school, both Mami and Baba would be waiting for her at home. After dropping her off, I made it three whole blocks before I had to pull over and let myself cry. I then prayed for the first time since I was sixteen that Tom would come home today and that I hadn't just lied to my daughter. No matter what I chose, I worried I was causing irreparable damage to her. How could she possibly grow up to have any sort of future when every day seemed to present some fresh new hell?

I'd spent most of last night obsessively reviewing what I knew of our finances in my head, and the only way to even consider paying our lawyer's ongoing fees would be to shut off all outgoing expenses immediately. Tom clearly wouldn't be bringing in any income, and getting my marketing firm on its feet had thus far been more expensive than I had imagined, with whatever income going straight back into the business.

The Barnes Marketing Firm might have been my baby, but it wasn't my family. As much as I hated the idea, I could go back to being an employee at some job I despised, but I couldn't survive without my husband.

I circled the block a few times, trying to cook up and repeat key phrases while staving off one of the hardest speeches I would ever have to make.

It was twenty minutes before I was able to force myself through the door, and when I did, it took every ounce of effort to be able to look my employees in the eyes. As I gathered Jen and Becky in the conference room, I couldn't help but think of Tom's motto and how I had never expected it to apply to everything I'd worked so hard to achieve. *Everything is temporary.*

"First of all, I want to thank the both of you for trusting me with your careers here at the Barnes Marketing Firm. I'm sure you're probably aware by now that some things have come up in my personal life that have forced me to re-evaluate and re-prioritize what's best for my family. It's with a heavy heart that, effective immediately, I'm going to have to shut down the Barnes Marketing Firm."

"Are you fucking kidding?" Becky said, clearly incensed. "I left Agle Media for you."

"I'm sorry to have broken your trust. I know that you both left steady jobs at established firms to take a risk on me. Don't think for a second that I take this decision lightly, or your dedication for granted. You know that this company has been the culmination of nearly two decades of work on my part, and I wouldn't be doing this unless I absolutely had to."

"So we're just out on our asses like that?"

"Becky, please," Jen mumbled, trying to defend me through red, glassy eyes.

Hearing Jen stand up for me, even as she was getting let go, was almost more painful than Becky's outrage. I tried to finish my speech, but Becky had already stormed out of the room to begin packing her things.

"Jen, I'm so sorry—" My words got cut off as Jen wrapped her arms around my neck and squeezed me in a tight hug.

"I understand," she said with a sniffle. "Take care of your family." She then left to pack her things too.

I sat in the conference room well after they had both left, mourning the life I almost had.

Once I finished killing my professional dreams, I had to head back home and go through the rest of our finances to figure out how else we were going to be able to pay these legal fees without becoming homeless. Tom wasn't a starving artist by any means, though he certainly wasn't famous either. Closing my business erased a lot of expenses, but it also meant I would have no source of income until I found another firm to hire me.

What felt most unfair was, I knew there was no way of covering these costs without completely draining the college fund we had been saving since Emma's birth. I hated myself for feeling like I was punishing our daughter for something she didn't do.

It wasn't until I pulled up to the courthouse for Tom's arraignment that I realized I hadn't eaten anything yet today and suddenly became ravenously hungry. There was a coffee cart about a half-block down. I inhaled a croissant and a coffee, then immediately regretted it when my stomach churned. The sick feeling only grew worse once I entered the massive building, getting lost several times on my way to where I was supposed to be.

At five minutes to one, I was approached by a slightly overweight man in his early fifties. He had salt and pepper hair, dressed in what looked like an expensive suit.

"Mrs. Barnes?" he asked, likely recognizing me by the lost look on my face while I tried to figure out which courtroom to enter. "I'm Eric Walsh. It's good to meet you in person." He stuck out a thick hand but was surprisingly gentle as we shook. Eric was older than he sounded on the phone. "We're going to have plenty of time to talk later, but right now, I just wanted to run through what's about to happen. In a minute, I'll walk you through those doors, and you'll take a seat in the front row, just behind the bar on your right. After that, a deputy will bring your husband through those same doors, to join me at the defense table. Your job here is to be supportive of Tom but also to remain as calm and quiet as you can. This will be difficult, but the deputy's going to be walking him right past you, close enough to reach out and grab him. I'm going to tell you the same thing I told him—while it's technically not allowed to touch or speak to each other, they'll usually let you get away with a statement of support, like telling him you love him. But if you bring up the case in any way, there's a good chance you'll be asked to leave. Do you have any questions so far?"

I felt like I'd had a million questions pop into my head over the last day, but in the moment, my mind went blank. I shook my head.

"Okay. In that case, just follow my lead, remember to keep quiet, and then later this afternoon, we can all sit down and go over the details of the case."

Eric walked me through the doors and to my seat, my heart racing. As hard as the last day had been, some small part of me still hadn't fully come to terms with what was happening. It all became excruciatingly real when the doors behind me opened and I saw Tom enter, wearing an orange jumpsuit and handcuffs. He looked ten years older, and his already thin face looked hollow. His eyes were dark, and we were only able to hold each other's gaze for a second before he turned away in shame.

When the guard brought him past me, I whispered, "I love you," remembering the advice Eric had given me.

Tom looked at me again. He didn't say anything, his face full of regret. Once he had been seated, the judge—a woman who appeared to be in her late fifties, with bright red hair—called the court to order and began to read from a document.

"Good afternoon. This is the arraignment in the case of the State of California versus Thomas Barnes. The defendant is charged with attempted murder by arson. Is the defendant present?"

Eric Walsh stood up, prompting Tom to do the same. "He is, Your Honor."

"Mr. Barnes, how do you plead to the charge of attempted murder by arson?"

Tom looked over to his lawyer, who nodded, then faced the judge again. "Not guilty."

The judge looked over to another man in a suit, sitting at the prosecutor's table. "Mr. Murphy, what is the state's position on bail?"

The prosecutor stood up. He looked young enough to still be in college. His face was narrow and pointed, reminding me of a wolf. "Your Honor, the state requests the defendant be denied bail. The state's preliminary evidence shows a willful, deliberate, and premeditated act of attempted murder. We suggest he remain in custody until a time when a verdict is delivered."

The judge nodded. "Thank you, Mr. Murphy. Mr. Walsh, do you have any response to the state's position on bail?"

"I do. Mr. Barnes is a family man with a wife and child. He has no history of criminal activity and acted in fear to defend his family's life. He poses no danger to his community. The defense requests bail to be set at five hundred thousand dollars. To prove my client is not a flight risk, he is willing to be outfitted with an electronic monitoring device to prove his dedication to remaining with his family."

The judge nodded, then consulted her chart once more. "I appreciate the offer, Mr. Walsh, but my number one concern as a judge in this proceeding is public safety. Based on the charges and arguments of both sides, I am going to set bail at one million dollars. In addition, the defendant is not to leave the San Diego city limits or have any contact with the alleged victim or any witnesses in this case. I'm going to set the preliminary hearing on November the sixth, two weeks from today, at which time both parties will discuss discovery and any pre-trial motions. Is there anything else that either of you would like to address at this time?"

Both lawyers shook their heads, and just like that, it was over.

Tom and I shared a hopeful glance as the deputy then ushered him out of the courtroom. The whole thing had gone by so quickly and without emotion, I hadn't known how to feel until he was already out of sight. But it was my understanding that everything had gone just as Missy predicted on the phone. At least for now, I was getting my husband back.

The timing was tight, but I was able to pay Tom's bail in time to get him home before the end of the school day.

"I'm so sorry," Tom said upon release as I threw myself into his arms. "I fucked up."

"It doesn't matter." I pressed my head into the space between his neck and shoulder. "I can't do this without you."

We had made it home with Eric Walsh following us. Just as we were all setting up to discuss the case on the dining table, the front door swung open.

"Baba!" Emma shouted, shedding her backpack and hoodie across the floor on her way to an embrace. Tom stood to catch her, but she hugged him so tightly she almost knocked him over.

"It's okay, honey. I'm not going anywhere," he said, getting down on one knee for her.

"You promise?"

"Promise. Remember, everything is temporary. This will all be over soon." As Emma buried her head in Tom's chest, he glanced over to the table, where Eric was sitting with a pile of documents. "Listen, Emma. Mom and I have some stuff we have to go over with the lawyer. Why don't you go to your room and get started on your homework?"

"No!" she shouted, squeezing him even tighter.

"Is it okay if she stays?" Tom asked.

"I'd generally advise against it, but it's completely up to the parents," Eric replied.

"Please!" Emma begged. "I promise I'll be quiet."

Tom looked over to me, the de facto boss of the house, to make the final call. After gaining some ground with her yesterday, I couldn't handle telling my daughter she wasn't allowed to spend time with her family at a time like this.

"For now, you can sit with us." I wondered if I was being a good parent or just further screwing up our child.

We all joined Eric at our oak table, and he opened up his folder. "All right, let's start with the basics. Normally, as a rule, I don't ask whether or not a client is guilty of the crime in which they're accused, but frankly, the evidence is already overwhelming. This means our defense needs to focus on the *why* instead of the *who*. In a case like this, the first thing police do in their investigation is track down evidence that could quickly disappear. This includes things like taking witness statements from neighbors and tracking down any security footage from nearby stores that may be automatically erased after twenty-four hours."

Eric shuffled through his pile of documents and brought out a series of grainy colored photographs. Each one of them showed Tom wearing the same paint-covered hoodie I'd last seen him in, riding his bike while wearing a green backpack.

"You were photographed in front of four different stores and one interior of the hardware store with you holding the can of lighter fluid that was found on your person during your arrest. We also have several witness reports in the neighborhood, sharing stories of a man fitting your description breaking into the home of one Carl Owens."

Emma's face blanched at the mention of Owens, and I immediately regretted letting her stay for the meeting.

Tom nodded, soaking it all in. "So, it sounds like you're saying I might be in trouble." He did his best to put on a smile, either for me or Emma—I'm not sure it was very convincing for either.

"I wouldn't have taken you on as a client if I thought your case was hopeless. We actually have quite a few tricks up our sleeve, depending on what gets turned up during discovery and how honest you are with me as we work together in the coming weeks. Our first potential positive is in taking a look at the judge and prosecutor assigned. I've known Judge Merlowe for years. She has a reputation for being lenient on first-time offenders, which already scores us some points. I'm not seeing any criminal history in your preliminary report, so this is your first chance to be honest with me. Both my team and the prosecution will be digging deep into your past, so either way, we're going to find the truth here. Have you ever been arrested or been in any legal trouble in the past?"

"No," Tom said, shaking his head. "A couple speeding tickets before I gave up my car, but that's it."

"If true, it should be very helpful in getting your sentence reduced, if it comes to that. There's a number of other things we have going for us as well. Arson is quite the tricky beast when it comes to the law. You'd be surprised how few arson-related cases end up going to trial. Ninety-five percent of prosecutors won't want to touch this, which means they'll be much more likely to try and accept a plea."

"I thought you said Baba wouldn't be going back to jail!" Emma said, her voice quickly rising in concern.

"Habibeh, please," I said.

"Emma, is it?" Eric's voice grew soft and sympathetic. "That's just *if* something happens. It's my intention—and strong belief—that we will be able to beat this. Of course, I can't promise anything, but it's my job to make sure your dad never spends another day behind bars.

"Now, like I said, when it comes to arson, you're either going to get a prosecutor who has little to no idea what they're doing, or you're going to get an arson specialist. I know the prosecutor, Jim Murphy. He's a very smart and capable lawyer, but he's never tried an arson case before. Because of his inexperience, he's going to try his hardest to keep this from going to trial. If he loses, it could really hurt the trajectory of his career. Again, it's something we can work with if the time comes for it."

"So he might make a deal that means Dad won't go to jail?" Emma asked.

The sympathetic look on Eric's face grew, and I braced for more bad news.

"My best guess is that either before or during the preliminary hearing, the prosecutor and I will sit down together and discuss options.

The alleged victim is unharmed and said in his statement that he never actually saw Mr. Barnes in the house. Because of this, Mr. Murphy's likely going to downgrade the charge from attempted murder—which carries a sentence of seven years to life—down to regular arson, which we call a two, four, six crime. That means, depending on how lenient the judge is, you're looking at a potential sentence of two, four, or six years in prison. But even at that, you would most likely only be looking at spending about a third of that sentence incarcerated. With a two-year sentence, you could be out in less than a year."

Tom shook his head. "That's not right. You said in the report that she didn't see me. That's a lie."

"And who is *she*?" Eric asked, looking back at his stack of notes.

"Sorry, I meant *he*. Owens. He came downstairs before I had even lit the fire. We had an argument."

"Well, that's very strange." A faint smile crept across Eric's face. He spent a minute reviewing his notes while scribbling things in the margins of the page. "According to the police report, Mr. Owens said he was asleep in bed and only woke up when he saw smoke coming through the door to his second-floor bedroom. By the time he got out, you were already gone."

"Why would he lie?" I asked.

"I don't know, though depending on the circumstances, it could potentially be very good for our case if we do end up going to trial. In the meantime, don't tell me any more of what happened. If you do, I'll have to share it with the DA's office."

"I can't take a plea deal," Tom said. "I have to be here to protect my family. He can't keep getting away with this."

Eric looked like he wanted to ask another question, then stopped himself. "I promise, we will have plenty of time to talk about whether or not we go to trial and what our defense strategy will be. For now, I'd like to focus on just the basics so that I can get a more clear idea of what the prosecution is going to try and throw at us. Besides, I'm sure you want to spend some much-needed time with your family, and the sooner I can get through these initial details, the better equipped I can be to knock down any potential evidence or arguments the prose-cution might bring."

"What kind of potential evidence?" Tom asked.

"Because this is your first time being arrested, they're going to try and find other things from your past to make you seem like a crimi-nal. Generally, when it comes to arson, one of their main plays is going to be trying to profile you as the type of person who would commit this kind of act. Basically, they're going to pour through your childhood and try to work up a psychological profile to try and paint you as a psychopath or sociopath. When it comes to arson, there's three signs they generally look for in a juvenile's history. The first is a pattern of defecating or urinating in places other than the bathroom."

Tom barked out a laugh, then his eyes went wide when we all stared at him. "I've never even wet the bed."

"So that's a no?" Eric asked.

"That's a no," Tom said, still with a little humor in his voice.

I grabbed onto his hand, feeling a semblance of the man I fell in love with sitting at the table. It was a small comfort, but one I desper-ately needed.

Eric checked off something on a page. "All right. Next, they're going to be looking for traumatic incidents and how you responded to them. Oftentimes, arsonists light fires because they feel like they have no control in their lives. Do you now, or have you ever, believed you were under the control of divine or demonic forces?"

Tom chewed on his lip and paused longer than I would have liked. "You mean, telling people that I was possessed or something?"

"Or just that you felt like you weren't in control of your own actions."

Tom shook his head. "No, I've never said that."

The way he worded it was slightly concerning. I would have felt a lot more comfortable if he'd used the word *thought* instead of *said*.

"Oh, my mom died when I was young. That's something that was out of my control."

"All right. Following your mother's passing, did you act out in any ways that might give the prosecution reason to believe you might be unstable?"

"I don't think so. I mostly kept to myself as a kid. I had a couple incidents with bullies and the like, but that's all normal stuff, right?"

Eric jotted a note on his paper. "We'll look into it. The last one—and this is a big one—is a history of torturing or killing animals. Anything there?"

"Um." Tom stared down at the table, hiding his reaction to the question. "What if there's context?"

"Well, that depends on the context. What happened?"

"Is it all right if we talk about it later?" Tom asked, clearly not wanting me or Emma to hear whatever he had to say.

I'd read a portion of his book, and I thought I knew what he was referring to. If I was right, I had a feeling it wouldn't be all that incriminating.

"That's fine, though the sooner you can give me all the facts, the better equipped I will be to try and knock it down in court."

Tom let out a heavy sigh, but his despair quickly shifted to one of almost manic hope. "The book! Sarah, did you find it?"

I nodded. "Yes, but—"

"Where is it?"

"It's still in your studio."

Tom leapt to his feet. "I'll go get it. This will clear up everything."

Once he'd run out of the living room, Eric turned his attention to me. "You're familiar with the book to which he's referring?"

I nodded. "Yes, sort of. When he called from jail, he insisted I find it and read it."

"And did you?"

"I started, but I'm not sure how it's going to help—"

"Here it is." Tom rushed back into the room and delivered the book to Eric. "This is it. This is my silver bullet."

Both Eric and Emma stared at the cover of his book, depicting an evil-looking Christmas tree grinning in front of a pile of toys. Above the tree sat the title: *Everything Is Temporary*.

EXHIBIT 1C: AN EXCERPT FROM EVERYTHING IS TEMPORARY, BY TOM BARNES

It was spring break, and Tim was spending the day with the only other friend he had outside of the Christmas House. Danny Chung had been his classmate and best friend since kindergarten. Growing up, the two had been nearly inseparable. They had even lived on the same street before Tim's mom died and he had to move to an apartment across town.

Danny and Tim had been in the same class at Dundie Elementary...until last year, when Larry Enholm carved "Fuck the Whites" into the fifth-grade announcement corkboard above the drinking fountain with a push-pin. Because Larry was on the school's Blue Team, he'd engraved what he intended to be school spirit by sending a message to his rivals.

The principal, Mr. Evans, took it differently. To put it lightly, Tim's school lacked diversity. Aside from the twins, Julia and Stephanie Diaz, the only other non-white student in his class had been Danny. The twins were beyond reproach, being the two highest academic achievers in their grade. With no further investigation, Mr. Evans concluded it must have been Danny who carved the epithet into the corkboard and promptly had him expelled.

Nowadays, Tim only saw Danny once or twice a month, always at the Chung's residence. He was too ashamed to bring Danny to his bare and dirty apartment, and on top of that, his old man had little patience for the ruckus two pre-teen boys could cause.

On this particular day, they were lying on their bellies in Danny's backyard. Danny's old man had given him a BB gun for his birthday and encouraged his son to use it on the seagulls that would bathe in his pool. According to Mr. Chung, the bird poop ruined the finish on the pool's floor, so in order to deter them, Danny would lie in wait for a bird to land, then pelt it with a BB. The rifle worked on a pump-action, building pressure with each cocking of the lever. While it was plenty dangerous enough to hurt the birds, they never went past four pumps. At that power, it was more of an irritant than anything. Upon being hit, the gulls would let out an annoyed squawk and fly off. Oftentimes, the same bird would be back within ten minutes, and the process would repeat itself multiple times throughout the day.

So far, they had only seen one bird circle the pool, but it never made the approach for landing. Instead, the boys had taken minia-ture Bic lighters and stuffed them inside the torsos of some robot models Danny had assembled. They each took turns blasting away at the toys, hoping to land a shot that would cause the lighter to blow up the figurine.

"Are you sure you're okay destroying these?" Tim asked Danny. Tim didn't have a lot of toys, and it made him a little uncomfortable to be taking pot-shots at his friend's stuff.

"Alex Song's dad works for Bandai. He gets tons of those things for free."

Tim didn't know who Alex Song was, though he assumed it was one of Danny's many friends at his new school. While Danny's depar-ture from Dundie Elementary had been devastating for Tim, Danny ended up being grateful for moving to a larger school, where he now had seemingly dozens of friends.

"How's things at the old alma farter?" Danny asked. "Did you ever get the balls to tell Julia you like her?"

Tim shook his head. "I asked her to be lab partners in science, but she told me she was already partners with Megan Cater."

"Did you call her Julia or 'wife'?"

"I haven't called her 'wife' in forever," Tim lied. In the fourth grade, their school had put on a production of *A Christmas Carol*, in which Tim and Julia had been cast as Bob and Mrs. Cratchit. During the run of the show, and for a month or two afterward, they had jokingly referred to each other as husband and wife. In the time since, the joke had seemed to lose its entertainment value for Julia. Tim knew it, but he always got so nervous when talking to her, he felt like he had to remind her of their fictional chemistry by continuing to call her either "wife" or "Mrs. Cratchit."

"I'm too busy for romance right now. I've got an after-school job."

"Dude, we're twelve. What kind of job could you have that keeps you too busy to ask out Julia?"

Tim immediately regretted using the Christmas House as his excuse. He wasn't sure how much he wanted to share about his time with Mrs. Claus or the bizarre magical creatures inside. The two boys were already growing apart so quickly, Tim was afraid if he told Danny what he had been up to, his friend would think he was crazy. Hell, even Tim wasn't sure about it himself.

"If I tell you, I need you to promise me that you won't think I'm insane."

Danny shook his head. "No way, José."

Tim decided to go for it anyway. He told Danny the whole story about Mrs. Claus, the house, and all the magic inside. Danny sat in rapt attention as Tim described Evergreen, the talking tree, and the Candy Stripers, who it had turned out were quite the mischievous little pack. He even explained about the sick kids who would come to the house, and how even though it was sad, he felt he was really making a difference to help give these kids one last great day. Once he was finished, he held his breath, eagerly waiting for Danny's response.

"Bullshit," Danny said, waving a dismissive hand at Tim.

"It's not bullshit! We're really helping kids."

"No, dumbass, I'm calling bullshit on the whole thing. If there was a house that was fully decked out like Christmas all year round, I think I'd know about it. Especially if it was full of living toys."

Tim felt his face get hot with embarrassment. The way his friend looked at him reminded Tim of the time he had snuck over to Danny's house to watch *X-files* a month after his mom passed, and by some crazy coincidence, the episode happened to be about Mulder's mother dying. Tim had ended up crying, and instead of comforting him, Danny just stared awkwardly at the show, then pretended nothing happened later.

"Fine. Let's go." Tim sprung up off his belly and clapped some fallen palm tree detritus from his hands and shirt.

"What, now?" Danny asked. "But we're blowing up Gundams."

Tim's old man had taken away his bike when he tried to run away after a particularly nasty disagreement a few months ago, but Danny let him borrow his old rusty bike for their ride to the Christmas House.

"No...," Tim said as soon as they turned onto Jacaranda, skidding to a stop in front of Mrs. Claus's house.

All the twinkling lights lining the roof were unlit, and the inflatable display of Santa and Rudolph on the roof must have been deflated—they were nowhere to be seen. The signpost advertising all to enter was gone, and the side path leading to the Winter Wonderland was closed off by a wooden gate.

"Wow. Magical. Someone forgot to take down their string lights," Danny said, trying to sound as deadpan as he could while being out of breath from pedaling through the neighborhood. "It's like Christmas morning all over again."

"It's not usually like this, I swear."

"Suuuure. Is this your way of trying to get back at me for convincing you I was an extra in *Jumanji*?"

"No, I'm serious, Danny. It's all real. I come here almost every day. It's always open." Tim dismounted his bike and ran up to the gate. It was locked. Feeling his heart race, he moved to the front door and rang the bell. "Hello! Mrs. Claus, it's Tim, your little elf! Are you home?"

Silence.

"Evergreen? Are you in there?"

Danny stared at Tim the same way he had during the *X-files* episode. "Little elf? Dude, this is getting weird. Are you having some sort of breakdown? Do you need me to get your dad?"

"No," Tim shouted, forcing his growing hysteria into anger. "I'm not crazy."

He ran up to the window, trying to peer through the slats in the shade. For a second, he thought he saw movement, a pair of small white orbs darting across the room. But as he adjusted his head to get a better angle, a cloud shifted overhead, causing a glimmer of sunlight to cut across the pane, making him question what he saw.

"Whatever, dude," Danny said, clearly bored and a little weirded out. "Want to go back to my house and see if any gulls are taking dumps in my dad's pool?"

The next day, Tim nearly had to shut his eyes before he walked around the corner onto Jacaranda, for fear he would be confronted by the same, boring, drag-and-drop house he'd seen after his bike ride with Danny. If there was no Christmas House here, then he would have to confront the growing worry that he was suffering some sort of prolonged mental breakdown.

But before he even made it fully onto the street, the bobbing white antlers of Rudolph the Red-nosed Reindeer were visible swaying in the wind atop the roof. The sign stood where it always had, welcoming everyone who wished to experience Christmas in all its glory.

In a flash, Tim's relief turned to anger. Where had all of this been yesterday? Why, of all the days he had visited this house, was yesterday the *only* day Mrs. Claus had chosen to take everything down? Tim stormed through the door, wanting to slam it behind him but stopping himself only when he saw Mrs. Claus sitting in a rocking chair, reading her copy of *Over the River* to a small pale boy in a knitted blue cap.

"Oh, hello, Little Elf," Mrs. Claus said in her always cheery tone. "I'd like you to meet Jeffrey."

The little boy turned to Tim, his face stark white and hollow, aside from the bright gleam in his blue eyes. Tim forced a smile and raised his palm, to which Jeffrey returned an emphatic wave.

"Sorry, is now a bad time?" Tim asked, putting his frustration on hold in front of the little one.

"Not at all." Mrs. Claus shut her book. "Jeffrey, why don't we take a little break from the story while I talk to my little elf here. How would you like to explore the Winter Wonderland outside?"

Jeffrey nodded with just as much enthusiasm as he had waved.

"All right, then. It's just through the kitchen. I'll meet you outside in a minute." Once the kitchen door closed, Mrs. Claus returned her attention to Tim. "All right, Tim, what's on your mind?"

"Where were you yesterday?" Tim blurted. The words came out as more of an accusation than he had expected. "I only have one friend outside of this house, and now he thinks I'm crazy because I tried to show him this house and you had literally taken down all the decorations."

"Oh, I'm so sorry. I left you a note on the doorstep. The wind must have carried it away. Do you remember little Sally from last week's *Over the River* event? She passed, poor thing, and her family asked me to attend the memorial."

Tim's heart was yanked in multiple directions at once. It wasn't the first time Mrs. Claus had been invited to a memorial service. Tim knew it was a sad part of her reality. But at the same time, he still wanted to hold onto the anger over the situation that had left him feeling alienated from his friend.

"But why take down all the decorations? It didn't even look like the Christmas House!"

"I never leave the sign up when I'm not home. As much as I wish I could let people enjoy the house while I'm not around, I'm sorry to say, you just can't trust people these days. And when it comes to

Santa and Rudolph on the roof, well, I hate to admit it, but I don't have all that much money. They do run up the electricity bill!"

Tim wanted to stay mad, but he was running out of things to be upset about.

Mrs. Claus's face softened, and for a moment, she looked at him with a warmth that felt just like the way his mom used to. "I'm sorry, Tim. I really didn't mean to upset you."

"It's okay." Tim let his anger melt into disappointment. "I'm sorry I got mad."

"No need to apologize! You're still my little elf, right?" Mrs. Claus opened her arms, welcoming him in for a hug.

Tim nodded and squeezed her tightly. "Thanks, Mrs. Claus."

With all of that over with, Mrs. Claus excused herself to the backyard to finish reading to Jeffrey. Tim was about to leave when Evergreen came to life.

"Say, Tim, I'm sorry to hear about your friend yesterday."

"That's okay, Evergreen. I guess I'll bring him by another time."

The eyeball lights on the tree slid from side to side, as if glancing around in a conspiracy. "You know, if you'd like to prove that Christmas magic is real to your friends, you could always borrow an ornament or two."

Tim furrowed his brow. "But I thought only special kids who believe in the true spirit of Christmas can see you?"

"Normally, that's true, but with your faith and even a little bit of belief from your friend, there should be enough Christmas magic in these to make a believer of him."

Evergreen's branches rustled around and presented a pair of turtle doves. The porcelain birds hung from his branch, intertwined with each other as they nestled their heads and gently cooed.

"Why don't you grab that red box over there, and I'll have them fly into it. That should give him quite the surprise!"

As soon as Tim grabbed the small red box, the two turtle doves flew around the room and settled inside.

Tim grinned, sure this would finally get Danny to believe in him.

10

SARAH

"Tom, I need you to talk to me. What's really going on with you?"

We pulled up to Eric Walsh's office a little early after dropping Emma off at school.

Last night after the lawyer left, Tom had sat in the shower for nearly two hours. When he got out, he refused to talk about anything related to the case, insisting we have one night where we pretended to be normal. As much as I'd wanted to indulge in his fantasy of pretending none of this was going on, I just had too many questions piled on top of a mountain of anxiety. And as a cherry on top of my worry sundae, there was a moment in bed when he tried to snuggle into me. My heart craved his warmth, but my body had reacted differently, squirming away. He didn't try again, and I was too embarrassed to cuddle back.

Tom had sat in silence during the whole car ride, only speaking up to tell Emma he loved her before sending her off to school, promising he would be home by the end of the day. When he turned to look at me, his eyes were unfocused, and I could tell he was deep inside of his own head.

"Sarah, I know I've put our family through a lot this week, and when we go into the lawyer's office, the things you hear are going to sound unbelievable. I just...No matter how bizarre it sounds, no matter how crazy you may think I am, I need you to understand that everything I've done, everything I'm doing, is for your and Emma's safety. I don't know how this is going to end, but whatever happens, I need you to believe that above all else."

I wanted to be supportive, wanted to believe there was nothing he could say that would drive us apart, but his words had managed to send a shuddering chill through me. I don't know what scared me more—the ominous warning he knew he was going to sound crazy, or his deep conviction that our family was in danger. I nodded my head in support.

"I'll do my best to stay open-minded."

He sat in silence for another minute before speaking again. "I'm aware there's a very real chance that I'm going to prison for this. If that happens, don't worry about me. Just promise that you and Emma will get as far away from here as possible."

"What do you mean?" I asked. "We're not going anywhere."

"Just listen to me!" he snapped, his eyes turning to stone. "Owens, or whatever she's calling herself these days, is more dangerous than you could possibly imagine. The only reason she's doing this is to hurt me, and even if I'm behind bars, it won't stop her. She'll keep coming until she's destroyed everything I love."

This was the second time he had called Carl Owens "she," and it worried me this could be just the tip of the iceberg of what was to come. I had been looking forward to our meeting this morning—or at least as much as any person in this situation could—but as the minutes ticked closer to our appointment, a knot in my stomach began to grow. By the time we reached the door to his office, a voice in my head started screaming at me to turn back if I wanted to preserve any shred of understanding of the man I'd dedicated my life to for the last fifteen years. I closed my eyes, gripped the door handle, and pushed through as if I were taking the plunge into an ice-cold pool.

"Tom, Sarah, good to see you both again," Eric Walsh said when we stepped into his office.

It was a smaller operation than I had expected. Most law firms I'd seen on TV had dozens of people in suits always rushing from one meeting to the next. This place looked more like a temporary workspace. There was little decoration on the walls outside of some framed law degrees and a few cheap paintings, like you'd find in a hotel room. A planter I suspected to be plastic took up a corner of the office, and the whole place had a grayness that tamped down my spirits even further.

"I'd like you to meet my team." Eric gestured to the only two other people in the office.

He formally introduced me to Missy, the woman I'd spoken to on the phone Monday. She was a petite brunette in her early thirties, with huge blue eyes and high cheekbones. Missy wore a bright red suit that felt like the only source of light in the whole office.

In a sharp juxtaposition to Missy, the man behind her didn't even seem to have his eyes open. They were small and beady, hidden under a heavy brow. His acne-scarred face was mostly obscured by a large beard. The man must have stood at nearly six five while hunched over. Eric introduced him as Angus, his investigator.

Once we'd met the team, Eric led us to a small room with plastic chairs and a scuffed gray table. He urged us to sit down and shut the door behind him. The table had a stack of folders, and on top of it sat *Everything Is Temporary*.

"Quite an interesting read." Eric set the book aside and opened the folders. "Kind of reminded me of that movie about the clown in the sewers." Eric let out a mild chuckle but cut it off when he saw the sheepish look on Tom's face. "Sorry. How about we get straight to business. Yesterday, we went over the preliminary evidence against you and what you might expect in terms of a legal battle. Today is all about getting your story and figuring out the best way to build a defense for your case. I know we talked while you were in jail, but I'd like to go over the whole thing again from the top, if that's okay. Let's start with what happened on Sunday."

Tom nodded solemnly and took several deep breaths. Underneath the table, I reached out and held his hand. It was only then that he began to speak.

"It started with the call from security. Emma had chosen to ride a Christmas-themed kiddie ride, of all things, and damaged it." He pointed to his book, as if it were an incredibly important detail. "As we entered the mall to pick her up, I passed by...Mr. Owens and recognized him." Tom paused mid-sentence, making sure he gendered Owens correctly.

"And how did you recognize him? Where had you seen Mr. Owens before?" Eric asked, his elbows on the table, fingers forming a tent over his documents.

"I hadn't. Not exactly."

"Then how did you know who he was?"

Tom's eyes shot up and to the ceiling corner, unwilling to look at any of us. "He was wearing a different skin."

My jaw nearly dropped when Tom threw out such a wild statement, but he quickly followed it up as if he were reading my mind.

"I know how insane it sounds. But even though he looked different, I could still feel *who* it was inside. Like, deep down, when you just know something in your gut and it's the most true thing in the universe. I just knew. Again, I'm aware this is going to be hard to believe, but I promise, if you let me finish the story, it will all make sense."

I was gnawing on my already torn-up cheek, praying Tom didn't look over to see whatever face of shock I'm sure was painted across it. Luckily, he kept his attention on Eric, who proved to have a much better poker face than I did.

"Go on," Eric said.

"So, after I had already seen Owens on the escalator, he appeared again on the security footage the guard showed us. At that point, I already had my hunch that he was targeting Emma. A few things clicked into place there. Emma was riding a Santa ride, which to me signaled she had been spending time in this new version of the Christmas House. It was just too big of a coincidence to ignore that Owens was there in the same footage as her riding Santa's sleigh. It also explained why she refused to introduce us to this mysterious friend she kept going on about. Even more importantly, it explained *why* she used the name Janice for this friend."

"This is because of the character named Janice in your book?" Eric asked.

Tom nodded, and at this point, he truly lost me with his story. I hadn't been able to make it more than a third through his novel before Tom handed it off to Eric. From what I'd read, no one with that name had shown up yet.

"I'm sorry," I interjected. "I haven't had a chance to finish the book yet, and this is all sounding very confusing to me. Who is Janice?"

Tom let out a sigh, clearly frustrated his lawyer had finished his book but not his own wife. "Janice was one of the victims in the book and part of the reason why I feel confident that Owens is targeting us. He's using the name Janice as a way to taunt me."

His explanation didn't do much to clear anything up, aside from making me feel stupid for not having had time to finish reading his novel.

Tom continued his story. "So, all of those things seemed pretty damning to me, but I still needed to be sure. It was all, um, circum-stantial evidence. Isn't that what you lawyers say? I had to find real proof. When we got home, I searched Emma's room. That's where I found this." Tom reached into a shoulder bag he had brought into the office and placed the red hat with the jingling bell on the table.

"And this constituted sufficient proof for you because..."

"Because it's almost exactly what she gave me."

"And by she, you mean..."

"Mrs. Claus. Mr. Owens."

I thought I had prepared myself as much as I could to understand Tom's story, but the further he got into it, the more I found myself feeling like I was on some sort of sick hidden-camera show meant to push me to the brink of insanity. The only thing holding me back from speaking up was that Tom and Eric were speaking with such sincerity, I somehow worried I would be the one being ridiculed by bringing up how bizarre this story was.

Eric nodded, just to further illustrate how seriously he was taking Tom's story. "So, you're saying that Mrs. Claus, a character from a novel, and Mr. Owens are the same person."

"That's what I'm getting to. The hat is almost exactly the same as the one I was given when I was a kid." Once again, Tom dug through his bag, then produced the ratty green costume I had found in Tom's junk box while searching for the book. "I knew at that point that I had to do something to protect our daughter. I know I said the book was fiction, and this is where I'm sure you're going to try to get me committed, but it's not actually a novel. It's a journal. Everything that happened in there is true. Every single word of it took place exactly as it's written."

"I see," Eric said flatly. "So tell me, what did you do, now that you had what you believed to be the evidence you needed to prove that Mr. Owens and Mrs. Claus were indeed the same individual?"

"I couldn't sleep that night, so I took my bike out and went searching for Mr. Owens's house."

"I think I know where you're going with this, but for my records, please explain how you knew what to look for."

Tom nodded. "I was looking for a house that had full Christmas decorations, something that either had a sign or a place for a sign that would encourage strangers to wander into their home. I was looking for the Christmas House."

"And you found it?"

Tom's eyes went wide. He let go of my hand and threw his own out to his sides. "I had to do whatever I could to protect my family." He turned to me. "To protect you."

I was trying so hard to keep quiet, to let him tell his story without jumping in, but something on my face must have shown him my exponentially growing concern.

"I'm not crazy."

"Honey...," I said, with nothing to follow it up with.

Luckily, Eric took the reins of the conversation from there.

"No one here is saying you are, Tom."

"But you're not saying you believe me either."

"No, I'm not because that's not my job. What I'm here to do is build the best defense possible to protect you from the prosecution. If you say this book contains evidence that helps prove that you were proactively acting in self-defense for you or your family, then that's what I have to run with."

"So you're going to use it as evidence?" Tom asked.

Eric unfolded his fingers, presenting open palms to the table. "I have to. The moment you gave it to me and told me that it was relevant to your case, it became a part of discovery. What I *will* tell you is the concern I have. When you gave me this book yesterday, you told me it was the silver bullet in your case. In that respect, I can't help but agree. The worry I have is whether it's a silver bullet for the defense or the prosecution. These characters in your book, you say they're all real people?"

"I changed the names a little bit, but yeah."

Eric nodded. "If we were to go to trial and bring them onto the stand, would they corroborate your story?"

Tom stared down at the table, clearly troubled by Eric's question. "I'd rather not bring them into this if possible."

Something about the way he said it gave me a shiver, like ice had just been poured through my veins.

"And why is that?" Eric asked.

"If you've read the book, you'd know I've already put them through enough. I don't want to bring them back into this again if I don't have to. I'd managed to put this out of my head for decades. It was the only thing I could do to find a way to live something resembling a normal life."

Eric placed his hand on top of the book, as if it were some sort of a holy tome. "If you want to have any chance at a jury believing the things you've written in this book, you're going to need at least some of these people to corroborate the details you're intending to convey as fact. Do you understand?"

Tom rubbed a pair of tired hands in circles around his eyes. "Fine. You can reach out to Terry and Julia. They might agree to talk if you reach out to them."

Eric scribbled the names onto a legal pad. "I'm guessing Terry is Larry from the book?"

Tom nodded.

"Can you give me their full names?"

"Larry Enholm is actually Terry Enbom. I think he owns a bunch of car washes in Santa Ana these days. Julia Diaz is actually Julia Dominguez. She's the CEO of some company in L.A."

"How do you know all this?" I asked.

"I follow them on Social," he said dismissively.

"Okay, this is potentially helpful information." Eric nodded, like he was finally getting somewhere. "The prosecution is likely going to be going after your psychological profile. Having character witnesses from your youth that will speak on your behalf could go a long way to convincing a jury that you had legitimate reason to believe your daughter was in danger. Now, I'm going to ask you something, and before you answer, I want you to think carefully about what this could mean for your case, as it could spell the difference between you walking away a free man or serving seven to life. Is it possible that Mr. Owens and Mrs. Claus from your novel are different people but have some sort of other connection?"

For once, it was Tom's turn to look confused. "What do you mean?"

"I'm asking if you think Mrs. Claus and Mr. Owens could be two separate people who perhaps knew each other, and as Mr. Owens grew up, could he have carried on her work?"

Tom started to shake his head but stopped himself short of speaking. "I don't believe that to be the case, but yes, it's possible."

Eric nodded. This time, he even smiled. "Good. That's very good. I'm going to have my investigator, Angus, look into both of their pasts to see if there's a chance they could have lived in the same town at the same time."

"But that's what I wanted to talk about before," Tom said, his eyes lighting up once again. "We had this exchange in his house when I was getting ready to light the fire. He knew who I was. He even invited me to do it."

Whatever small victory Eric thought he'd won quickly evaporated, and his face soured. "You're saying that Mr. Owens openly asked you to start a fire in his home?"

Tom nodded. "Absolutely. That's how I knew it was the same person as Mrs. Claus."

Eric sat in silence for a minute, clearly trying to come up with a response. "Unfortunately, because there are no witnesses to this conversation, it's your word against his, regardless of what you claim happened. I don't see how we can use this in the case unless Mr. Owens recants his initial claim that he was in bed at the time."

Tom looked like he had something else to say. He seemed frustrated, like he'd just won a gold medal, only to have the award stripped away from him at the podium.

"Let's move on," Eric said. "Now, I know you changed the names of your friends in the book. Did you ever learn the real name of Mrs. Claus?"

Tom shook his head. "The best I ever got was Sandra Claus."

"That's okay. We have other ways of learning about her. Do you remember the address she lived at when you were a kid?"

"Not the numbers, but it was on Jacaranda. On the right side of the street. I'll never forget that."

"Okay. This gives us a few leads to track down. I'll have Angus investigate her as well as your childhood friends."

"I want to talk to them," I heard myself say. "Terry and Julia. If it's all right, I'd like to meet with them."

At my suggestion, it was suddenly as if I were looking at the two theater masks representing comedy and tragedy. Eric seemed pleased, but Tom looked horrified at the suggestion of me meeting figures from his past.

"Maybe they'll be more willing to talk if they're approached by someone who really knows Tom." My point seemed cogent enough, though in reality, I think I volunteered because I was starting to feel afraid to be around Tom.

While there were a number of similarities in the stories he'd told, particularly about the house and program for sick kids, his utter conviction that there were people masquerading in the skins of others was frightening to me. I needed to find out for myself whether Tom's mind had created some wild story to cope with a traumatic incident in his childhood or if he was actually in the midst of some sort of psychotic episode.

"All right. One last thing before we break for today," Eric said. "Your daughter, Emma. She's admitted to spending all this time with Mr. Owens, correct?"

The reminder of my daughter spending any amount of time with this stranger sent my nerves into full fight-or-flight mode. "Yes. She told me everything after she heard me mention his name," I replied. "She says Mr. Owens has done nothing inappropriate and didn't mention anything out of the ordinary."

"I hate to bring this up, but if we do end up going to trial, one of the biggest plays we have in your case is the fact that this man lured a minor into his home for a period of months without your permission or knowledge."

"Absolutely not," Tom and I said simultaneously.

We both knew where Eric was headed, and there was no way either of us were going to put our daughter through any more trauma than necessary. No matter what I thought about Tom at this moment, at least we could both agree nothing was more important than keeping our Emma as far from this as possible.

She would not testify, under any circumstance.

EXHIBIT 1D: AN EXCERPT FROM EVERYTHING IS TEMPORARY, BY TOM BARNES

Tim stared at the clock, watching the seconds tick by until class would be excused for lunch. He already had his backpack open, with the ham sandwich he'd made sitting in a brown paper bag on top. As hungry as he was, he had a more pressing matter to attend to first.

The second Mrs. Callahan let them out, Tim gunned it to the bathroom to relieve himself. By the time he re-emerged, there was a large congregation of kids, all laughing and cheering. They'd formed a circle in the middle of the quad. He couldn't explain how, but he had a feeling in his gut something terrible was about to happen. It was at that moment Tim realized he'd stupidly left his backpack sitting on his chair before running to his bathroom break and remembered the comment Larry had made weeks ago about stealing his lunch.

Tim approached the congregation of not just sixth graders, but also fifth and fourth graders, all sharing the lunch period. As he got closer, kids noticed him and began to point and laugh, making his heart feel like it was beating a million times a second. He pushed through the crowd, and what he saw, what he heard, was so much worse than he could have even thought.

Larry Enholm was dancing in the center of the circle. Tim's backpack sat beside him, and Larry was wearing Tim's pointy green elf hat, singing his own song to the tune of *Holly Jolly Christmas.*

"Have a merry fairy Christmas. It's the wrong time of the year. It never snows, and Tim's a psycho. It's why his mom killed herself last year."

Larry's song cut off once he noticed Tim watching. He grinned, showing off the massive gap between his front teeth.

"Look! Here he comes! The little fairy prince himself! You gonna jingle some bells for us?"

Everyone was laughing. Tim's stomach flipped over, and he felt hot tears stream down his face. He tried to think of something, anything, to say, any way to defend himself. His lungs had no air in them, except to hiccup out the first of what was sure to be a full-on crying fit. He shoved his way through the jeering crowd and sprinted across the field to the utility closet, where the PE teacher stored all the sports equipment. Tim shut the door behind himself.

It was pitch-black in there, but he didn't care. He sank to the floor, curled into a ball, and sobbed. About a minute later, someone knocked on the door.

"Go away!" he shouted.

"Tim, are you okay?" a muffled girl's voice called through.

"Just leave me alone," he pleaded.

"Are you sure, Mr. Cratchit?"

A confusing wave of emotions crashed over him when he realized the voice on the other side of the door belonged to Julia Diaz, the girl he'd had a crush on since forever. It took him a few seconds to try and calm himself down enough to not look like even more of a total fool in front of her.

He opened the door just a crack. Even though Julia and her sister, Stephanie, were identical twins, Tim never made the mistake of confusing the two. To most people, the only way to tell the difference between them came down to a tiny pair of freckles on Julia's chin. To Tim, they couldn't have been more different.

"I got your backpack and hat back from Larry."

"Thanks."

"Can I come in?"

Tim let out what he hoped to be the last sniffle of his crying episode, wiped his eyes with his sleeve, then scooted himself over to let her in. He watched as Julia slid through the crack in the door and sat across from him. She had dark skin, with straight black hair that looked like the softest thing in the world. Her face was long and narrow, with a chin that stuck out a little, reminding Tim of a crescent moon.

"Unfortunately, during his dance, Larry seemed to have stomped on your lunch. It's beyond saving. If you want, you can have half of mine. It's turkey. I have some apple slices too."

Tim nodded. "Thanks. You didn't have to do that."

"I know. I'm just so sick of the way Larry picks on you."

"It's okay. I always have to remind myself that everything is temporary. I just need to make it through the end of the year and hope that we end up at different middle schools."

There was an awkward silence as the two ate their sandwiches. This was the longest conversation he'd had with Julia all year, and he had no idea what to say.

"So, why *do* you have a Christmas elf outfit in your backpack, if you don't mind my asking?"

Tim's face flushed, and he was thankful to be in such a dark room. "I got an after-school job, sort of. It's at a house that lets sick kids experience Christmas if it doesn't seem like they're going to make it to the end of the year."

"Are you serious?" she asked.

Tim could feel his embarrassment double. For better or worse, everyone had treated him differently after his mom died, and he worried that telling Julia of his after-school activities would make her think he was morbid, or sad.

Instead, she said the last thing he expected. "That's the most incredible thing I've ever heard."

Tim lifted his head in shock. "Really?"

"That must be so hard. I couldn't imagine the strength it must take to keep your spirits up in a situation like that. Especially when

—" She stopped herself from finishing the sentence about his mother's death. "I just thought you'd hate Christmas after what happened."

"That's how my old man sees it. I don't know. Being around Christmassy stuff kind of keeps her alive for me, in a weird way. It's hard to explain. I just have so many happy memories of her at Christmas, I want to feel like she's around all year. If I can help anyone else feel good...it makes me feel good too."

Julia listened to him with her full attention. Something about her eyes made him feel more than just heard; he was understood.

That was the biggest difference between Julia and her twin. Julia was thoughtful with her words and caring in a way that made her the most beautiful girl in the world. By comparison, Stephanie was an outspoken know-it-all who never missed an opportunity to show off her superior intellect.

"Can I tell you something else weird?" he said.

Julia nodded.

"My old man doesn't know this, and if he found out, he would probably take away my TV. My mom and I used to watch *A Christmas Story* every day of December. Ever since...that day, I can't sleep unless I have it playing on my TV. I've watched it almost every night for over a year now." Tim cringed as he spoke, afraid he'd once again overshared.

Julia smiled.

"What? Is that too weird?"

"No, it's not that. It's just funny," she admitted. "I sort of have a similar habit. It's not just one movie, though. I can't stop watching romantic comedies. I think I've seen *You've Got Mail* at least a hundred times by now."

"Does Stephanie like it too?" Tim asked, assuming the two girls shared a bedroom.

Julia laughed. "She can't stand it. I think I was able to bring her around to *She's All That* for a while, but she doesn't like anything that isn't going to make her smarter. She basically only watches documentaries with my parents."

"Why do you like romantic comedies so much?" Tim asked.

Julia sat in contemplative silence, trying to find a way to properly articulate herself. "Now it's your turn to keep a secret, okay?"

Tim nodded, feeling a piece of his heart melt as the only girl he'd ever liked prepared to entrust him with something personal.

"I love my sister, and in a lot of ways, we're very much alike. But sometimes, I think she might be a robot."

Tim couldn't help but laugh. "What, do you have to plug her in at night?"

"No," she said with a smile. "I just don't think she feels emotions the same way as most people. And we're so alike in so many other ways, I worry that maybe..." Julia winced, then took another second to rephrase. "I keep having this nightmare that I'm in *The Wizard of Oz* and I'm the Tin Man, but Dorothy never shows up. It makes me worry that I don't have a heart. At least, not like other people. So, I watch romantic movies like *10 Things I Hate About You* to see what it's like to be in love. Talk about crazy." She let out a nervous giggle.

"Don't take offense at this, but you're nothing like your sister. You have the biggest heart of anyone I know."

An idea sprang into Tim's mind, quickly followed by a streak of panic. He clutched at his backpack, feeling for the small red box inside his front-zippered pocket. It was still there and, thankfully, still intact. "What are you doing after school today?"

"Just homework, why?"

"Do you remember Danny Chung?"

"Of course." Julia nodded.

"I'm going to his place to show him something special that I got from the Christmas House. Do you maybe want to come with me?"

———

Danny's eyebrows nearly lifted off the top of his face when Tim showed up after school with Julia by his side. As they walked down the hallway to his room, Danny elbowed Tim several times in the ribs. Tim worried Julia would notice, but she seemed busy looking at all the family pictures along the wall. It gave Tim a moment to quickly flash Danny a goofy grin of pure excitement.

"All right. Time to put up or shut up. Let's see it," Danny said.

"Hold your horses. I got 'em right here." Tim gently placed his backpack on Danny's bed, then unzipped the front pocket and removed the small red ornament box. "Okay, so before I open this, I need you both to promise you won't freak out when you see inside."

"I will never make that promise," Danny said in his trademark deadpan humor.

"What do you have in there?" Julia asked.

"There's something I didn't tell you about the Christmas House. You know how people throw around the term 'Christmas magic' in movies and stuff?"

She nodded.

"Well, as it turns out, it's actually real, as long as you believe."

Tim lifted the lid. Inside were a pair of ceramic turtle doves entwined so the head of each dove rested on the back of the other.

"Wow. Mind blown," Danny said in an ongoing monotone voice.

"Just give them a minute to wake up." Tim carefully lifted them out of the box and placed them on Danny's bed.

The ornaments remained perfectly still. As the moments passed, an anxiety rose from Tim's chest. Doubt started to creep in. What if they didn't do anything? What if the magic that brought all these little figurines to life only worked inside of the Christmas House? Or worse, what if Tim actually *was* crazy?

"Oh my God," Julia gasped as one turtle dove's wings slowly began to flap, speeding up until it had taken flight and started soaring around the room.

Relief poured through Tim. Ever since he met Evergreen and the rest of the magical ornaments, he worried he had been experiencing some extended form of hallucination. But now, there was no denying it. The ornament was flying in front of both of his friends. Christmas magic was real.

"Hang on a second." Danny picked up the other turtle dove. "Nice try, dude."

"What do you mean?" Tim's heart began to sink just as quickly as it had inflated.

"Look at this. It's a frickin' wind-up toy."

"No, it's not!" Tim argued, his voice rising several octaves.

"Look here. You can see the joints in the wings. Alex Song's sister has a set just like these. They're like Littlest Pet Shop, but they can fly around and stuff."

Tim snatched the ornament from Danny, scouring the figurine. "What are you talking about? There's no wind-up crank, no battery compartment. It's flying on its own!"

"Look here." Danny pointed to a small seam separating the wings from the body that Tim had sworn wasn't there before. "I don't know how it's powered, but this is just a toy, dude."

As if on cue, the other turtle dove flying around the room suddenly smacked into a wall and came crashing to the floor. Despite the bird's collision, its wings still flapped endlessly and aimlessly.

Julia bent over and picked up the ornament, inspected it carefully, then gave Tim a soulful look with her big brown eyes. "To be fair, it does look really *convincing*," she said, attempting to show understanding.

Tim recognized it as pity.

He opened his mouth to try to explain what Evergreen had told him. Only kids who had faith in Christmas could see the magic. If only they'd believed, *truly believed*, then they'd see.

But they didn't. They couldn't. How could they? Julia and Danny hadn't been through what Tim had. They hadn't seen what Tim had. They hadn't been tormented, like Larry had done to him, neglected by his father, or abandoned by his mother. They had other things to hold onto, grounding them in this world. All he had left was Christmas.

Tim turned away from them, forcing himself to calm down. Somewhere in the distance, he swore he saw the same two floating white balls that had been inside of Mrs. Claus's house the day he brought Danny over.

He wanted to mention it but couldn't bring himself to face the fallout of them failing to recognize that anomaly as well. Instead, Tim forced himself to pretend like he was letting go of it all and turned back to face them, nodding in agreement. "I guess I just really wanted it to be real and got too excited."

Danny patted Tim on the shoulder. "Don't worry, buckaroo. I'll still visit you at the funny farm."

11

SARAH

On the way home from the lawyer's, Tom didn't speak except to say the one thing I was dreading.

"You think I'm crazy."

"No," I replied. I meant to follow it up with something more convincing, to let him know that I would be his rock during his darkest hour, but I struggled to find the words. I'd been trying so hard to keep myself together, I hadn't spent enough time thinking about how much worse this must be for him. I wanted to do whatever I could to help him feel better, but at the same time, I couldn't see how I could lie and tell him I believed the increasingly unbelievable claims he'd been making.

"You know I love you more than anything in this world, and I will always be here for you. I think that something happened when you were young, that for some reason you felt like you couldn't share with me. And now, it's coming out in a way that you've been unprepared to handle."

"So you don't believe in the book."

"I haven't had a chance to read the whole thing yet. I had to hire your lawyer, deal with your bail, and take care of our daughter. I want to talk about it, but you refuse to tell me anything until I've finished your book. How about this—as soon as we get home, I'll read the rest of it, and then we can talk."

Eric Walsh had scanned and made several copies of *Everything Is Temporary* for his own investigation, as well as to share with the prosecution. He had held onto the original as evidence and provided me with one of the print-out copies.

Tom nodded, slightly at first, but quickly growing in assurance. "Okay."

Hearing that I would read the rest of his book seemed to calm him, at least for the time being. When we pulled into the driveway, Tom immediately went to his studio, claiming he wanted to give me privacy to read. But the first thing I did when I got into the house was call my parents to see if they were available to come help look after Emma while I was away for a day or so to interview Terry and Julia. I'd kept them somewhat in the loop, trying mostly to downplay the situation as a misunderstanding. This time, I had to admit things were serious, I was afraid to leave Tom alone, and I needed their help. They said they would pack up from their home in Palm Springs and be here by dinner time.

Before sitting down to read the rest of the story, there was one last thing I needed to do. I went to our family desktop computer and did some searching for Terry Enbom and Julia Dominguez. I started out on Social, since that's where Tom said he had kept up with them. The browser was already logged into his account, so I figured it would make it easier to look them up.

Terry was easy to find. Like Tom said, he owned a number of car washes around Orange County. His photo seemed almost identical to the man described in the book, except he was bigger and his hair was thinning. But when I went to look up Julia, her name didn't pop up under Tom's friends list. I tried to do a general search for her but couldn't find anyone even remotely matching Tom's description, or who listed their occupation as CEO.

I started to type in a Google search for "Julia Domiguez CEO Los Angeles," but by the time I had typed JUL, the search auto-populated the rest for me. The results page brought up a purple link at the top, meaning it had already been viewed. It was a *Techbounce* article about a company called WatAir, started and run by one Julia Dominguez. Her company's mission was to make a cheap and portable device that created purified drinking water out of moisture molecules in the air. It sounded like her, but there were no pictures.

I couldn't explain why I did it, but I logged out of Tom's Social account and signed into mine. Once again, I searched her name, and a woman who matched the description in the book popped up immediately, also confirming her position at WatAir. This set off multiple alarm bells in my head. First, she looked shockingly similar to me, with the exceptions that her skin was a bit darker and her chin came to more of a point. What worried me even more was my realization that the reason she didn't pop up on Tom's Social account was because she must have blocked him.

I then went back into my browser and looked up the computer's search history. As it turned out, Tom had searched for both Julia and Larry the night before he got arrested.

My quest for answers had only led to more questions. Tom had said he didn't want them involved but had been looking them up in the middle of the night. I found phone numbers for both businesses and called to try and set up appointments with each of them.

Because of my new concerns regarding their relationships with Tom, I called using my maiden name, posing as a potential franchisee for Enbom Car Wash and Detail. It was my hope to meet with Terry to discuss expanding to San Diego. The man on the other end of the line was more than happy to set up an appointment for mid-day tomorrow.

Julia was harder to reach. I told the receptionist at WatAir I was working with an environmental group looking to use their product in combination with other quality-of-life improvements in developing countries. The woman sounded skeptical, and when she asked for the name and website of my company, I froze and hung up. I would need to find another way to reach Julia.

I was about to step away from the computer but then decided to search for one last thing. I typed in "Year round Christmas houses, childrens hospital" into the search bar and hit enter. I was shocked to find dozens of results chronicling houses that did exactly what Tom described in his book. As it turned out, there were Christmas houses operating year-round in nearly every major city in the country, and almost every one seemed exactly like the one described in his book.

I spent the next hour and a half finishing *Everything Is Temporary*, but the more unbelievable the story got, the more difficulty I had concentrating. There was no way anyone in their right mind would believe any of this was true. If it went to court and the media somehow got involved, it could turn our whole lives even more upside down than they already were. I thought of Emma and how she would have to carry the weight of her father's mad claims following her for the rest of her life.

There was another idea I had, one I'd been fighting to entertain even for a second, but upon finishing the book, I just couldn't help myself. I gathered my car keys and made my way to Tom's studio. When I tried to open the door, it didn't budge. He'd locked himself inside.

In the fifteen years since we had been married, not once had he ever locked the door while he was in there. I knocked.

"Did you finish the book already?" Tom asked from inside.

"I did," I said, dreading what would come next.

"Hang on a second."

I heard him madly scramble around in his gallery. By the time he opened the door and ushered me inside, his work table was completely covered in a large brown canvas tarp.

"Listen, before you say anything, I want to show you something." He hurried over to the cardboard box marked "Tom's Junk" and pulled out a small red ornament box.

"Tom, please, you don't have to—"

"I promise, it's fine. Here, look." He opened the box, and sitting inside were two toy turtle doves. "They're not real. I know they're toys. I know there's no such thing as Christmas magic."

A tentative wave of relief washed over me, enough for me to

unclench my jaw, which I had just realized I'd been doing ever since our meeting with the lawyer.

"I know there's a lot of crazy shit in that book, and I know it's not all real."

"But in the meeting, you were so sure. You said it was a journal—"

"I know what I said, and I can't explain everything fully, but you know me. You know the way that my brain works. I have a tendency to take things and internalize them in a way that might feel a bit more...whimsical than most. I'll be honest with you, I don't remember a lot of the things that happened back then. I know that something bad happened. Mrs. Claus, Mr. Owens, whoever they are, they hurt me and my friends in a way that I've had to find a way to cope with."

This was not what I was expecting to hear. He was finally opening up in a way that sounded like my husband.

"I don't know what to say."

"You don't have to say anything. It was unfair of me to put all of this on you while I was in the midst of a monumental breakdown." His eyes rolled up to the ceiling, and he bobbed his head a few times. "Let me rephrase that—while I *am currently* in the midst of a mental breakdown. I wish I could tell you the real story, all the details of what actually happened, but ever since the mall incident, I've been having a lot of trouble seeing things clearly. I've been reliving some trauma that I've spent a lifetime trying to lock away."

I reached out and grabbed onto him, holding my husband in a tight embrace. "Whatever it is you're going through, just know I'm here for you. Even if you do believe in magical turtle doves, I'll be right by your side, as long as we can work our way through it together."

When we had finished with our embrace, he stepped back and held me by my shoulders, his eyes suddenly growing serious. "Whatever happened, whatever *happens*, there is one thing that I do need you to believe. I may not remember exactly how I recognize him, but I know with all my heart that Carl Owens is dangerous. I know I really messed up by going about things the way I did. I panicked. But you have to believe me when I say that we need to do everything we can to keep Emma away from him. Okay?"

I nodded, feeling a twinge of guilt for what I was about to do. "Okay. I believe you," I said.

Tom blew out a breath of air, making him look like an anvil had just been lifted off his chest. "Oh, thank God." He pulled me in again and gave me another hug.

"Listen," I said, while we were still in the midst of our embrace, "I have to run out to get a few groceries for dinner. I asked my parents to come down to help out with Emma while I'm away and—"

Tom disengaged, and for a moment, all I could see was hurt on his face. My pulse started to pound as he looked at me. Finally, he nodded with acceptance.

"You're right. I...*We* need some help right now. I understand." Tom nodded again for emphasis. "Is it okay if I stay here for a bit?" he asked, like I had suddenly become his parent.

"Sure," I replied, then headed out of his studio for the car.

"Hey, I love you," he said when I was about halfway down the driveway.

"I love you too."

I wanted more than anything to believe everything he had just told me, but as I got in my car, I watched him shut the door, then heard the lock click shut again. I hated the thoughts running through my head. In the book, he had done almost the exact same thing to appease his friends when they started to look at him funny. Did he really mean everything he just said? Could I actually believe him?

I hadn't been sure if I was going to go through with my plan, but after talking to Tom, I just needed to know.

I started the car, and made my way to do the one thing he had begged me not to.

12

SARAH

The house I was looking for was incredibly easy to spot. It was a two-story cottage-style home with plastic icicles running across the roof's edge. A candy-striped pole sat in front of a side gate; however, it appeared to be closed. There was no sign welcoming me, like the one from Tom's book. No inflatable animals on the roof.

I rang the doorbell. My heart immediately began to race.

This was a bad idea.

What was I doing?

Eric had specifically told all of us to have no contact with Mr. Owens, and I didn't want to do or say anything that could hurt the case. Furthermore, I felt horrible for betraying Tom's only wish. As I waited at the door, I couldn't help but replay the one point he had emphasized in our conversation.

Owens is dangerous.

I was about to lose my nerve, turn around, when a voice called out from inside the house. "One minute!"

The door opened slowly. The first thing I noticed was an almost overwhelming smell of chocolate chip cookies. Standing before me was a rather meek-looking man. He was shorter than me, overweight, with little hair on his head and almost pink skin. The man looked anxious, as if he were opening the door to a SWAT team ready to take him down. From his appearance, I could see nothing threatening, with the exception of a milky glaze over one eye that I would describe as more off-putting than frightening.

"Can I help you?" he asked in a small voice.

"Hi, my name is Jen Walsh," I said, stealing the name of my now-former assistant. "Are you Carl Owens?"

He gave me an almost imperceptible nod.

"I'm with the *Union Tribune*. We're doing an article about leaders in the community. We recently became aware of your program with the local children's hospital and were hoping to do an interview."

"Oh, no, thank you. I'm not looking for any recognition," he said with clear discomfort.

"Are you sure? From what I understand, you've helped a lot of kids. An article like this could make other hospitals in the area aware of your efforts. More exposure could allow you to do more good."

Carl looked at his feet and made a face like he was trying to dry-swallow a mouthful of pills. "I'm honored that you would want to talk to me, but I'm afraid I had a small house fire recently, and my home's not really in any shape for visitors—"

"I'm not here to take pictures. If now's not a good time, we can always have our photographer come another day. We could just talk today, maybe get a few quotes?"

He considered me for a few moments, and I worried that maybe he had seen right through my cover story. "Okay, but please watch your feet. I'm still cleaning, and I'd hate to have you step on a nail or something." Carl stepped back and opened the door fully to usher me inside.

When I entered his home, the smell of cookies was marred by an invading odor of burnt wood. The house *was* Christmas-themed, but it certainly wasn't the over-the-top extravaganza described in *Everything Is Temporary*. To my immediate right, there was a cheap plastic tree with nothing but some string lights adorning its otherwise bare branches. Scorch marks licked the side of a wooden cabinet which had some decorations on display. It was mostly covered in plates that looked like they had been decorated by kids with crayons. On one shelf, there were some ceramic Hummel figurines—maybe a dozen in all.

The fire damage looked to be mostly superficial. Almost everything in the room had char marks, but it didn't look like there was any real damage to the staircase or walls. The carpet seemed to have suffered the worst of it, exposing a blackened wood floor underneath.

It was impossible not to notice *some* similarities, but then again, I'd known dozens of people who collected Hummel figurines in my lifetime. They were a fairly ordinary Christmas decoration. And for that one similarity, there were more things dissimilar than matching. The majority of the decorations were tinsel and string lights. No candy canes, nutcrackers, train sets, or gifts piled around the place where a tree should be.

"Again, apologies for the mess. I'm hoping to have the floors redone soon, but I'm trying to find a quote that I can afford. Can I offer you some cookies? I've been trying to get the burnt smell out using air fresheners, but the only thing that seems to do the trick is baking." When Carl spoke, he often paused to inhale in the middle of sentences. It was as if the simple act of talking caused him to need to catch his breath. He turned his back and headed for the kitchen, walking with a slight limp.

"No cookies for me, thanks." I followed him into his kitchen. It was a cramped room with a small table tucked into the corner.

"Well, let's head in here anyway so we can get some distance from the smell. You said you heard about me through the children's hospital?" Carl put on a pair of green oven mitts, then bent over and pulled a tray of cookies from the oven.

"They said you work with terminally ill children and bring them a lot of joy. How long have you been running this program?" I asked, keeping enough distance between us so I could make a quick getaway if needed.

"I'd been working seasonally as a mall Santa for about a decade, and every year, I was shocked by the number of sick kids that came to visit. It broke my heart a little. I'll never forget the child that gave me the idea in the first place. She was so brave. Mary was her name. I asked her what she wanted for Christmas, and most kids, even the sick ones, usually ask for toys. But Mary, she told me all she wanted was to live long enough to see me again next year. I briefly spoke to her parents, who told me that the doctors were expecting her to pass sometime early the following year.

"Once the season was done, I couldn't stop thinking about poor little Mary, and I realized that there were so many kids out there who wanted nothing more than to see another Christmas. I couldn't stand knowing how important the holiday was to them and how many would never get a chance to sit on Santa's lap again, or eat ginger-bread cookies, or open gifts. That's when I decided to keep the deco-rations up year-round and do whatever I could to make at least one of their last wishes come true."

He sounded sincere, but then again, what kind of abuser doesn't? On its surface, the ritual of having kids over to celebrate one last Christmas sounded like Tom's book, but in my research, this seemed pretty standard for the dozens of establishments running this exact kind of program across the nation.

I decided to start moving into the more probing questions. "Have you lived here all your life?"

Carl shook his head. "I grew up in Utah, then moved here in the early nineties. Been living here ever since."

I pulled out my phone and pretended to type notes. "Can you walk me through your average visit from the hospital and how you started working with them?"

"Sure. It started with me visiting the children's hospital directly, dressed in my Santa suit and carrying a sack full of gifts. I started making a habit of coming around several times a month and got to know some of the staff. I told them about how I'd decided to keep my house decorated year-round, and pretty soon, they were orga-nizing trips for many of their patients to come visit my house. Hospitals are a scary place. Even with the suit and gifts, it didn't really feel like Christmas. The hospital knew about other houses that did this sort of thing and suggested that it wouldn't do any harm to let them have a field trip to get away from there, at least for a few hours.

"We only take small groups at a time, so each child gets a chance to feel special. I give them a tour of the house, do the Santa routine—where they each sit on my lap and tell me what they want. I'm not a wealthy man, but I do keep track of what toys are popular and try to have a few on-hand so that I can grant their Christmas wishes. After that, we all sit in a circle and sing Christmas songs."

Carl Owens suddenly turned away from me as he began to cough, then cleared his throat several times.

"Sorry, the smoke is still getting to me a little. Is it all right if we finish this conversation outside?"

I nodded, fighting off alarm bells warning he was leading me further away from the exit. "Of course."

We went through a backdoor to a small garden. There was no babbling brook or bridge, or fake snow like the Winter Wonderland in the book. But it did still seem festive, with more of the tinsel and string lights from inside and a single nutcracker who stood at least four feet tall.

There was one other detail about the backyard that made my heart leap into my throat. Emma's bicycle was parked along the back wall. I had to fight off a shudder and pretend to continue admiring his decorations.

"Can I be honest with you about something? And please don't get upset," Carl said, interrupting my thoughts of Emma. "You're Sarah Barnes, right? Emma's mom?" He nearly winced when he said it.

Another chill passed through me, this time actually forcing my limbs to quiver. Apparently, I wasn't so good at acting after all. I opened my mouth to try and keep up the charade, but we both knew the jig was up. "How did you know it was me?" I asked.

"The *Union Tribune* already did an article on me last year," he said, almost apologetically. "Besides, you kind of look just like Emma."

I felt my lips tighten into a thin line when he mentioned my daughter's name, but he hadn't made any sort of move toward me. His demeanor hadn't grown aggressive. If anything, he was giving me more space, speaking with more sympathy. He shuffled over to a wooden bench and took a seat.

"It's okay. I won't tell anyone you came here. I'm actually glad you did. I'd love to have the opportunity to explain myself. To be completely honest, I suspected who you were the second you arrived, and I really don't feel comfortable lying."

"I'm just trying to figure out what happened," I said, keeping myself near the opened door to the house.

"That's totally understandable, and the last thing I want to do is hide anything from you. First of all, I want to assure you that I really only had the best intentions. I know in this age it's hard to trust strangers, and if you ask Emma, I'm sure she'll tell you that I had asked her several times to meet with you. She begged me to keep it a secret, and against my better judgment, I reluctantly agreed. I'm not expecting you to take my word on this, so before you go, I'll give you the number of my family to verify this."

"How do you know my daughter?"

Carl nodded, resting his chubby hands on his thighs for support. "I first met Emma when she came here about six months ago with her friend Maya. After poor Maya passed, Emma showed up again, asking questions and just looking for someone to listen.

"Mrs. Barnes, you have to understand, I was raised in the Mormon Church, but I knew from a very young age that I was a homosexual. But because of my faith, I've chosen to live a life of abstinence. It's been a struggle, to say the least. Coming out to my parents —even though I never acted on my desires—was enough for them to kick me out of the community. It's why I moved here in the first place. I'm not a pedophile. I'm not interested in women. I don't swear, drink caffeine, and to this day, I remain a virgin. All I ever tried to be was a person that she could feel safe talking to.

"I'm sure you're already aware of this, but Emma is having a really hard time processing Maya's passing. When children come here and they're nearing their transition, they bring their whole families. Parents, siblings, sometimes even best friends. I hope you believe me when I say I've dealt with this sort of thing a lot. There's no wrong way to grieve, especially for a child of Emma's age. For whatever reason, she felt comfortable sharing her feelings with me, and I want you to know, it has nothing to do with your approach to parenting. From how she tells it, she has a wonderful, loving, and supportive family. I hope that you won't blame her for coming to me to help her with this. What I'm trying to say is that if you need to blame anyone, please, blame me."

I wanted to believe him. From what he said, it sounded like he was a profoundly sad and lonely man who, instead of allowing himself to live his truth, chose to bottle it all up and surround himself with a bizarre combination of death and Christmas. But at the same time, he was saying all the right things. To use an apt metaphor, he had gift-wrapped for me the best possible explanation and tied it off with a perfect little bow.

"What about my husband?" I asked.

A look of sadness overtook Carl, and he stared down at his red flannel slippers. "I don't blame him for what he did. I think, given the situation and lack of context, he was doing what he thought was best for his child. The love of a parent is a fierce and primal thing, and sometimes, it makes people act in ways that surprises even them."

There was still something niggling at me in the back of my head. "Can I ask you one more question?"

He smiled as warmly as he could. "Anything."

"In the police report, you said that you never saw him in the house, but the way he tells it, the two of you had some sort of exchange."

I couldn't be sure, but I thought I saw just the slightest twitch in his milky eye when he spoke, almost as if he were wincing. When he spoke, he paused for breaths even more than before. "Like I said before, I don't like to lie. We did speak. I tried to explain to him the same thing I just did to you, but he had already made up his mind, so I moved to safety out here and called the fire department. I even asked the police when they came not to press charges, but they told me that your husband had committed a felony crime, and it wasn't up to me. I figured if I told them I hadn't seen him, I couldn't identify him in a potential lineup. I just wanted this whole thing to go away."

This conversation had gone so differently than I had expected. It left me feeling more conflicted than ever. Emma had sworn that Carl Owens had never done anything even approaching inappropriate with her. And though it was hard for me to believe the words of a stranger, I *did* trust my daughter.

"I should let you go. I've already taken up too much of your time."

"Not at all," Carl said. "For what it's worth, I hope everything works out with your family." He led me back through his charred house so I could get back to my car, but something stopped me along the way. Among the group of Hummels, I noticed a pair of elves working on a rocking horse that reminded me of a description from the book.

"You sure you don't want a cookie?" Carl interrupted my inspection.

"I'm sure," I said, heading for the door.

He reached into a drawer and pulled out a candy cane. "Well, at least let me give you this, for the road."

I took it and thanked him. "You've been extremely understanding, Mr. Owens. I'm sorry for the distress and damage our family has caused you."

"I appreciate it, but you've got enough on your plate right now without having to worry about me. I'll be fine, and soon enough, I'll be back to having a holly jolly home."

He nearly closed the door as I began to cross the street to my car, then opened it again, remembering something.

"I believe in the end, Mrs. Barnes, it will be all right. Everything is temporary."

EXHIBIT 1E: AN EXCERPT FROM EVERYTHING IS TEMPORARY, BY TOM BARNES

It was a beautiful day in June. Tim had just finished attending the memorial service for a kid named Anthony he'd met only a few days ago at one of Mrs. Claus's *Over the River* visits, as they liked to call them. He had passed the very night Tim had met him, and they were asked by the family to attend. Anthony's mom explained through tears how much the visit had meant to her son. It had been all Anthony could talk about until he passed in his sleep that night.

Anthony hadn't been staying in the children's hospital, which was fairly common for these visits. Many families felt more comfortable keeping their kids at home with them for as long as possible. It was Tim's understanding that, while Anthony's condition had been terminal, he had been expected to be able to stay home with his family for at least another month or two before needing to make the difficult move to the hospital.

Even though Tim had now been to about a dozen memorials, they never got any easier. While Tim felt a real sense of doing good, it also felt like every time he put on his suit and tie, it was as if someone were hanging a weighted chain around his neck—like Robert Marley described when he visited Ebenezer Scrooge on that fateful night in *A Christmas Carol.*

Once the service let out, Tim made his way around to the back of the church, where he'd parked the bike his old man had finally returned to him as a graduation gift for surviving elementary school. He changed out of his suit and stuffed it into the backpack hanging off the handlebars, trading it for a T-shirt and shorts. From there, he rode to Hart Park, where he was meeting Julia for a lunch picnic.

Tim still wasn't clear exactly what their relationship was—dating, boyfriend/girlfriend, friends hopefully on the verge of something more. In any case, he was just happy to be seeing her. Even after the embarrassing turtle dove incident, she'd been there for him whenever he told her about the memorial services he occasionally attended. After each service, they would meet up and spend the afternoon together. One time, they went for a walk, and she even held his hand.

Whatever weight he felt during his ride lifted as soon as he saw her sitting on a beach towel under the shade of a large oak tree. Little glimmers of white light danced across her black hair when the wind caused the leaves to rustle overhead. She was wearing a yellow sundress that exposed her shoulders, and in front of her sat a picnic basket and a couple of cans of soda.

"How was it?" Julia asked.

"Sad, but good. The family was happy to see us there."

"But how are *you*?"

"Better now," Tim said, and he meant it. "What do we have for lunch today?"

"I know you'd rather have a ham sandwich," she said, which usually meant all her family had was sliced turkey. "So...I made ham sandwiches." Julia flashed Tim a devilish grin, knowing from the look on his face she'd successfully subverted his expectations.

She opened the basket, and as they dug around inside for their sandwiches and bags of chips, a new shadow loomed over Tim's back.

"Yoink!" Larry said, appearing from seemingly nowhere and stealing a can of soda from the blanket next to Tim.

"Oh, come on. Can you just leave us alone already?" Tim complained. It had been his hope, ever since school let out for the summer, he wouldn't have to deal with Larry anymore. But if anything, things had gotten worse without having a teacher around to stop some of his crueler antics. It didn't help that the apartment where Tim and his dad lived was literally across the street from the affordable housing community where Larry and his family lived. Tim sometimes wondered if that was a reason why Larry had honed in on Tim as his favorite target. From his third-floor apartment, Tim literally looked down on Larry's house.

"Look at you two lovebirds. Set a wedding date yet?"

Julia blushed, clearly uncomfortable at Larry's insinuation.

"We're trying to enjoy a nice day," Tim said. "I'm asking nicely. Can you please just leave us alone?" Julia hated swearing almost as much as she disliked conflict, and Tim had practiced pushing his patience to the absolute limit in order to try and be someone Julia could one day call her boyfriend.

"Does it seem hot out here to you?" Larry asked, queueing up some new horrible trick. "How about I help cool you off?" He shook the can of soda violently, then pointed it right at the picnickers and cracked the tab. Carbonated foam exploded out of the can.

Tim caught a portion of it; however, it was Julia who got a direct hit. Her yellow sundress turned black with the brown syrupy soda.

"Oh my God, I just got this for my birthday!" she whimpered, looking down at her sticky stains.

That was it, Tim decided. Ever since the "Rebel training" incident, he'd worked so hard to contain his anger. But now, as he looked up at Larry, all he could see was Scut Farkus, the bully from *A Christmas Story*. And much like Ralphie Parker, something inside of Tim snapped.

He charged at Larry, catching him by surprise when he slammed his shoulder as hard as he could into Larry's stomach. The two boys went down, and Tim wailed on Larry with a flurry of fists. He might not have had much strength, but he had speed and a bottomless pit of rage to fuel him.

However, unlike in the movie, Larry did not stay down and just take it. Tim had maybe landed a dozen micro punches before the much larger kid swung a fist at his face. It connected with Tim's jaw and sent him sprawling back into the grass.

"You think you can play hero in front of your crush?" Larry climbed back to his feet and kicked Tim in the ribs. "You're just a pussy."

Julia rushed to her feet and tried to pull Larry away from Tim, but she was significantly smaller. Larry swatted her away like a fly. As she fell to the ground, her arm clipped against the wicker of the basket. It drew blood, quickly followed by tears.

"Julia, run!" Tim gasped, trying and failing to get up.

Julia looked hesitantly between the two, then did just as Tim said. She didn't need to see the pounding he was about to receive.

Once she had made it over the hill, Tim curled into a ball to protect himself, preparing to wait out the pain until Larry would eventually get bored and leave. He expected some kicks to the ribs, maybe a few to his back. What he did not expect was the full force of Larry's foot slamming into his head, so hard it made white fireworks explode around Tim's eyes. His body went limp, and he was no longer able to control his limbs. His head roared with pain, and the world around him swirled. It was only a matter of time before Larry finished him off with a blow that would knock him out for good.

Only, the next hit never came.

"What the fuck?" Larry shouted, his voice filled with a terror seemingly wholly inappropriate for the current situation.

Tim forced all his energy into lifting his throbbing head and decided to hazard a glance at what had spooked Larry. The bully was stumbling backward, nearly tripping over his own feet as he tried to get away from a pair of small floating objects. At first, Tim thought they were the turtle doves, but they had no wings. They were round and mostly white, with the exception of two black circles in the center, pointed directly at Larry.

Eyeballs.

Floating in the air, completely of their own accord.

Within seconds, Larry had turned tail and was running as fast as he could away from the park.

Now that he got a good look at them, Tim was sure he had seen them before. They had been outside Danny's house, watching him when the turtle doves failed to impress. And they were inside the Christmas House on the day everything was dark.

By the time Tim climbed to his feet and wiped the blood running from his nose, the eyes had vanished.

He wanted to chase after Julia but worried about how she would react to seeing him, with his quickly growing bruises, bloody nose, and torn shirt. After only a few moments on his feet, he started to feel woozy, like he was on a ship and the whole world was rocking back and forth.

It hurt to climb onto his bike, and with each pedal, his right leg ached, presumably from one of the many blows Larry had landed before retreating. Tim began to ride but only made it a few feet before he lost his balance, fell to the ground, and vomited.

Tim needed help, and there was only one place he could think to find it.

"Mrs. Claus?" Tim called, bursting through the front door of the Christmas House.

"Little Elf, is that you?" she said from the kitchen. The smell of fresh cookies hung heavy in the house, as always, and it made his stomach growl since he'd just thrown up what little he'd eaten today.

"Have you been spying on me?" he said, forcing his quavering voice to sound as firm as he could.

"Tim, are you okay?" Evergreen's red-bulbed eyes turned blue as he looked the boy over.

"Not now, Evergreen."

Mrs. Claus stepped into the living room, wearing a look of shock and concern. "Oh my goodness! Little Elf, what happened to you? Let me get my first aid kit. We'll have you cleaned up in no time."

"Please, can you be honest with me? I just got saved by a pair of floating eyes. I need help."

Mrs. Claus let out a sigh, her shoulders sagging. "I'm not spying on you, Little Elf. I'm just trying to look after you."

"My name is Tim," he said, trying to stay angry in the face of the woman who had helped him so much in the last few months. "Do you really not see any of the living Hummels? The talking tree?" He collapsed onto the floor, his shaky legs finally giving out on him. Tears dripped from his eyes onto the carpet, next to blood droplets coming from his nostril. "Am I going crazy?"

Mrs. Claus frowned, her eyebrows drooping. "No, Tim. You're not going crazy. Yes, I know all about the Christmas magic."

"Why would you lie to me?" Tim asked between gasping breaths.

"I'm sorry for lying. I wanted to share something special with you, but I was afraid."

"Afraid?"

Mrs. Claus knelt and pressed some gauze against Tim's bleeding nose. "I was afraid that if I told you the truth, you would bring others over to see me, and then my secret would be out. You have to understand, Christmas magic is a very special thing. It's not for everyone."

"That day, when I brought Danny over. Were you home?"

Mrs. Claus chewed on her lip for a second. "Yes."

"And the turtle doves? Why?"

She shook her head, casting a dirty glance at the tree in the corner. "That was all Evergreen's idea. Believe me, he's been thoroughly reprimanded for that."

"Sorry, Tim," the tree said. "I was trying to help, but she found out and took away the turtle dove's light."

"What about the eyes?" Tim asked.

"I just wanted to look after you, make sure you're doing all right. I care about you, Tim. You're the closest thing I have to a family."

"How?" he asked, only able to gasp out a single word. He pushed through another wave of nausea, his world nearly flipping upside down.

"Please, if I show you, don't be afraid. I promise, I'm only trying to help." She sucked in a deep breath, then let out a long slow sigh, bringing her hands to her face. A moment later, she held two fists in front of her, and her eyelids were shut. She opened her hands, and a pair of eyes floated up about six inches from her palms.

"What are you?" Tim asked, feeling horror bubble up behind his dizziness.

"That's...a complicated question. I was human once. I had a husband, children, and community. There was an accident a long time ago, and I lost everyone close to me, on Christmas Eve of all days. I can't explain how exactly, but I made a wish, a Christmas wish, and that very night, I was visited by Santa—"

"Santa Claus isn't real," Tim slurred, interrupting her.

"You're so sure of that, are you? Just like everybody knows that trees can't talk? Or that the Humble Hummels aren't alive?"

Tim's head was spinning, so badly he had to lie down. He didn't know what to believe. Mrs. Claus took his silence as a cue to continue with her explanation, her eyes hovering in front of her face.

"My family was gone, and while Santa couldn't bring them back, he was able to give me a different kind of gift. Something that allowed me to never be alone, ever again. But it didn't just let me bring my trees and ornaments to life—the magic changed me too. One of the reasons I invited you into my life was because I could see you were suffering, much like I was. You had a special connection with Christmas, just like me. If I'm being completely honest, you remind me of the son I lost all those years ago. I promise, I wasn't trying to spy on you. I just care about you, and perhaps I crossed a line. For that, I truly am sorry."

As she spoke, she slowly pressed her eyes back into their sockets, blinking several times as she re-acclimated.

Tim felt his heart ache and his terror subside, if only a little. He missed his mother, and Mrs. Claus had been the first person to show him any sort of kindness in over a year. "How old are you?"

She blew out a breath of near-silent laughter. "Can we just say I'm older than I look and leave it at that? Now, you lie back and rest. We have another group of kids coming to visit this week, and we don't want you to scare any of them, do we?"

Tim started to get sleepy. His head was pounding, and he could barely keep his eyes open. "Why were you in the park?" he asked, his words blending together.

"I know it's hard to ignore bullies, especially ones as persistent as Larry, but you have to remember, everything is temporary," she replied, repeating the catch phrase she used almost daily. "I know you have your doubts, but believe me when I say, Larry will be receiving a rather large lump of coal for Christmas this year. Sooner or later, people like that always get what they deserve."

Fireworks exploded around Tim's vision again, and in the periphery, everything started to grow dark. "What do you mean?" he tried to ask, but his words came out as mush.

He closed his eyes, only for a second, but when he reopened them, he was alone, in his own room at home, and it was dark outside.

13

SARAH

Tom barely spoke throughout dinner. By the time my parents had arrived, it was as if our heart-to-heart in the art studio had never happened. He seemed almost like he was embarrassed to be around us, and it made me worry that everything he'd said in there *had* just been an act to keep me from being afraid of him. He only put in energy to talk to Emma, and even that seemed like it was a strain.

He picked at his plate and hardly thanked my parents for making baklava for dessert—a favorite in our family. At least Emma seemed to enjoy it, along with having her grandparents over for a couple of days. When I'd first broken the news to her that I would be leaving town, she'd burst into tears, wrapping herself so tightly around my stomach that it nearly knocked the wind out of me. Tom hadn't been himself since coming home, and I had become her new point of stability in the family.

It was only when I announced that her Teta and Jido would be here that she loosened her grip enough for me to catch my breath. Traditionally, Emma only saw her grandparents once or twice a year, and they would always shower her with attention and spoil her with gifts. When they'd promised to take her shopping after school, her mood finally shifted, and she actually seemed excited for tomorrow.

At least that made one of us.

After dinner, once my parents were situated in the guest room and Emma had gone off to her room to do homework, I asked Tom what had gotten into him.

"I don't know if I want you to go tomorrow," he said, wandering into the master bathroom and arbitrarily reorganizing all the pill bottles.

"What do you mean?" I watched him fidget with everything in the room to avoid engaging directly with me.

"I'm just worried is all. I know I told you I don't really believe that any of the stuff in the book happened. But...what if I do? What if you talk to Terry and he says it's all real? What if he says I'm a fucking lunatic?"

I put my hands around his shoulders, trying to calm him down. "I'm not married to Terry, and if he's anything like the guy in your book, I'm pretty sure he's going to be an asshole."

Tom sighed, and his shoulders tensed up with anxiety. "I'm serious. This is my childhood you're about to run headfirst into. Why can't you just leave this alone and let the investigator do it?" He shrugged me off and huffed over to the bed.

I'd tried my best to be supportive and understanding, but something about the way he was acting made a flame rise in my chest.

"I don't know what to tell you. You've never once mentioned a single thing about your life before we met, and in the span of a half a week, you've managed to throw your whole family's life into a blender. Do you know what I had to do just to be able to afford our lawyer? You haven't even asked me once how I've been dealing with this. I had to close down my marketing firm, the one thing that I'd spent my entire adult life working toward."

He shook his head. "I didn't ask you to do that."

"You didn't give me a choice! Do you know how much this lawyer is going to cost? And maybe if you'd have opened up to me about what was going on, I could have talked you down before you tried to fucking kill a man! Honestly, Tom, if the situation were reversed and I suddenly went out and tried to murder a stranger, then blamed it on a book about magical Christmas trees, what would you say?"

"I'd do whatever I could to support you. That's what married couples do."

I let out a grunt of frustrated skepticism and followed him to our bed. Of course, it was easy for him to say that about a hypothetical situation. I'd told him everything about my childhood, about my parents escaping Beirut for our safety. He knew about the sound of my mother wailing on the phone when she found out her sister and brother-in-law had been killed in a bombing. I told him about how, even as a child, it stuck with me, and that still to this day, I would occasionally have nightmares about the sound of my mother screaming, learning her worst fear had come true. I had childhood trauma too, but instead of cooking up some fantasy, I'd told him about it, about how it had affected me as an immigrant child, and how it still affected me today.

"Tom, I want to support you. I do. But you have to let me in. If there's something that I'm going to hear from these people tomorrow that's going to fuck up my life any further, I need to know now."

"So you do think I'm crazy." He ripped a decorative pillow off our bed and threw it to the ground.

"I'm not saying you're crazy. Like I said before, I think you had something traumatic happen to you as a child, that you are trying to process." I moved toward him, and he shrunk away. I didn't let it stop me and pushed forward again, grabbing his bony hand and holding it in both of mine. "Whatever happened, I'm here for you. For our family. No matter what happens at the end of this, I will always be by your side, and I will always know that whatever it is that you did, you did it because you thought you were trying to protect us."

"Then why do you have to go dig up the past? Just let me deal with this."

I shook my head at his stubbornness. "What, like the way you dealt with Carl Owens? Since you've been home, you've locked yourself away in your studio. You've barely talked to your daughter. I can't trust you to take care of things on your own.

"Don't forget, you're the one who told me to read your book. I'm doing the best I can to support you here, but you have to give me the space to do it in my own way."

He clenched his fists, and his jaw ground back and forth, but his eyes told a different story. All at once, it was like he was a marionette whose strings had been cut, and he completely fell apart. "I just wish I could go back to that day. I wish none of this ever happened," he moaned, falling onto the bed. "I'm so sorry for what I've put you all through. I want to take it back." Tom began to sob.

As hard as this ordeal had been on me, I had to remind myself that this whole thing was centered around him. I sat on the bed and rubbed small circles in his back. "Nothing Terry or Julia say to me is going to change the way I feel about you. You know that, right?"

Tears cascaded down his eyes as he looked up at me. "It might."

"It won't. I love you. I love our family. You chose one way to fight for us. Now you need to trust me to find my own way to do the same."

He shook his head, looking completely lost. "If you say so."

"Whether you believe me or not, I'm going tomorrow to help you build your case. Whatever happens, I'm going to do whatever I can to convince them to come help you so that you can stay here and watch our daughter grow up from our home, instead of through a plexiglass window in a prison somewhere."

"I'm so sorry for putting you all through this. I'm sorry for making you close your business."

"I know. It's going to be okay," I tried to reassure him, bringing his head into my lap.

Eventually, once we'd both shed all the tears we had inside of us, the emotional exhaustion hit me like a ton of bricks, and I fell into a deep and dreamless sleep.

When I awoke, the clock read 3:14 a.m. Feeling a chill, I rolled over to nuzzle into Tom, but he was nowhere to be found. I checked out the window, but the lights to his studio were off. A wave of terror swept through me, and I wondered if he'd gone back to Mr. Owens's house to finish the job.

I threw on my nightgown and headed out of the bedroom but

slowed myself when I heard mumbling coming from downstairs, along with a flickering of lights. From the landing of the stairs, I saw Tom sitting on the floor in the living room with his legs crossed. He was barely a foot away from the TV, and I recognized the movie playing. It was *A Christmas Story*, but the volume was turned all the way down.

"Oh fudge," I heard Tom say. He was reciting the movie as it played, perfectly synced with the action happening on screen.

As quietly as I could, I sat down on the top stair and watched for nearly fifteen minutes as he continued to narrate the entire film, word for word.

"It was all over, I was dead. What would it be? The guillotine? Hanging? The chair? The Rack? The Chinese water torture? Mere child's play compared to what surely awaited me."

EXHIBIT 1F: AN EXCERPT FROM EVERYTHING IS TEMPORARY, BY TOM BARNES

Tim arrived at the Christmas House early so he would have time to talk with Mrs. Claus about what had happened the previous day.

"Good morning, Little Elf!" Mrs. Claus said, organizing a plate full of cookies. As soon as she saw him, her face dropped into one of shock and worry. "Oh my goodness, what happened to you?"

It hurt for him to squint his eyes. He was still dealing with the queen-mother of all headaches. "What do you mean? I came here yesterday."

Mrs. Claus shook her head, looking confused. "I'm sorry, Tim, I haven't seen you since last Friday. Are you sure you're feeling all right?"

Tim's heart skipped a beat, then made up for it by jackhammering in his chest. "What are you doing? We had a whole conversation about Evergreen, your eyes, Santa..."

"I'm sorry, Tim, I honestly can't say I know what you're talking about." Mrs. Claus advanced toward Tim with the back of her hand out, as if she were going to press it against his forehead to feel his temperature, but he staggered back.

"Come on! You finally admitted to seeing all the Christmas magic.

I promise, I won't tell anyone. Just please, acknowledge that we had the conversation. Tell me I'm not crazy."

Mrs. Claus shook her head, giving what Tim thought was a very convincing act of pretending to be concerned. "I think that maybe you should go home and rest. We have some very special guests coming today, and if you're going to behave this way, I don't think it would be appropriate for you to be here."

Tim's face felt hot. He was about to turn and leave when the doorbell rang. Through the window next to the door, he saw a parked bus and about a dozen children standing outside, along with their families. He turned back to Mrs. Claus, staring at her with a mix of confusion and anger. Finally, he said, "I'm going to go put my elf costume on."

He spent a few minutes in the bathroom, putting on his green suit and convincing himself anything he had to say to Mrs. Claus could wait until after the *Over the River* session. Right now, the kids were what was most important.

Tim ran out to the bus and offered to push wheelchairs or for the arriving children to use his arm as a crutch to help them walk. After that, he waited for cars to pull up, belonging to the families whose children still got to sleep in their own beds at night.

It wasn't until the third car pulled up that Tim had his second shock of the day. A man dressed in dirty mechanic's overalls stepped out of a beat-up Honda Civic, then opened the back door. Two kids emerged.

One of them was Larry Enholm.

The other was an emaciated little girl in a pink dress that looked like it hadn't been washed in weeks. The two boys locked eyes. The way Larry stared at Tim made him feel like Larry was trying to kill him with his mind.

Mrs. Claus had mentioned special guests. This must have been what she meant.

"Go on. Get in there." Mr. Enholm brought a lit cigarette up to his mouth. His fingers were nearly stained black with oil, or maybe tar.

Larry didn't immediately respond, either because of his surprise or unwillingness to approach. His hesitance was met by a smack in the head, almost as hard as any time Larry had hit Tim.

"The fuck did I just tell you, boy? Grab Janice and get in there."

"Can you please come with us, Dad?" Larry asked, finally turning away from Tim.

"You stupid or something? I got shit to do. Now, grab your sister and move your ass."

"When are you going to be back?"

Tim couldn't be sure, but he thought he heard a trace of fear in Larry's voice.

"Keep asking questions and you'll be carrying her home. I'll be back when I'm back." Mr. Enholm was already back in the driver's seat of his car. He sped off before Larry could even help his sister off the curb.

"Come on." Larry held Janice by the arm and helped her slowly across the street. He supported her gently and made sure each of her steps were complete before trying to advance her any further.

Despite their rivalry, Tim couldn't help but approach, offering to help.

"Don't touch me. Don't look at me," Larry said, and almost instantly, Tim understood where Larry had learned his attitude. While he was distracted by chewing out Tim, Larry failed to notice a slight pothole in the ground, which Janice stepped into. Larry was able to catch her before she fell. "See? Look what you did! You almost made her fall, fucking gay-ass elf bitch."

Tim turned and ran back into the Christmas House, slowing himself only when he got to the door to make sure no one inside saw his hurry. He crossed the living room while Mrs. Claus chatted with a group of parents and their children, then ducked into the closet under the stairs, where dozens of the latest toys sat in perfectly gold-wrapped boxes. Leaning against the far wall were a collection of child-sized crutches, wheelchairs, and other mobility-aids. He grabbed a four-post walker, with a pair of wheels on two legs and cut up tennis balls covering the others, then snuck it outside before Mrs.

Claus noticed him. By the time Tim returned to the street, Larry and Janice had only made it a couple more feet.

"Here. We have a bunch of extras in the house, so if you want it, you can have it. Just act like you already had it when you come in, and Mrs. Claus won't ever notice."

Larry's eyes narrowed, and his nostrils flared, but he didn't say a word.

Tim turned his attention to the little girl at Larry's side. "My name is Tim the Elf. What's yours?"

"I'm Janice," she said, her eyes bright.

Tim taught her how to lean onto the walker with her forearms to keep herself stable as she used it to find her own footing on the pavement.

"Do you like Christmas, Janice?"

Her face lit up like Evergreen's bulbs. "I *love* Christmas!"

"Well then, we have a great day in store for you! Santa's up at the North Pole, but he sent me and Mrs. Claus to wish you the most merriest Christmas of all! We have cookies, hot chocolate, gifts, story time, and more lights and decorations than you can shake a stick at."

Tim kept his attention on the little girl, worried that if he looked up at Larry, it would cause him to falter from his always-chipper elf persona. It seemed to work. Janice quickly got the hang of the walker and picked up the pace. They finished crossing the street and headed into the Christmas House.

There were parts of these days when it was hard to keep his smile, but Tim's favorite moment was seeing the kids' reactions when they first crossed that threshold and found themselves instantly transported to the morning of December 25. It didn't matter what time of year it actually was—as soon as you were in the Christmas House, it was impossible to imagine it being any other day of the year.

Janice was no different. Her eyes sparkled, and her jaw dropped open in gleeful surprise. She even stood up a little taller, feeling a sudden rush of energy as excitement took over.

"How would you like a cookie and some hot chocolate?"

The little girl in pink nodded excitedly, but Tim was quickly side-lined by Mrs. Claus calling out to him.

"Little Elf, Little Elf! Mother Christmas needs your help!"

"I'll have those cookies in just one minute. You and your big brother can feel free to explore the house and Winter Wonderland out back. I'll find you soon, okay?"

Again, Tim made sure to keep one hundred percent of his focus on Janice as he spoke. She nodded, already overwhelmed by all the decorations. Tim broke off and helped Mrs. Claus serve cookies to some other children who had arrived earlier and were already waiting for their snacks.

The Treats and Tours portion of the day ran for the first hour as a few more families trickled in. This was unstructured playtime, where kids could explore the grounds at their own leisure, enjoy sweets, and even make a friend or two. Tim's job was to bring around trays of chocolate chip cookies to kids and their families. He did his best to steer clear of Larry, though he did overhear him actually being very sweet to his little sister, telling her a story about how he once caught Santa sneaking into their home and nearly stole his hat. It made Tim feel good to know Larry at least had the capacity to be a decent person, even if he had only ever been a rotten piece of shit to Tim.

After the tours were complete, it was time for everyone to gather in the living room for the Singing Circle, where they would all take turns performing the kids' favorite Christmas carols. They let the children choose which songs to sing, though by the end of Singing Circle, they always managed to cover the same ten or so songs.

The Singing Circle also helped to settle the kids down a little bit for Story Time, which was Tim's least favorite part of the day. Mrs. Claus would fetch two copies of her picture book, *Over the River*, and read it aloud. She made sure to pause between each page to make sure each child got to see the illustrated pictures of the story's main characters slowly saying goodbye to the lives they once had, while preparing for a magical sleigh ride to the fabled land on the other side. Sometimes, it was hard for everyone to see with just a single book, so Tim would follow along, showing off the pictures to the rest of the kids. He wasn't sure if most of them were old enough to understand exactly what the book was trying to convey, but the siblings and parents sure did.

Over time, he had learned that in order to make it through this part of the day, he had to put in extra effort to ignore the adults. As hard as they would try to stay strong for their kids, the book was oftentimes overwhelming for them, and many would silently shed tears and step outside for a breather while their kids focused on the story.

Today, Tim came the closest he had ever been to breaking his rule. He'd heard Larry be kind to his sister, but part of him was desperately curious to see if Larry would cry too. It took everything he had to force the thought out of his head, as he couldn't be sure if he was looking to see humanity in the young man or gain some sort of sick satisfaction in seeing his bully in pain. That wasn't what the Christmas House was about, and he was afraid of what he would have to confront inside of himself if he did choose to look.

Thankfully, the book was fairly short—only twenty-four pages—with most pages containing only two to three sentences. After Story Time concluded came the final part of the day, when Mrs. Claus would cheer up all the kids by having them each take a turn sitting on her lap and telling her what they wanted for Christmas. It was then Tim's job to hurry to the gift pile either under Evergreen's branches or in the closet under the stairs to fetch whatever toy they mentioned. There were piles of Furbys, Tickle Me Elmos, Bop Its, and even a few Nintendo 64s. Mrs. Claus seemed to anticipate every gift request; Tim could count on one hand the number of times they had to give out a consolation prize because they didn't have each child's wish on-hand.

That's why it seemed so strange when it was Janice's turn to sit on Mrs. Claus's lap.

"And what do you want for Christmas, little girl?" Mrs. Claus asked.

"I want a Tamagotchi!" Janice said with excitement, and for good cause. She'd been around the fifteenth child in line to ask for a gift, and so far, everyone had gotten exactly what they'd asked for.

"Oh, I'm so sorry," Mrs. Claus said. "I think Santa just ran out of those. How about we get you a nice teddy bear instead?"

"Um, Mrs. Claus, I can double-check. I think we may have one in the back." Tim knew there were at least a dozen piled up in storage.

"No," Mrs. Claus said with an uncharacteristic harshness to her tone. "Let's not get little Janice's hopes up too much. I think a teddy bear will do."

Tim tried to process the disappointment on the little girl's face, along with the stern look coming from Mrs. Claus. While his conversation with her had been hazy yesterday, he specifically remembered her saying she was going to punish Larry. The way she was treating Janice felt like it was Mrs. Claus's way of hurting Larry by extension and only furthered Tim's resolve in believing he was not crazy, that the conversation had indeed happened.

"One teddy bear, coming right up." Tim rushed into the back room and grabbed a small gold-wrapped package without hesitation. "Well, what do you know. It turns out Santa may have left us one extra special surprise, just for you." Tim handed Janice the package and watched the light return to her eyes when she ripped into the paper.

"A Tamagotchi!" she squealed.

"And it's pink, just like your pretty dress," Tim added.

"Thank you, Mrs. Claus!" Janice hugged the old woman tightly. As she pressed her head into the old woman's shoulder, Mrs. Claus glared at Tim, her lips curling up into a sneer.

Tim glared right back.

By the time the festivities had wrapped up, it was nearly dinner time. The bus to the children's hospital had left, and one by one, parents profusely thanked Mrs. Claus for everything she had done.

"Little Elf!" she called Tim over in her saccharine-sweet voice. "Can I have a word with you?"

"Of course." Tim put on the same cheerful act. "Let me just make sure this little one gets a ride home first." He gestured to Janice.

Mrs. Claus's eyes narrowed as he helped Janice out the front door on her new walker. Outside, the sun was slowly being swallowed up by the hills in the distance. Janice was enraptured by her new digital egg-shaped pet and sat with her brother on the curb outside of the house.

After about five minutes of silence, Tim couldn't help but break the tension.

"You know, my old man's a real hard-ass too," Tim said, extending an olive branch to the bully who'd made it his life's mission to bring Tim as much pain as possible.

"Don't act like you know me just because you have a shitty dad. This doesn't make us friends."

Tim couldn't help but laugh at the suggestion. "No offense, but I think the friendship between you and me set sail a long time ago. But that doesn't mean I can't be friends with Janice, right? How do you like your new Tamagotchi?"

"It's evolving!" she said, smiling with her whole face. "Thank you, Mr. Elf!" She reached up to hug him, and as they did, a shiver ran through her.

The last of the day's heat slipped away, and a chilly evening breeze rolled in.

"Are you cold? I have an extra jacket in my backpack." Tim shrugged the bag off his shoulder and pulled out a purple hoodie.

"We don't need any more of your *gifts*," Larry said, as if it were a bad word.

"Well, you know where I live. How about you give it back to me next time I see you? It seems like ever since school got out, we can't stop running into each other."

Tim held out the jacket, glaring into Larry's eyes like he was playing a game of compassionate chicken. The hoodie sat in space for a few seconds before Larry snatched it and put it around Janice's shoulders.

"Thanks," he grunted.

Tim decided he couldn't in good conscience leave without making sure Larry and Janice had a ride home. Technically, their homes were within walking distance, but soon it would start to actually get cold, and he didn't know if Janice could make it the mile or so on her feet, even with the walker.

With the little girl fully absorbed by her digital pet, Tim hazarded an actual conversation with Larry. "How long has she been sick?"

"Around March," Larry said after chewing his lip for a few seconds. "She just woke up having no energy, and after a few weeks of staying home from school, I took her to the minute clinic at CVS. They sent us to the hospital and—"

"Early March or late March?" Tim felt his heart suddenly race, and an almost painful tingle spread through the back of his head.

"What's it fucking matter to you? Jesus, you really *are* a freak."

Tim didn't know how—or even if—he wanted to explain when he'd started visiting Mrs. Claus. On the first day they'd met and for many days after, he'd complained to her about Larry. The timeline seemed to match up almost exactly to the period Janice got sick. It seemed like an insane correlation, but Tim thought about the way Mrs. Claus had treated Janice today and remembered what he'd heard her say to him about Larry getting a lump of coal for Christmas. It had to just be a coincidence, right?

"Sorry, it's none of my business," Tim finally said. "Listen, I know that after today, you're probably going to go back to making my life a living hell, but let me ask you one question."

Larry's nostrils flared, but he didn't turn away. "Fine."

"Yesterday, when you were beating me up, something scared you away. What was it?"

The boy sneered at him. "Oh, fuck you. What, you want to hear me say it? Yeah. I'm allergic to bees, okay? I didn't want to get stung."

Bees.

Tim's head started to spin again. Was Larry telling the truth, or could he be covering for the fact he saw something as bizarre as a pair of floating eyes? Could Mrs. Claus's magic disguise the eyeballs as bees to everyone else but Tim?

He wanted to ask a follow-up, but before he could, a rusted clunker of a car turned the corner and parked. Larry started to help his sister up. Seeing that they finally had a ride home should have alleviated Tim's fear, but instead, it only ramped up the feeling like he was about to have a panic attack.

As they drove off, Tim turned back to the house and saw Mrs. Claus standing in the window, staring at him with unblinking eyes. At that moment, he decided it was the last time he would ever visit the Christmas House.

Tim decided to break his own rule for once and asked his old man if he could have a couple of friends over for the night.

"As long as you keep it down. And stay in your room," his disheveled father said as he spread mustard onto a bologna sandwich, then took it, along with a pair of beer bottles, into his bedroom.

Danny was surprisingly easy to convince, given they hadn't hung out much since school ended. All it really took was Tim asking that he bring his BB gun and be ready for action. Julia was a little more difficult. Her parents were very strict, and though he couldn't say for certain, Tim suspected she'd told her parents there was *something* going on between the two. The only way Julia had been able to convince them to let her have a sleepover at Tim's apartment was by explaining it was a last-minute birthday party. She ended up being allowed to come, under the one condition her twin sister, Stephanie, join in too.

Stephanie was a know-it-all, a firm believer in science, facts, and the natural world as explained by the *Houghton Mifflin Social Studies* textbooks. Tim knew his plan for the night would be a hard sell, especially after the turtle dove incident. It would be another matter entirely, having Stephanie in the mix.

Danny scarfed down dinner at his parents' house, then sped on his bike straight to Tim's apartment. He surprised Tim with a Tupperware of leftover meatloaf and mashed potatoes, for which Tim was incredibly grateful.

Even with the gifts of alacrity and sustenance, Tim refused to explain the purpose of their impromptu sleepover until the whole gang was there. They played card games, killing time and compulsively peering out his bedroom window at the street below until Julia and Stephanie were dropped off by their parents a little over an hour later.

Tim's heart raced the minute he saw the girls step out of the car, and he wished he'd spent more time cleaning up the bachelor pad he and his old man had lived in for the past year and a half. Even if he had, there was no covering up the depressing state of the apartment. The walls outside of Tim's bedroom were bare. There was no dining room—just a couch with a coffee table facing the TV. The kitchenette provided little in the way of snacks or drinks. The best he could offer them were glasses of water and stale pretzel sticks.

Just to further illustrate the difference between the two girls, he paid close attention to their reactions upon entering the apartment. Stephanie looked around with clear disgust and judgment, hesitant to touch anything and nearly gagging at the permanent smell of rotting food in the overflowing trash bin. Meanwhile, Julia looked almost heartbroken to see the conditions in which Tim lived. Honestly, he wasn't sure which made him feel worse.

"So, are you ever going to tell us why we're here?" Danny said as soon as Tim had ushered the twins into his dingy bedroom and shut the door.

Tim quickly realized, from Stephanie's reaction, the smell in here wasn't much better. While he'd done his best to throw all his clothes in the hamper, he was only allowed to do laundry when his dad went down to the laundromat. There was little he could do about the smell of his BO radiating off his dirty pile of shirts and socks.

He'd been thinking about his plan all evening, though when the time came to explain, he had no idea how to put it into words in a way that would sound realistic. Even if he did, Tim wasn't sure he'd be able to bring them onboard, given the nature of the ask.

"Mrs. Claus isn't human," he blurted out, getting straight to the point.

"I don't get it," Stephanie said. "Is this for a game or something?"

"I know you all think I'm a little crazy. And after tonight, if it turns out I am, you guys can all never speak to me again. To be totally honest, it would actually answer a lot of questions for me if I *did* turn out to be a nutbag. But if I'm right, I think we have a chance to save someone's life tonight."

All three of them stared at him in stunned silence. It hurt, knowing they wouldn't believe him, but he'd already lost so much and his grip on reality was pushed so close to the brink, he'd nearly convinced himself he didn't care.

"Stephanie, did Julia tell you about the Christmas House and what Mrs. Claus and I do for terminally ill children?"

Stephanie nodded, clearly unimpressed. "Yeah, so?"

Tim was almost afraid to put his thoughts into words. "I think she might be making kids sick."

"On purpose?" Danny asked. "Why?"

Tim shook his head. "I don't know. That's what I'm hoping we can figure out tonight."

"What makes you think this now? You've been spending time with Mrs. Claus almost daily for months," Julia said.

"Yeah, since late March. That's actually part of it. Something weird happened today, and I just can't shake the feeling that something bad's about to happen."

"To who? You?" Danny asked.

Tim shook his head and nearly cringed when he explained his reasoning. "Okay, so, remember yesterday at the park, when Larry ruined our picnic?"

"How could I forget?" Julia said with a groan.

"He was just getting warmed up to kick the crap out of me, when a pair of floating eyes appeared in the park and scared Larry away. When I confronted Mrs. Claus about it, she admitted to being some kind of witch and then made some semi-vague comments about how Larry would be punished soon. Then today, we had an *Over the River* session at Christmas House with kids, and Larry showed up."

"What did that asswipe do this time?" Danny asked.

"That's just it, he didn't *do* anything. He was bringing his sister. It turns out she's really sick, like *dying* sick. And the whole day, Mrs. Claus was kind of awful to her, which I've never seen before. I asked Larry when his sister first got sick, and he told me it was right after I started working at the Christmas House. Like, probably within a couple weeks. One of the first things I ever told Mrs. Claus was how horrible Larry had been to me."

"You think that because Larry's sister got sick somewhere around the same time you gained an unhealthy fixation with an old woman, that makes her a child killer?" Stephanie asked.

"I have other evidence, sort of. We've been to a few funerals after some of the kids passed away, but it's almost always the ones who weren't that sick. I mean...Crap, I'm saying this all wrong. Some kids come straight from the hospital, where they have their own rooms and stuff. But almost every time we have an *Over the River* day, someone dies who didn't seem that bad. More importantly, every single time, they were still living at home with their parents."

"I don't think you know what evidence means," Stephanie said in a clear tone of condescension.

Tim ignored her and kept going with his explanation. "I think she goes after kids in houses because it's easier to get in. Everyone would notice if someone came into the hospital and started killing children, but if she could somehow get into their homes..."

"No one would notice a Christmas witch murdering kids?" Stephanie said. "Don't you think people would still be suspicious if a bunch of dying children were covered in defensive wounds?"

Tim shook his head. "Not if she's, like, stealing their life force or something. Then it just looks like natural causes. I already told you, she knows how to use magic. There's no telling what she's capable of. And because her victims are already sick, people just assume they're dying because, well, they are."

"I think *you're* sick," Stephanie said.

"Leave him alone," Julia demanded. "He's been through a lot."

Tim didn't know how to take Julia's comment. He was glad she was defending him, but it mostly sounded like it was out of pity.

"She did tell me she was old. Like, really old. And she admitted straight up that she's not human. Maybe she lives off the life force of children or something."

"Let's say, for the sake of argument, any of what you're saying is true," Stephanie began. "What are we doing here?"

"So, like I said earlier, there's almost always a death the night of these special visits. I think she's going to go after Larry's sister, Janice. And the thing is, Larry sort of lives right across the street from me." Tim pointed to the glorified trailer park right outside his window.

"So after everything he's done to us, you're saying you want us to actually *help* Larry?" Julia asked.

Tim nodded. "Yeah."

"I'll be honest," Danny said, "of all the bonkers shit you've said so far, that may actually be the most coo-coo bananas. Why would any of us ever try to actually help that psycho?"

"Because his sister is innocent. Mrs. Claus is trying to punish Larry by killing a little girl, and we have a chance to at least try and stop it." Tim felt his face get hot again, and he did his best to focus on the one detail everyone should be rallying behind. What did they have to lose by just believing in him for one stinking night?

"But you already said she's terminally ill," Stephanie noted. "She's going to die either way."

Tim expected pushback on his plan—actually, he expected a *lot* of pushback—but not on this part. "How can you be so heartless? This is a person we're talking about."

Next to her, Julia's chest heaved up and down, her focus entirely on Tim. She looked like she was nearly hyperventilating. "If you truly believe this, why not call Larry and warn him?"

Everyone stared at Julia like *she* was the crazy one.

"Okay, point taken. Fine. In that case, I'm with you."

Tim looked over to Danny, who let out a half-smirk. "Screw it. Let's do it. What's the plan, man?"

A wave of relief poured over Tim. Even if Stephanie didn't believe him, he had the support he needed from his friends. By the end of tonight, they would either truly believe he'd lost his mind or would prove, once and for all, he had been right about everything. Tim could live with those consequences. He had to.

"Basically, the plan is to keep watch outside the window, like a stakeout. If we see Mrs. Claus, we try to stop her."

"Let's say, for the sake of argument, you're *not* having a psychotic break...How would we even stop an ancient witch?" Stephanie asked.

"I have no idea. Danny's got his BB gun. My dad has a kitchen knife we could use."

"Oh, so the idea is murder?"

"I don't know! I just can't sit back and let another innocent child die when I could have potentially done something about it. I wouldn't be able to live with myself."

Julia stepped in close to Tim and took him by the hand. All at once, he felt both steady in his belief and shaky in the legs.

"Then we'll stay up all night if we have to."

The four of them decided to take shifts looking out the window, while the rest kept themselves awake by having a movie marathon on Tim's TV.

"What flicks do you have?" Danny asked.

After another embarrassing moment of showing off his DVD collection, which consisted entirely of Christmas movies, Julia decided to start off with the pairing of both *Home Alone* films. Tim took the first shift, and they traded off at the conclusion of the movie, with Danny taking the second watch.

Nearly two hours later, *Home Alone 2* was winding down, and Kevin McCallister had just electrocuted Marv to the point where the viewers could see his actual skeleton.

"That's so unrealistic. That would totally kill him," Danny said.

"Well, yeah," Tim replied. "Any of these traps would kill a person. They'd be dead like two hundred times over by now if this were real." Tim then realized something. "Wait. What are you doing looking at the movie, Danny? You're supposed to be on watch?"

Danny shrugged. "Sorry, I got a little distracted."

Tim peered out the window. "How long have the gates to the trailer park been open?"

Danny turned around. One of the tall black iron gates had been pushed inward. "Shit, it wasn't like that a minute ago, I swear."

Julia pricked up her nose, sniffing at the air. "Do you guys smell cookies?"

Chills ran down Tim's neck. "It's happening. She's here." He felt the triumph of vindication, quickly countered by the terror of realizing his theory held water. Now they actually had to do something about it.

"Oh my God, I can't believe this," Julia said.

Their eyes met, and it steeled Tim's resolve.

"Let's lock and load." Danny pumped the lever on his BB rifle nearly ten times to build up maximum pressure.

"Hold on, everyone. Before we go storming the gates, can we at least consider the possibility that someone in the complex is just baking cookies?" Stephanie objected, finally bringing her head out of her book.

"If I'm wrong, what's the worst that can happen?"

Against Stephanie's complaints, the foursome snuck out of the apartment, Tim grabbing the one mustard-stained kitchen knife his old man owned on the way out.

As soon as they stepped into the night air, Tim had to push down a shiver he convinced himself was because of the sudden exposure to the cold. They hurried across the street and into the small community.

"Which house is Larry's?" Danny asked.

"I'm not entirely sure. I've only ever seen him coming through the gate. I know it's not the first row of houses, but that's about it."

"So we don't even know where we're actually going?" Stephanie said.

"Hold on." Julia put up a hand. "The smell is getting stronger. This way."

Julia pointed to the right of the gate, leading deeper into the park. Each of them nodded, even Stephanie.

"This is what her house always smells like," Tim said.

The smell made it significantly easier to follow her tracks, growing stronger with each oversized mobile home they passed. Finally, they found a trailer with a window sitting wide open and an overwhelming odor of chocolate chips wafting through.

"This has to be it. She must have climbed through the window," Tim suggested.

"It's pitch-black in there. How do you know we're not just breaking and entering into some stranger's home?" Stephanie asked.

"This is it. I just know." Without any further delay, Tim climbed through the window as quietly as possible and found himself in a living room/kitchen only slightly smaller than his apartment. He looked around in the darkness, searching for movement.

A sound came from his right, and on instinct, he brought the knife up, ready to defend himself. Sprawled out on a couch, surrounded by a small collection of crumpled up beer cans on the floor, lay Larry's father.

He was snoring.

In a moment of relief, Tim became aware his hand holding the knife was shaking and his breathing had nearly doubled. His heart pounded in his chest so hard he could feel it in his temples. A moment of reality hit him like a ton of bricks as Stephanie's words echoed through his head. He had just broken and entered into a home, intent on potentially killing the woman who had shown him nothing but kindness for the last three months.

"Hey!" a voice startled him out of his own head. It was Danny whispering from outside. "What's the sitch?"

Tim crept back over to the window. "It's definitely Larry's house. Stay quiet. His dad looks like he's passed out on the couch in here."

Danny climbed through the window, then Tim helped Julia and Stephanie through. Once they were all inside, they discovered a door cracked open, with a dim glow seeping out into a tiny brown hallway. Tim put his finger to his lips and pointed in the direction of the door.

When he crossed the threshold, Tim found he no longer had to worry about staying quiet. In fact, he tried to scream, but the best he could manage in his shock was a pathetic whimper.

Larry was sleeping in a bed to Tim's immediate right, but on the far end of the room hunched a figure no force on this earth could have prepared him for. His first realization was, it had no legs. Instead, a long green scaly tail coiled up to a pair of feminine hips. He forced his confused eyes to scan up what looked like a vaguely female body to something resembling a head. It was green and serpentine, with long stringy white hair running down its back. Hovering above the scaly green head were a pair of eyes. They were focused on Janice, who lay in bed, staring up at the creature hunched over her in muted terror.

The snake woman held the girl down with its hands, which had impossibly long fingers ending in sharp claws. The creature's mouth was filled with jagged teeth, though that was far from the most horrifying thing about its face. Protruding from the monster's eye sockets slithered a pair of snakes that had shoved their way down little Janice's gasping mouth. The pair of writhing creatures created obscene bulges in her throat, and something inside of her mouth glowed red.

Tim stood, frozen in terror, while the monstrous serpent sucked the life out of Janice Enholm. He couldn't move, couldn't make a sound, until he heard the loud snap of something behind him.

"Holy guacamole," Danny said, then fired his BB rifle directly at the creature's head. The BB bounced off like it was a Nerf dart, and without moving anything else, the floating pair of eyes whipped over to stare at the four of them.

A long, forked tongue lashed out of her fanged mouth, then she hissed at Tim. "Little Elf, Little Elf, how dare you intrude while I'm feeding myself?"

The way she spoke confirmed everything for Tim.

Somehow, this beast *was* Mrs. Claus. He tried to throw himself at the snake-woman, to slash and stab at her with all his might. But he couldn't seem to get his feet to respond to what his brain—and adrenaline—were telling him.

A doll went whizzing by his head, pelting the creature with as much effect as the BB. Julia appeared next to him, searching for anything else on the ground to throw. Mrs. Claus let out a chirping sound Tim thought might be some twisted rendition of a laugh. He watched as the floating eyes shifted their attention to Julia, and at that point, his body finally caught up to the message in his brain.

The time to act was now.

Holding the knife in front of him like a sword, Tim charged at her, thrusting it forward as soon as he got within striking distance. With seemingly little effort, Mrs. Claus backhanded Tim with a clawed hand. He felt the air burst from his chest as he flew backward, dropping the knife and landing on Larry's bed. The bully opened his beady eyes and blinked a few times in utter confusion.

"Tim? What the hell are you doing in my room?" His eyes then widened when he looked past his prey and saw the monster straddling his sister's bed. "Holy shit! What the fuck is that?"

"Help us. She's trying to kill Janice," Tim wheezed, trying to catch his breath.

Without a moment's hesitation, Larry reached under his bed and pulled out a baseball bat.

"Get the fuck away from my sister!" he yelled, leaping out of his bed wearing nothing but boxer shorts.

Tim scrambled to reclaim the knife and mount a second attack, hoping a team-up would increase the odds of landing a blow. Danny's BB gun let out another crack, this time hitting her in the neck and causing her to flinch.

Larry was the first to reach her, but Mrs. Claus saw him coming and wrapped her slender, reticulated fingers around his neck. She lifted him off the ground, but Tim seized on her distraction and drove the knife into her arm. As hard as he stabbed, the blade only seemed to make it an inch or so into her thick scaly hide.

It might not have been enough to really hurt her, but at least it forced her to re-prioritize her attack. She dropped Larry, then reared back, pulling her eye-socket snakes out from inside Janice's throat. The snakes hissed at the kids. They had no teeth. Instead, their mouths were like gummy suction cups glowing in alternating pulses of red and green.

In the bed, Janice coughed violently, then threw up onto the carpeted floor.

Larry swung the bat, connecting with Mrs. Claus's face and sending the little snakes reeling back into her head. Mrs. Claus reached up and grabbed the eyes hovering above her, reinserting them into the sockets. She then focused her attention back on Tim.

"You've just made my naughty list, Little Elf. I'll have your soul, right after I kill your little bitch girlfriend." Mrs. Claus slithered off the bed, rising on her tail so her head almost reached the ceiling.

Larry took another swing at her with the bat, but she ignored it completely and set her sights on Julia.

She snapped forward, moving past Tim in a flash, but then reared back when the room lit up. A burst of flames met her halfway between the bed and Julia. She shrunk back, screeching in pain and covering her eyes with her hands. In less than a second, Stephanie had pushed to the front of the group, holding a can of Axe body spray and a lighter.

"Stay away from my sister!" she shouted, tapping the nozzle of the aerosol and sending forth several more blasts of flame.

Mrs. Claus cried out again, this time more in frustration than pain. In a split-second, she spun around and smashed through the closed window next to Janice's bed, disappearing into the night before anyone could even get to the window to see where she went.

"Oh my God, you're bleeding," Julia said, after we'd all had a moment to catch our breaths and check on Janice.

Tim looked down. The entire front of his black *Volcom* shirt was shredded. When he felt the sudden sting, he realized he had four long slashes across his chest.

Through gasping breaths, Larry snarled, "Does anyone want to tell me what the hell just happened?"

But before anyone could answer, a man's voice called out from the living room, "Shut the fuck up in there. I'm trying to sleep, goddammit."

14

SARAH

I had expected some resistance from Emma while I prepared to make the drive to Tom's hometown, but when the time came for me to go, Emma went into full histrionics. She begged me to stay through shuddering tears, shouting that I was going to abandon her too. It was already hard enough, leaving her behind, and seeing her react so strongly made me nearly crumble and ask the lawyer's investigator to just go instead. Lord knows it would have made Tom happy.

But I had to know. I needed to find out for myself what really happened all those years ago. Eventually, her Teta and Jido were able to help calm her slightly with the promise of homemade pita and zaatar for breakfast.

Tom had already locked himself in his studio by the time I was up, and when I knocked on the door to say goodbye, he came rushing out, squeezing me so tightly I could barely breathe. After his behavior yesterday, this was not what I expected.

"Please be safe, and come home soon," he said.

"I will." I tried to phrase my next words as gently as possible. "I know this has been especially hard on you, but while I'm gone, can you please help my parents take care of Emma?"

He nodded, then rubbed his hands down his eyes and dragged

them over his cheeks. He looked tired, like he hadn't slept in a week. "I'll do better, I promise. But right now, there's also something I have to work on."

"Just don't lose yourself in there. She needs you."

"I know, I'm sorry. I love you."

"I love you too."

I'd planned for the trip to Orange County to take a little under two hours, but traffic was light, and I ended up arriving with nearly forty minutes to kill before my meeting with Terry Enbom, a.k.a. Larry Enholm.

Thumbing through Tom's photocopied book, I looked up the street where the Christmas House was supposed to have been. Jacaranda was a short street overlooking a canyon, ending in a cul-de-sac. While I didn't expect to find a house covered in Christmas decorations, I had hoped maybe a new owner hadn't changed the color and I would be able to find the odd green house amongst all the beige and eggshell homes. It seemed whoever owned the place now *had* repainted, and I eventually gave up after seeing five nearly identical homes that could have once been the Christmas House.

Of course, it's possible the house never even existed in the first place, a creeping cynical voice whispered into my ear.

Even with the detour, I still arrived at Enbom Car Wash and Detail a good fifteen minutes early but was quickly ushered into an office by a man in a crisp polo. I had a slightly guilty conscience about my fib in order to get the meeting. The cashier seemed excited by my arrival and offered me coffee and donuts while I waited for Mr. Enbom to arrive.

No more than five minutes later, a man walked in who was somehow both everything I expected yet completely a surprise. He was tall, with a bulk that suggested quite a bit of muscle hidden under a mild layer of fat. What little hair he had on his head had been buzzed into a neat crew cut. His eyes were small and hard to read. I don't know why I expected him to be covered in grease like a mechanic, when in fact his business was in keeping cars clean. He wore a short-sleeved baby-blue button-down with a tie that gave him an air of self-made success story.

He put out a huge hand and shook mine enthusiastically, introducing himself. Based on his legendary temper, I felt a kettle of anxiety rise to a boil when we settled into chairs on either side of his office desk. I worried how he would react to learning I'd set a meeting under false pretenses and was even more nervous about what he would do when he learned who I was—or rather, who I was married to.

"Listen, Mr. Enbom—"

"Please, call me Terry," he said, maintaining a squeaky-clean grin.

"Terry. I have to apologize in advance. I wasn't exactly honest when I first made this appointment."

His grin faltered for a beat but quickly recovered. "So, you're not looking to open up your own Enbom franchise?"

"No, sorry. I'm actually here to talk to you about my husband. The two of you knew each other a long time ago." I took a breath, dragging out my admission for no reason other than my fear of a harsh or even potentially violent reaction. "Do you remember a kid you went to school with named Tom Barnes?"

I watched his ruddy cheeks drain of all color. His eyes sauntered away from mine, staring into dead space. He blinked a bunch of times, as if he couldn't get his eyes to focus.

"I'm sorry. Did you say 'Tom Barnes'?"

"I'm actually his wife, Sarah. I wanted to talk to you because—"

"Tom fucking Barnes?" His breath grew heavy, and he pressed his massive thumb and forefinger into the bridge of his nose. "You're his wife?"

I nodded, then remembered his meaty fingers were covering his eyes. "Yes. I wanted to talk about something that happened when you were kids."

"Jesus Christ. Tom Barnes." He kept repeating his name in a way that did nothing to allay my fears.

"I know you had some bad blood in the past—"

"Are you kidding me?" He lurched forward, not quite slamming his palms onto his desk. "Let me tell you something about Tom fucking Barnes." His voice grew loud, forceful in a way that made me shrink back in my chair. "In my lifetime, no one—and I mean no one —has done more for me than that man."

I was so shocked by the end of the sentence, I actually felt my jaw drop. "Come again?"

"I haven't heard from him in, what, twenty-something years? Sorry, you'll have to forgive me here. This is just throwing me for a big fucking loop right now."

"So you're not mad?"

His palms slapped against the table so loudly they made me jump. "Mad? At Tom? He was the best friend I've ever had in my life. He helped me through some serious shit all through high school until I shipped off for the military at eighteen. He took care of me when everyone else had long-past given up on me. I don't know that I would have even survived high school without him."

Now it was *my* turn to be confused. I tried to push forward to the matter at hand. "The reason I'm here is that Tom's actually in some trouble now, and I came to talk to you about something that happened—"

"Fuck!" he shouted, making me nearly jump out of my seat as he cut me off again. "This is about that book, isn't it?"

A shudder ran down my spine when he mentioned it. "Actually, yes. I'm guessing you've read it?"

"Fuck no. I mean, he sent me a copy years ago. I didn't get it until after I got back from Iraq. I couldn't read more than the first twenty pages." Another realization seemed to dawn on him. "Oh Christ, you must think I'm a monster, considering the way I treated him back then. Listen, you gotta understand—and I'm not trying to make excuses or nothing—I had a real shit childhood, and it left me with a lot of anger that I didn't know what to do with. My mom took off when I was five. Pops couldn't have given less of a shit about me and my sister." He sighed, diving deeper into the rabbit hole of his memories. "Fuck. Janice. When she first got diagnosed with Leukemia, my dad acted like it was my fault, like somehow I had failed to look after her and cancer was something you caught from playing out in the yard too late. He resented every penny he had to spend on her treatments." Terry shook his head and stared down at his desk. "Selfish asshole."

"So, about the book...I have to ask...The things Tom wrote about are pretty out there. Are you saying that it was true?"

He shook his head. "From what I read? If anything, he was actually going easy on me. The absolute shit I put him through. I can't apologize enough."

While it was nice hearing what a stand-up guy my husband had been to Terry, he had been dancing around the matter at hand, and I was here to get answers. "I meant more about the Christmas House. In the book, he describes a woman who was some sort of monster."

Terry nodded, then blew out a huge breath that reeked of coffee and cigarettes. "Mrs. Claus. Look, can I be honest with you for a second, Mrs. Barnes? Jesus, that sounds weird to say...Mrs. Barnes."

"You can call me Sarah."

"Sarah." He nodded. "My sister, Janice, died some time when I was in seventh grade, and then my dad basically took off. By that time, I was already pretty heavy into drugs, you know? I'd started sneaking beer and pot from my dad in something like fourth grade. By junior high, I'd graduated to harder stuff and already almost failed out a bunch of times. If it wasn't for Tom, I don't know where I'd be. Probably dead from an overdose, if I'm being honest with myself."

He had seemed to dodge the question entirely, so I tried again but more directly. "Tom was recently arrested for attempted murder. He says he did it to protect our teenage daughter from this monster that he claims you all fought as kids. I honestly don't know what to think at this point."

"You're going to have to forgive me. I've worked really hard to forget pretty much everything that happened to me before getting clean. My memory is not so good."

"But you'd remember if you and Tom got together to fight some sort of supernatural creature, right? The things he describes in this book, they're not real, are they? Living trees and ornaments, an old woman that transforms into a snake?" I felt stupid even saying all of this to a stranger, but I was too deep to back out now.

"Can I be completely honest with you? I don't remember exactly what happened. I wish I could tell you, but it's taken a lifetime of therapy and sobriety to get to the point where I can even look myself in the mirror and see a human being. I don't know what was real, but I will tell you this. I remember Tom being there for me and my sister when no one else was. When you're young and as fucked up as I was, it's hard to know the difference between a memory and a nightmare. I feel like I remember some really fucked-up shit going down, but I honestly couldn't tell you much beyond that."

The ball of worry inside my gut hardened into a knot of frustration. I'd come here expecting Terry to either fully corroborate Tom's story or—what seemed much more likely—kick me out the minute he heard who I was. I didn't know *what* to do with what he was giving me now.

"Sorry, you were telling me Tom needs help?"

I nodded. "He believes that everything he wrote in this book was true and that something that attacked you all as kids is back and trying to hurt our daughter."

"Oh shit. What do you need me for? Whatever it is, I'll do it. Everything I have today, I owe to him."

I nodded. "Well, it seems likely that he's going to be headed to trial for this, and he's using this story from your childhood as the crux of the argument. Our lawyer thinks if we could have some witnesses testify to Tom's character—"

"Just tell me when and where. I'll say anything you want to help get him off. It's the least I can do. Seriously, you just tell me what to say, and I'll say it. I'll even swear on a Bible. Lord knows I'm already going to hell for the shit I've done. Any time, day or night. You give me a call, and I'll come running."

Larry extended a hand to me, and I reached out to shake it. He hesitated to let go until our eyes met in an uncomfortable stare.

"I mean it. Anything Tom needs. I'm there."

EXHIBIT 1G: AN EXCERPT FROM EVERYTHING IS TEMPORARY, BY TOM BARNES

Despite seemingly saving Janice's life, Tim couldn't help but think he'd made things a whole lot worse by confronting the monstrous Mrs. Claus in Larry's home. Or, to be more accurate, he felt a tremendous amount of guilt for bringing the twins and Danny into this. Last night, she had specifically called out Julia as her next victim, and he could only imagine the rest of his friends weren't far behind on her list.

To make matters worse, Julia and Stephanie's parents had taken off that morning for a weekend conference out of town, and their house happened to be located right on the other end of a canyon that ran along the backside of the Christmas House. Mrs. Claus could come at any time in the night and not even need to cross streets to get there.

The one silver lining in this mess was that Tim had added two more members to his team to help protect Julia. Stephanie couldn't deny what she'd seen last night, nor could Larry. The rage he felt toward the beast that had tried to kill his sister seemed to eclipse any hostility he had toward Tim, and after seeing what they were up against in action, having someone as big and tough as Larry on their side seemed like it could significantly increase their odds for survival.

In what was maybe the most shocking moment of this whole ordeal, Larry apologized to Tim for everything he had done and promised he would do whatever it took to make it up to him.

Even crazier than that, it sounded totally sincere.

Once the twins' parents had left, Tim, Danny, and Larry all made their way to the Diaz house—a massive, two-story adobe-style home with a huge backyard and even a jacuzzi that had a waterfall effect into the pool. Compared to the rest of his elementary class, Julia's family was considered super rich.

"What if we just go in there, guns blazing, and catch her off guard?" Danny suggested as they sat around a living room larger than Tim's entire apartment, on leather couches probably more expensive than all his home decor combined.

"What do you mean, guns blazing?" Stephanie asked, her eyes squinted in condescension. "You have one BB gun, and it didn't seem to do anything more than tick her off."

"Aha, but now I have these!" Danny pulled a blue box from his backpack. "Hollow point high velocity pellets. I didn't realize we were dealing with an actual monster before. These have pinpoint tips designed to pierce through even the toughest hide, and then once inside, they turn into shrapnel, messing up everything."

"Still, that only leaves us with one weapon, and we don't even know if her body can be hurt like a normal animal," Tim said. "Plus, she's got an entire army of living toys at her disposal. If we took the fight to her, she'd have a clear advantage."

"What if we burned her house down?" Larry suggested. "We don't even have to go inside. Just douse the outside with lighter fluid and set the whole bitch on fire."

Stephanie nodded slightly, then twisted her mouth into an uncomfortable smirk. "Fire did seem effective, but it might be a little too obvious if a gaggle of pre-teens show up and start squirting lighter fluid from a suburban sidewalk. A neighbor could call 911, or Mrs. Claus could catch us in the act. Plus, to really be effective, we would need to hit multiple points of structural integrity to ensure the house actually burned, which is hard to do from the outside. You can't just squirt lighter fluid around randomly and expect to knock the whole place down."

"What if we snuck across the canyon and came at it from her backyard?" Tim asked.

Stephanie shook her head. "Then we risk causing a brush fire across the canyon. It could burn down other homes, possibly even crossing through the canyon and reaching our house. It's out of the question.

"Also, if she really is a snake, she'd likely sense us coming. Real snakes actually have terrible eyesight and hearing. Instead, they have these holes in their nose that are basically heat sensors. In fact, over eighty percent of the average snake's movements are based on tracking heat sources."

"So what do we do? Just sit around and wait for her to come suck our souls out with those weird glowing eye-snakes?" Danny asked.

"Actually, you might be onto something," Tim said.

"Who, me?" Danny said, with just a hint of surprise.

Tim nodded. "You would all agree the odds are fairly high that she's coming after us here, right? She seemed to take it pretty personally when we stopped her feeding last night. At this point, I'm guessing she's not just mad. She's hungry."

"I'm still not seeing the part where I had a good idea."

"What movie did we all watch last night during our stakeout?"

Julia and Stephanie's faces both scrunched up in the exact same motion. "Please don't say what I think you're saying." Julia looked concerned.

Tim nodded. "I think it's our best bet."

"I don't get it," Larry said. "What movie did you watch?"

Tim grinned. "Let's *Home Alone* the shit out of this house."

Julia leaned forward anxiously, resting her elbows on her thighs and holding her chin in her hands. She then blew out a breath that sounded like a hooting owl. "Our parents are going to be so mad when they get home."

Tim looked over to Stephanie, ready for her to dismiss the idea. She sat in silence, squinting her eyes in the same way she did in school when she was in deep concentration. Finally, she nodded in a rare instance of approval.

"I think it could work. If she really does have an army of toys at her disposal, we would be especially well served to have a strong defensive position."

"So you believe in those too?" Tim's heart swelled at the notion even Stephanie was fully buying into his story.

She rolled her eyes, seeming like she was trying to diminish Tim's statement, but in the end, she had to agree. "After what we saw last night, I think it would be willful ignorance to rule anything out."

The five kids quickly got to work. They drew up plans and came up with a list of things they would need from the store to help build traps. Tim outlined each of the possible threats Mrs. Claus might bring with her—Evergreen, the Candy Stripers, the Humble Hummels, the Nutcracker Suite, even the dancing marshmallows, just in case. Julia and Stephanie came up with methods of creating controlled blasts of fire. The challenge was in finding ways to use it against an enemy in a way that wouldn't result in burning their house down.

Larry found a box of nails in the garage and pounded them into his baseball bat, while Danny practiced firing his upgraded pellet gun at some plastic bottles in the backyard.

Once they completed the list of supplies, everyone pooled their money together and handed it off to Larry, since he was the strongest and could load up multiple bags and still ride his bike. Julia and Stephanie had at least one hundred dollars each. Danny handed over five dollars and sixty-two cents.

Tim handed his current life savings—a pair of twenty-dollar bills —to his former bully. "Keep the change, ya filthy animal."

"What did you just call me?" Larry said, stepping toward Tim and puffing out his chest.

"It's a line from the movie. Forget it. Just make sure you get everything on the list."

Once Larry had left, everyone split up to keep working on the plan. The twins and Danny focused on the inside the house, while

Tim scouted out the backyard leading down into the canyon for any possible entry points he could sabotage. There was a fence running along the property line that was obscured by a cluster of trees, and he wondered if there was anything he could do to force Mrs. Claus into entering from one place in particular. He'd opened the back gate and started to wander through a thicket of bushes, when a voice surprised him from behind.

"Need any help?"

He spun around and watched Julia approach.

Tim smiled. "Shouldn't you be inside with the rest?"

She reached forward and grabbed him by both his hands. He didn't know that he still had it in him to feel adrenaline after last night, but as soon as their skin touched, his pulse quickened, and the back of his neck grew hot.

"I wanted to spend some time with you. Just the two of us."

"Okay," Tim said, maybe just a little too eagerly. "What do you want to talk about?"

"Well..." Julia looked down at her feet, which were twisting back and forth, crushing dead leaves in the dirt. "I just thought you should know, I guess officially, that I like you."

All the worries about the Christmas House and Mrs. Claus vanished in that moment, and he—for once—got to experience a real moment of normal adolescence. "I like you too."

"If we make it through this thing—which, of course, is a big if—do you think you'd maybe want to be boyfriend and girlfriend?"

Tim's heart fluttered in his chest, and he couldn't even tell if his feet were still on the ground. "I'd love that."

Her lips eased their way into a warm smile, and her big brown eyes locked with his. Time slowed to a crawl as she inched her face closer to his.

Oh my God, this is actually happening, Tim thought, preparing for his first kiss. After what felt like a century of anticipation, their lips finally connected. She was soft and warm, and every nerve in Tim's body buzzed with exhilaration.

"Tim!" a voice called from somewhere far, far away.

Julia didn't break off their kiss, so neither did he. If anything, she pulled him in tighter. Their lips smacked once, then reconnected again for a second kiss. Or was it a continuation of the first kiss? Was this how kissing worked? Julia's mouth opened slightly between little kisses, and her tongue tickled against him. He opened his mouth slightly too, following her lead.

"Tim, you want a soda?" the voice called again, and this time, he could hear footsteps tromping through leaves. "Oh my God!" the voice screamed.

He finally broke away and looked to see who was approaching. It was another Julia. Tim turned back to the girl in front of him, and all of his tingles turned into an electric shock.

Her chin was missing two tiny signature freckles.

"Stephanie?" Tim gasped, then looked over to Julia, who had dropped the can of soda and already had tears welling in her eyes.

"Julia, wait. I didn't know!" Tim shouted.

It was too late. Julia took off, rushing through the trees and down into the canyon at full speed, sobbing as she sprinted.

"Stephanie, how could you?"

He tried to pull away, but Stephanie's hands held him tightly in her grip. Her lips curled into a malicious grin. As she licked them, her tongue split and ended in two sharp little points.

"What's the matter, too much tongue?" she said in the old crone voice of Mrs. Claus.

Tim kicked the imposter as hard as he could in the chest, and she fell to the ground, laughing maniacally.

"Better go after her. She's next!"

"Danny, help! She's here!" Tim screamed at the top of his lungs before he sprinted after Julia.

She already had a lead on him, but he pushed as hard as he could to catch up to her. Julia had been the fastest runner in the school but only by a fraction. It took him a few seconds to catch the back of her head as she ran down the side of the hill. He called out for her to stop, wanted to explain, but he needed to save his breath to keep up with her.

Julia was fast but careful not to trip over brambles and leaves. Tim sprinted with full abandon, allowing each hurried stride to help him close the distance by a matter of inches, until he could finally see her whole figure running through the woods.

And then, she was gone.

In an instant, he saw Julia's long black hair fly upward along with her hands, and she plummeted into the earth, followed by a loud thump and then a squeal of pain.

"Julia!" Tim called. "Are you okay?"

Echoing sobs rang out from somewhere in the mess of bushes ahead. He slowed his pace a little to make sure he didn't fall down the same hole, eventually coming to a gap in the earth leading down into an underground cavern. He squatted down on his hands and knees, spotting Julia on the rocky floor. Down and to her left was another opening he could walk through without having to fall through.

Tim slid down a patch of dirt nearby until he saw the yawning mouth of a small cave. Inside, Julia sat on the ground, her knees scraped and bleeding. He ran to help her up, but his heart stopped as soon as he saw what lay just behind her.

"Julia, don't turn around," he begged. He should have known that, of course, telling a kid not to do something was the only way to ensure they did just that.

She swung her head behind and let out an ear-piercing scream that exceeded the shock of her fall.

Propped up against the stone wall of the cave was the decomposing corpse of what looked like an old woman. Thin white wisps of hair hung down a maggot-infested skull, with small rotting patches of meat still clinging to the cheeks. Her jaw was gaped open in terminal shock, and a tattered red dress was draped over the body, turned mostly black from blood and the filth of putrefaction. Her arms lay at her sides, shriveled and brown like a mummy, with filthy bones revealing themselves in large patches.

"Julia, take my hand." Tim reached out for her.

Julia gagged and retched but remained in place.

"Come on, we have to go *now*." He took another step toward her.

When she finally turned back to look at Tim, her wet eyes gleamed with a new terror, somehow greater than the already traumatizing combination of falling into a cave and discovering an old woman's corpse.

"Behind you!" she cried.

This time, it was Tim's turn to refuse an order. Whatever it was, he didn't want to know.

His breath rattled in his chest and came out as a series of hiccups. In the cave's entryway echoed the grunt of something large...and wild.

Tim finally turned, and that's when he saw it.

It was the inflatable reindeer from the roof of the Christmas House, but it was alive, twisted, and angry. Its nose and eyes glowed a deep red, and as it peeled back its lips, it revealed a mouth full of real teeth. Not just that, the antlers on its head were a branching cluster of bone, each coming to a razor-sharp point. The reindeer let out another chest-rattling grunt, and steam hissed from its big red nose.

Tim quickly searched the ground around him and found a stick roughly the size of a baseball bat. He picked it up and held it in both hands, ready to strike.

"Julia, can you stand?" Tim asked.

She quickly clambered to her feet, holding onto the rocky wall for stability. "Yeah."

"Keep pressing yourself against the wall. I'm going to lure it over to the other side of the cave. When I do, you run for the exit."

"But Tim—"

"Get ready."

The reindeer clomped a very real hoof against the ground several times, kicking dirt and rocks behind it and preparing to charge.

"Come on, Rudolph. Let's go down in history."

Tim ran at the beast. The reindeer charged as well, tucking its head as it ran. Tim made a move like he was going to take a swing with the stick, but it was a feint. Instead, he dove to his right, landing on his stomach. The beast charged past him, scraping its antlers against the rock wall. The sound made his teeth clench, like a dozen nails raking against a chalkboard. His chest ached where Mrs. Claus's claw had slashed him the night before. He quickly climbed to his feet again, hoping to see Julia by his side at the mouth of the cave.

She hadn't moved. Julia was completely frozen in fear and now stood between Tim and the beast with nowhere to go. The girl and the reindeer caught each other's eyes, and before it could make a move toward her, Tim ran at the thing, this time swinging the stick for real. It connected with the reindeer's neck, then bounced back as if he had just smacked an Astro Jump.

Oh no, Tim realized.

The antlers, teeth, and hooves were real, but the body was still made of inflated plastic. He swung again, but it was about as useful as kicking a tire.

The one thing he did manage to accomplish was the reindeer had redirected its attention back on him. Tim used it. "That's right, Rudolph. Look at me, not her."

"Hey!" another voice called from nearby. It was Danny.

"Down here!" Tim shouted, standing in the mouth of the cave.

The reindeer roared, and the reverberation of the cave made it so loud, Tim almost had to drop the stick to cover his ears. It lowered its head and prepared to charge Tim once more. He didn't know what else to do to stop it. The stick ended in more of a nub than a point, and he doubted he could pierce its plastic skin, even if he did stab it.

There was no time to plan. Rudolph came charging for him, and once again, Tim dodged to the side to avoid it. Only this time, it wasn't a narrow miss. In fact, it was almost as if it wasn't aiming for him at all.

That's when he realized he wasn't the intended target.

Danny had made his way down the bank and was about ten feet behind Tim. He stood aghast, holding his rifle at his side and gaping at the charging creature. The reindeer's antler gored itself right into Danny, then it whipped its head, sending him flying at least ten feet away from the cave. Danny screamed, soaring through the air, then went silent as he landed on the ground with a hard thump.

"Oh God," Tim said.

The reindeer slowly made its way to Tim's fallen friend. Huge red stains were forming on Danny's shoulder and leg. He wasn't moving. Any second now, the reindeer would make sure to finish the job it had started, making good on one of Mrs. Claus's promises to kill all Tim's friends.

Tim searched the ground for the pellet rifle, finding it lying a few feet away. He scrambled for it, nabbing it and aiming for Rudolph's body. He squeezed the trigger and heard two cracks. The first was the pellet rocketing from the air rifle's barrel, quickly followed by the loudest pop Tim had ever heard.

The pellet had pierced the inflated plastic skin of the reindeer, causing it to explode like a balloon.

15

SARAH

I sat on a bench, pretending to stare at my phone while I waited for the workday to end. Upon first pulling up to the L.A. corporate offices for WatAir, I was lucky enough to find that employee parking was in a separate structure across a small open-air business park, not directly under the building. It was already crazy enough that I was planning on accosting Julia Dominguez on her way home from work. I didn't need to get pepper-sprayed while hiding behind a car in a creepy basement lot.

Even still, there was no denying my plan *was* crazy. I was at least four hours into my stakeout—I couldn't be sure since my phone's battery had run out of juice as I sat and killed time on it. While the meeting with Terry had gone well enough, I felt like I was no closer to getting a straight answer on what the hell had happened, and it made me more desperate than ever to find the truth.

Eventually, five o'clock rolled around—or at least, I assumed as much without having a working phone. People in business suits started shuffling out of the building and across the walkway toward the parking structure. A rush of adrenaline surged through me as I surreptitiously tried to spot Julia amongst the crowd. I figured she, as the boss, would be one of the last to leave, which would probably work to my advantage if either of us ended up creating a scene.

I rehearsed the talking points in my head on repeat, both to calm myself down and so I wouldn't forget them.

As it turned out, no amount of preparation could have made me ready for the moment she exited the building. I had a pretty good idea of what she looked like from the picture I'd found online, but seeing her in person was almost a surreal experience. She looked so much like me, it was almost as if we could have been cousins. Her skin was much darker than mine, and her narrow face came to more harsh points at the cheeks and chin, but otherwise, it was almost uncanny. Even her formal gray blazer looked similar to my style.

As she approached, a thought burst into my head that I hadn't considered until just now, and it made me lose track of all the talking points I had planned. Nearly everyone else in the book had their full names changed, except for Julia. He'd only altered her last name. I remembered how she'd blocked him on Social, and a vise grip of insecurity grabbed me by the throat. I wondered if I had just been some sort of proxy for Julia. What if the real reason Tom didn't want me on this trip was that I'd realize I was just his silver medal?

I was so in my head, I almost let the opportunity to grab her attention slip by.

"Excuse me, Miss Dominguez?" I called out, rising from the bench to catch up with her.

She walked fast, with purpose, and didn't slow down.

"Not interested," she said, dismissing me without even looking.

"Julia, I just need a minute of your time."

Something told me people didn't often use her first name, especially strangers on the street. It gave her pause, if only for a moment.

"My name's Sarah Barnes. Do you remember a man—Well, he would have been a boy back then..." I was tripping over myself, blowing the only chance I had. "Tom Barnes?"

She stopped dead in her tracks. Her eyes turned into a pair of daggers. "What do you want? Is this some sort of sick joke?"

I shook my head, over-widening my eyes and softening my brows to seem as non-threatening as possible. "I just wanted to talk to you. Five minutes and then I'll leave you alone."

Her jaw clenched, and she considered my offer. "What's he done now?"

The word *now* clamped onto my heart, making me wonder what else he might have done that I was unaware of. I didn't want to jump straight to the charges, so I tried to push forward to find a soft opening. "We have a daughter. She just turned twelve. Her friend died last year, and she's been going through a hard time and—"

"Get to the point. What's this have to do with me?" she said impatiently.

"Our daughter's been hanging around this man. He's got a house—"

"Spit it out," she said, giving me what felt like a final warning.

"It's Christmas-themed. Tom tried to burn it down with the man still inside."

Julia nodded, as if none of this information came as a surprise to her. "You want my advice? Take your daughter and get as far away from that lunatic as possible before he gets one of you killed." She turned and started to walk away. Clearly, she was finished with me.

But I wasn't finished with her.

I grabbed Julia by the arm, trying anything to get her to stay. She ripped herself from my grasp, but at least she had stopped moving.

"Please, I'm just trying to understand what's happening. He gave me this book that he swears explains everything, but I don't know what to make of it."

"*Everything Is Temporary*," she said. Simply producing the words made her look like it left a rotten taste in her mouth.

I nodded. "You've read it?"

"No. I've spent a lifetime trying to forget he ever existed. The last thing I want to do is further indulge in a psychopath's delusions."

"Please," I begged once more. "Can we just sit for a minute? I feel like I'm going crazy. I'm just looking for an explanation."

She considered me once more, then pulled out a phone from her pocket and checked the time. "Fine. You have three minutes."

"Thank you."

We sat down on the bench, and Julia finally looked me up and down.

"He really has a type, doesn't he?" she said, with just a hint of disgust. She was clearly noticing the same similarities as me.

I chose not to address it and pressed on. "In the book, he claims that this woman he calls Mrs. Claus was some sort of a monster and that she came after you all. I just want to know what really happened."

Julia pursed her thin lips and nodded to herself, much in the way Tom described Stephanie doing whenever she was deep in thought. "You want to know what really happened? Tom was a deeply troubled boy who suffered some sort of psychotic break after his mother died on Christmas Day. I had the misfortune of feeling sorry for him and decided to try and be his friend. He developed an unhealthy obsession, then manipulated me and anyone else unfortunate enough to pity him into torturing an innocent old woman. During his delusional crusade, I lost my twin sister in a horrific accident of his design, to which he never admitted culpability. He ruined the lives of everyone around him and then suffered no consequences for any of it."

My heart sank lower than I ever thought possible. I'd stopped breathing after she began her explanation and had to hold onto my knees, dizziness threatening to send me to the floor. This wasn't a story of confusion. I wasn't sitting next to an ex-addict with a fuzzy memory. This was a sharp, rational, powerful woman explaining to me how my husband broke her.

"I'm so sorry," I said, instantly losing a battle to hold back my emotion.

"Does that clear things up for you?" Julia said, more as a demand than a question. "I don't even know what he did to poor little Douggie."

I looked back at her, confused.

"Sorry, you probably know him as Danny."

Through my spiral of despair, something odd snapped into my head. "Wait, how did you know he called him Danny in his story?"

Julia scowled. "Fine. Yes, I read the book. God knows I wish I hadn't. You want to know what he doesn't include in there? After he killed my sister and nearly destroyed my family home, my parents blamed me for everything. They acted like the wrong sister died, sent me off to boarding school, and then basically never spoke to me again. It took years of therapy to try and forgive myself for what happened, and right when I was finally getting my act together, suddenly this book showed up on my front door. It read like the sad manifesto of an untreated schizophrenic, who, instead of seeking help, doubled down on his delusions. He used our trauma as material to write a fucked-up fairy tale to make himself feel better." She opened her purse, pulled out a piece of paper, then started writing an address on the back. "Here. You want further evidence of just how full of shit Tom is? Rather than dealing with the consequences of his own actions, he chose to kill Douggie off in his book instead of telling the truth. If you really want to see what Tom is capable of, you go and pay *him* a visit."

She folded the paper over, then passed it to me. Her hand was trembling.

"As far as I'm concerned, whatever trouble Tom's in now is coming twenty-five years too late." Julia rose to her feet, let out a breath, then turned back to me one last time before walking away. "If you or Tom ever try to contact me again, I'll have you arrested for harassment."

16

SARAH

By the time I reached my car, my whole body was shaking. I wanted to call Emma, to call my parents. Julia had rattled me, and suddenly, I felt like I didn't know Tom at all. I wanted to see if everyone was all right, but my phone was still out of battery. Plugging it into my car charger, I then set it in the cupholder next to the candy cane Carl Owens had given me.

Thinking back on my meeting with him, he'd seemed sad and lonely but not threatening. Terry hadn't been able to confirm anything beyond Tom's capacity to forgive, which was only a consolation if he wasn't secretly the delusional—and possibly dangerous—person Julia had described.

The address she had given me was in Orange County, a short detour on my way back home to San Diego. The name above it read "Douggie Chin." I'd need my phone to navigate to the house, but I knew well enough how to get to OC on my own, and it would have enough juice by then to take me the rest of the way by the time I'd reached Tom's hometown.

About ten minutes into the drive, my phone jingled to life, and I immediately called home. My mother answered, and I felt a slight loosening in my chest when she told me there was nothing to report.

Apparently, since Emma had gotten home from school, she had been making them watch *The Sandman*, as they hadn't had a chance to see it a dozen times yet.

"Didn't you used to read books about this when you were a kid?" my mom asked.

I commended her for her good memory, then forced out a laugh to try and keep her from worrying about me. She laughed too, meaning I'd successfully managed to hide my fear.

"What's old is new again. Maybe next she'll start listening to that moody band you loved so much next." She was referring to *My Chemical Romance*, which I had been obsessed with as a teenager.

Mom actually raised a good point. I remembered one of their albums, *The Black Parade*, was all about coming to grips with dying of cancer. If Emma didn't want to listen to me talk about Maya's passing, maybe some angsty emo-pop about the subject could help her work through her grief.

"Can you put her on for a minute?" I asked. I heard groaning in the background, then my mother telling her she would pause the show until she got back.

"Hi, Mom." Emma sounded put-out for having to talk to me. This morning, she had made it seem like she couldn't even survive a day without me around, and now, she didn't want to have anything to do with me. Such is the life of a pre-teen.

I tried to manage small talk with her, checking in on how she was doing.

Fine.

I asked if her father had come in from his studio at all.

Not really.

I knew she wanted to get back to her show and that she was punishing me for what she believed to be me abandoning her, but I couldn't stop myself from asking the question that had been on my mind ever since reading Tom's book.

"Listen, habibeh, there's something I want to ask you. And I need you to tell me the truth, no matter how embarrassing it may be."

She groaned again on the other end of the line.

"Did Mr. Owens ever show you anything unusual while you were at his house?"

"Ew! Mom, that's gross! I already told you, he's not a pedophile."

"No, that's not what I mean," I said, truly believing she was telling the truth. "Has he ever shown you anything that seemed like it might be—I don't know how to describe it—Christmas magic?"

"What?"

"Has he ever introduced you to any decorations that may have seemed like they were alive? Maybe a talking tree?"

"What the hell are you talking about?" Emma said, like I was the crazy one. "You know I'm old enough to know there's no Santa, right?"

I didn't like her using the word *hell*, but I let it slide for now.

"Of course, I know you are. But if anything ever did happen that was weird, you know you can always talk to me, right?"

"Yeah, Mom," she said, sounding bored.

"I trust you, habibeh. I just want you to know that if you ever feel like sharing anything, even if it sounds crazy, I'll always believe you."

"Okay," she said after a long pause. "When are you coming home?"

"I just have one more stop, but it looks like I won't have to spend the night after all. I should hopefully be home before bedtime."

"Cool. See you then."

"I love you," I said, but she had already hung up.

Rush hour traffic had set in by the time I got on the 5 freeway, and it took me twice as long to get back to Orange than it did to make the trip up to L.A. By the time I reached the address on the paper, the sun had already set. I worried about ringing a stranger's doorbell after dark and thought it would have probably been better to try this during the day, but I'd already promised Emma I'd be home tonight.

The house was small and looked to be in a state of disrepair. The screens on the windows were torn between black security bars, the roof was missing shingles, orange paint was chipping off the front facade, and an ominous black-barred metal gate stood in the frame, guarding the actual front door.

I got a bad feeling just looking at the house, but I'd already come so far. There was no turning back now. I grabbed my phone from the cupholder and stuck it in the pocket of my blazer, then made my way to the house. As I rang the doorbell, I had an odd moment of panic.

As a child, everyone had apparently called him Douggie, but that was over twenty-five years ago. Who was I supposed to ask for now? Douggie? Douglas? Doug?

The door opened, and an elderly Asian man stood in its frame behind the security gate.

"Can I help you?" he asked.

This wasn't Douggie, or whatever he called himself these days. I figured it must have been his father.

"Hi, sorry to bother you. You don't know me, but my husband was a childhood friend of Doug, erm, Douggie. Is he home?"

"Who's your husband?" the man said, with just the slightest trace of a Chinese accent.

I wanted to turn around, tell him this was a mistake, and run back to my car as fast as possible. Instead, I said, "Tom Barnes?"

The old man muttered something that sounded like a harumph, twisted a lock to open the gate, then walked back into the house. "Come in. I'm Rich. This is Liya." He pointed to a woman on a couch around the same age, with more salt in her hair than pepper. "Can I get you something to drink?"

I shook my head. "No, thanks." The house smelled stale, like the inside of my mother's closet.

"So, little Tom got married, eh?" Rich asked, leaning against the couch next to his wife.

"Yes, sir. Fifteen years now."

"Ah, time flies."

"Is your son here?" I asked after a long and awkward pause.

"He's in his room. May I ask why you want to talk to Douglas?"

I considered telling the truth, but the story was insane enough already, and I didn't want to risk it. "I was in town for business, and Tom just wanted me to send his best. I know it's been a while since they spoke."

Rich let out a single bemused laugh. "Yeah, you could say that. You sure you want to see him?"

The question made me nervous. "I won't be long. I have to get back to San Diego tonight. I just wanted to say hello."

"From Tom," Rich said.

"Yes." Clearly, I was missing something, an important detail Julia had chosen not to share. Had they read the book? Did they even know about it?

"Well, come on. I'll show you to his room. Not sure how thrilled he'll be to see you."

I followed Rich down a hallway filled with family photos on the wall. A much younger Rich and Liya sat with a little boy I had to assume was Douglas, and I became acutely aware none of the pictures seemed to date past the age described in *Everything Is Temporary*.

Rich opened the door.

I immediately understood why there were no photos, why Julia sent me here, and it made me sick to my stomach.

A shaggy-haired man lay in bed, dressed in flannel pajamas. He was propped up on one of those electric beds reserved mostly for hospitals, with off-white metal bars attached to the sides. Behind him were several machines displaying digital information I couldn't decipher. At least a half dozen wires emerged from under the bed sheets, connected to these machines, and an IV bag hung from a pole. The room smelled sour, and it felt stuffy, like someone desperately needed to open one of the barred windows to let in fresh air.

Douglas's mouth was gaped open, a small amount of drool running out the side. His eyes were fixed on a cartoon playing on the TV, something to do with *Star Wars*.

"I'll leave you to it. Try not to get him too excited. His bedtime is at eight." Rich stepped back and shut the door behind him before I could ask any more questions.

I don't know what I expected to find here, but this wasn't it. I wanted to understand what had happened. More importantly, I wanted to know why Tom had killed Douglas in the book when he was clearly alive. A flash of anger snapped inside of me.

This would knock down any possible argument Tom could make about the contents of his novel being factual. It's one thing to change some names around, even to personify an abusive woman as an actual monster, but to declare a child to be dead who was actually alive—especially when it clearly had something to do with the events from the story—that was something else. How could he possibly build a case around even the delusion that any of the so-called facts in the book were real when there was clear evidence lying in front of me he had intentionally changed major details to fit a narrative that suited him more.

A second spark of anger chained itself to the last, and I tried to reason why he would make such a radical change intentionally. None of it helped Tom, either in his criminal case or my personal trial of whether or not I could believe him. It made me nauseous, wondering why Tom lied.

Did he change Danny/Douglas's fate to appease his own conscience? Had he killed him off as a way to avoid confronting the consequences his actions had led to? The ongoing destruction of a family? Or was it something worse than that? Could Tom have done this to him directly?

Whatever the reason, the move felt cowardly, regardless of what Tom believed actually happened.

"Hi, Douglas? Douggie? My name is Sarah. I wanted to ask you a couple of questions, if that's all right?"

If he could hear me, there were no clear indications given.

"Do you remember Tom Barnes, from your childhood? What about Julia and Stephanie Dominguez? Or Terry Enbom?"

He blinked several times, though I couldn't be sure if it was in response to my question or just a biological function.

"Tom told me a story about something really bad that happened to you when you were kids. Do you know what I'm talking about? I've talked to the others, and nobody's been able to confirm what Tom's been telling me. I know this sounds crazy, but do you know anything about a woman who claimed to be Mrs. Claus, who turned out to be some sort of monster?"

Douggie's eyes went wide for a second, and I thought I'd broken through. From the TV came the sounds of lightsabers clashing and characters shouting, and I realized he might just be reacting to the show.

I didn't know if he could hear me or if he even knew I was in the room. Nearly everything today had felt like one soul-crushing dead end after another, and even though I knew I should just leave the guy alone, an almost feverish desire to get a reaction from him took over. I crossed the room, kneeled at his side, and peeled his sheets back to hold his clammy hand.

"Please, Douggie, if you can hear me, I really need this right now. I'm so sorry for what's happened to you, and I'm worried that whatever happened back then is happening again but to my daughter. I need to know if my family's in danger. I need to know if Tom is dangerous."

The man finally turned his eyes away from the screen, slowly drifting across my face and down to where our hands met. His eyes widened again, and this time, it was accompanied by panting—soft at first, then quickly growing more urgent.

He moaned something quiet and indecipherable.

"What is it?"

He moaned again, trying to form a word. It sounded like "diapers."

"I'm sorry, I can't understand you."

Douggie started chanting it, his voice rising in tone and urgency each time but not making himself any clearer. Tigers? At one point, I might have even heard Red Ryder as his mumbling escalated into shouting. I backed off, afraid at the terror in his eyes while he continued to shout at me. Through his white sheets, a yellow stain started to spread.

In my retreat, I bumped into a dresser drawer. It startled me and forced out a little yip of fear.

The door swung open, and Rich hurried in to comfort his son. He pet his hair and held him around the shoulders as Douggie kept repeating the word.

"I think it's time for you to leave," Rich barked.

I wasted no time, apologizing profusely as I hurried out of the house and back to my car. Slamming the door behind me, I breathed almost as heavily as Douggie was when he started to yell. He was clearly terrified of something. I could still hear his garbled moan, and the urine-stained sheets led me to think he was, in fact, saying "diapers." Was he so afraid of simply being reminded of the past that it had caused him to wet himself?

I reached into my blazer pocket to grab my phone and find the fastest route home, when my hand connected with something else. The candy cane I had thought I left in the car was there, the hook clinging to the outside of my pocket. Could I have grabbed it by mistake along with my phone when I snatched it from the cup holder?

Another frightening theory hit me.

What if he saw the candy cane, and that's what triggered him? I thought back to the name Tom had given the living candy canes in his book.

Could that have been what he was saying? Stripers?

EXHIBIT 1H: AN EXCERPT FROM EVERYTHING IS TEMPORARY, BY TOM BARNES

"Danny, wake up. Are you okay?" Tim hunched over his best friend, shaking him gently.

Dark pools grew around Danny's shoulder and leg.

"Oh my God, what happened?" A girl who looked like Stephanie came rushing down the embankment, finding Tim with his fallen friend.

Julia was crying nearby, curled up into the fetal position.

"Stay back!" Tim shouted, scrambling for Danny's Daisy air rifle.

"Whoa! What the heck are you doing?" Stephanie raised her arms and froze in place. "What happened to Danny?"

"You tell me, Mrs. Claus," Tim said.

Stephanie's brows furrowed. "Does somebody want to explain what's going on? I just went to the bathroom and heard shouting, then it sounded like the Goodyear Blimp burst. Julia, what is this?" She took a step forward, and Julia scrambled away from her, crab walking across dead leaves and dirt until her back pressed against the mouth of the cave. "Tim, can you put the gun down for a second and explain what's going on? Is Danny okay?"

"Nice try," he said, keeping the gun trained on Stephanie. "What do you want from me? Why can't you just leave us alone?"

"You asked to come over to my house. Can someone please stop acting like I just ran over their puppy and tell me what the heck happened?"

"Julia," Tim called over to her, but she couldn't stop whimpering. "Julia, you know I thought I was kissing you just now, right? We were both fooled."

"You kissed my sister?" Stephanie asked, finally raising her voice.

"No, you kissed me."

"I did not!" Stephanie protested, looking offended. "Like I said, I just went to the bathroom."

Tim looked over at Julia, who was still crying but seemed to be getting a grip on herself. "Julia, what's the last thing you remember in the house? What happened before you came outside?"

Julia nodded several times, the same way her sister did when concentrating. "She did say she was going to the bathroom. That's why I decided to take a break and bring you a soda."

Tim narrowed his eyes at Stephanie. "Can you prove it's really you and not Mrs. Claus in disguise?"

"How on earth could I prove a negative? You want to try and rip out my eyes? Because that's not going to happen."

"What's Julia's favorite movie?" Tim asked.

Stephanie shook her head and shrugged. "I don't know. It seems to change by the day. She was obsessed with *Clueless* last week. Before that, it was *Never Been Kissed*, though it sounds like she's trying to change that."

Tim looked to Julia for confirmation. She nodded her head meekly.

"So, let me get this straight. You're saying Mrs. Claus just disguised herself as *me*?"

"Or she killed Stephanie and we're talking to Mrs. Claus right now." Tim gestured his head into the cave, where a corpse sat rotting. "We found a body in the cave, of an old woman. How do we know you haven't stashed the real Stephanie somewhere and stepped into her skin?"

"Then ask me anything else, and I'll prove it's really me," Stephanie demanded.

Tim shook his head. "How do we know she can't steal your memories?"

"Oh, come on, guys, seriously? We don't have time for this."

Tim didn't know what to believe, but a more pressing matter emerged when Danny let out a groan of pain beside him.

"Danny, are you okay?"

"Did I just get attacked by a blow-up doll?" he mumbled.

"Can you feel your arms or legs? We need to get you to a hospital. Julia, can you help me carry him back up to the house?"

Stephanie took another step toward Tim in an effort to help, but he refocused the rifle on her. "Not you."

Julia slowly rose to her feet, then joined Tim by their injured friend. "Oh God, this looks bad. We should call his parents."

"No!" Danny shouted. "I'm okay, I think." He tried to sit up but gritted his teeth in pain.

"Danny, you're hurt—"

"Tonight is our only chance to take out this monster. If you call my parents, they'll call the twins' parents, and we'll miss our chance. Help me back inside and bandage me up. I'll be fine."

"You don't look fine," Julia said, wiping her forearm across a trail of snot and tears on her face.

"After we beat this bitch, you can take me wherever. But until then, I don't know...Lock me in an upstairs bedroom with the air rifle and let me help."

"Who was my first crush?" Julia asked Stephanie, narrowing her eyes.

"In school, it was Sean Mitchell, but if you mean your *real* first crush, Freddie Prinze Jr."

Julia pursed her lips, considering her maybe-sister. Finally, she nodded. "Good enough for me. Come on, let's get him inside."

If Stephanie was trying to play some sort of trick, she was doing an excellent job. Once the kids got Danny into the house, they set him on top of the kitchen island counter. Stephanie cleaned and dressed his wounds with a first aid kit.

"How do I look, doc? Am I gonna survive?"

"I'll be the first to admit, my medical knowledge doesn't go much past the first aid badge I got in Girl Scouts. From what I can tell, you got extremely lucky. Your shoulder and leg are going to need real medical attention in order to heal properly, but it doesn't look like you got hit in any vital organs or arteries. This could have been much worse."

"All right. So until tonight, we're on the buddy system," Tim said. "We keep the doors locked, and nobody goes outside alone."

Stephanie had finished bandaging Danny and was staring off into the distance.

"Stephanie, everything all right?" Tim asked, still feeling nervous to be around her. "Maybe we should check around the house for a body, just in case."

"No...I mean, sure, if that's what you want," Stephanie said. "I just thought of something, though it may sound a little out there."

Tim let out a nervous laugh. "Believe me, I deal in crazy. What are you thinking?"

"You said you found the body of an old woman in the cave. Do you guys remember the module we did on Greek myths in school?"

Tim crooked his mouth to the side. "Sort of," he said, having already forgotten basically everything he'd learned during his tenure at Dundie Elementary.

"I'm just thinking about all the things we've seen, and it sort of sounds like a figure from one of the myths. Do you remember Lamia?"

"The guy from *The Emperor's New Groove?*" Danny asked, sprawled out on the island.

"Not llama. Lamia. She was a woman who had an affair with Zeus, but Hera found out. To punish her, Hera murdered her children and removed her eyelids so she could never sleep again. As a result, she went insane and turned into some sort of shape-shifting snake monster who lured children into caves and ate them. Part of the myth was that she was able to remove her own eyes and that she could transform into all sorts of shapes in order to lure her victims to their death."

"Well, there we go," Danny said. "Case closed. Sounds like we got Lamia on our hands."

Stephanie shook her head, like she was talking to a room full of idiots. "I wasn't actually saying it was Lamia. I'm just pointing out how myths can sometimes be used as the basis for things in reality, or vice versa. The myth of Dracula came from Vlad Dracul, a man with porphyria who drank the blood of his enemies. What if we're dealing with a creature, or even a breed of creatures, that have been around for so long, people made up myths to explain them."

Tim thought back to his first meetings with Mrs. Claus, how she said she had been running the Christmas House for years, and then thought about the decomposing body in the cave. This Lamia creature could have killed the original Mrs. Claus, stashed her away, and stolen her life in order to feed on kids without suspicion.

And she used him as her accomplice.

A wave of nausea passed over him, and he wondered if he'd ever actually met the real woman or if he'd been dealing with the monster this whole time.

Across the house, a door echoed as it slammed shut, making everyone jump. They all turned to look at Larry, strutting in with several bags full of supplies.

"What's going on, fuckers? Did I miss anything good?"

17

SARAH

It was past ten by the time I pulled into our driveway, and it took everything I had not to immediately confront Tom before going into the house. Instead, I had to keep my cool. I greeted and thanked my parents for staying with us and checked in on Emma.

"It's about time," is all she said, clearly still upset with me for having left in the first place. "Can I go to bed now?"

It seemed like everyone was exhausted. Everyone except for Tom, who was shut away in his studio. Once everyone else was in their rooms for the night, I knocked on Tom's door until he opened up. He was paler than I had ever seen him. His eyes had dark circles, and his cheeks were gaunt.

"How did it go?" he asked timidly, as if he already knew the answer.

"Why didn't you tell me Danny was alive?"

He'd entered the conversation looking like he was afraid I might smack him, but he seemed totally unprepared for this.

"What? How did you—"

"Julia told me, which is a whole other can of worms that I don't want to get into right now."

"You met Julia too..."

"I met all of them."

"How's Terry?" He tried to change the subject.

"Why would you kill a child in a book you're claiming is fact? How fucked up are you?"

Tom opened and closed his mouth several times, attempting to come up with an answer. "Because what happened to him is my fault. I felt like I'd already put his parents through enough. I don't know, it just felt easier to let him go. I thought if any of this ever came back, like it has, I just wanted to leave his family out of it."

"Well, it was a real shit thing to do. And by the way, I hope you realize this destroys your entire case, right? Even with all the supernatural shit aside, you've taken a real person and altered their fate."

He didn't answer and instead stared at his feet, refusing to meet my eyes.

"Did you even come into the house to check on our daughter after school? What are you working on in there?" I tried to peer behind him, but he angled himself in the doorway so I couldn't see anything past him.

"I came in to grab a quick dinner. It sounded like she was having fun with your parents. I didn't want to interrupt. I'm working on some stuff that I think might help with the case."

"Well, I'm glad you're finding it so comfortable, with whatever it is you're doing in there, because you're not coming into our bedroom tonight. I can't even look at you right now."

He hung his head but accepted my verdict. Tom stopped me just as I was turning to leave. "Wait. The lawyer called. He has some new information and wants to meet tomorrow."

"Good. That way I won't have to repeat myself when I explain everything that happened today."

I went to bed angry and quickly found that sleep was impossible. Every hour or so, I would look out the window, and each time, I saw the lights to Tom's studio were still on. Whatever he was doing in there, he'd put his whole self into it, letting everything—including his family—fall to the wayside. Eventually, I managed to doze off, if only for a couple of hours.

When morning rolled around, the lights were off in the studio, and as I headed down the stairs, I saw him fast asleep on the couch. He almost looked like a stranger, and it reignited all the fears I'd had over the past week. I snuck past him, not wanting to re-litigate any of our arguments, and headed down the hall to the guest room, where my parents were staying.

Thanking them for everything they'd done in the past day, I informed them that we had a meeting today with Eric Walsh. Once that was finished, they could feel free to head back home. Of course, they offered to stay as long as we needed, but I didn't want them to see any more of the mess Tom and I had become.

Emma was still acting sullen when she came down to breakfast, offering almost no reaction when I said her grandparents would be taking her to school and then heading back to Palm Springs.

"Cool, so now they're abandoning me too," she said, picking at her breakfast.

I tried to explain that no one was abandoning her, that everything we were doing was for her, but it was like talking to a wall. Once this was all over, I would find some way to make it up to her. I had to.

Tom and I didn't exchange words, with the exception of him offering a reminder of the meeting with Eric. The two of us stood on opposite sides of the closet, putting on our suits.

The last thing I wanted to do was hurt Tom by explaining my findings, but at the same time, I couldn't help but feel like I was just bringing to light things Tom should have already known. And furthermore, I was growing even more afraid there was a piece of Tom he had never shown me, a side capable of doing horrible things. Even after fifteen years, you can never really know what's going on inside someone's head.

On the ride over, he tried to conjure up a number of apologies and explanations, but I repeated to him that he could save it until we were in the meeting. He stared out the window, like a kid waiting to be called into the principal's office.

When we entered, Eric greeted us with as grim a face as the one I was sure I had. There were no cordial greetings or reassuring gestures. He simply prompted us to join him in his office.

"You lied to me," he said, once we'd all taken our seats around the table. "Do you remember the one thing I told you when I first agreed to take you on as a client? As long as you're completely honest with me, I would represent you to the absolute best of my ability."

"What does that mean? You're dropping me?" Tom asked, on the verge of panic.

"I should," Eric said. "Remember when I said your book would be a silver bullet but didn't know for whom? Well, I can confidently tell you now, you've basically handed over your own guilty sentence."

"I didn't lie," Tom tried to protest, though he was met with cold looks from both me and the lawyer. "At least about important things."

"So you didn't think it was important to mention that you nearly hospitalized a student dressed up as Santa during your sophomore year in college?"

I was hoping Eric was talking about Douglas, but this was an entirely new incident I'd had no idea about. Once again, I felt a sickening, sinking feeling settle into me and wondered what else he could possibly be hiding at this point.

"What?" Tom almost sounded offended. "Why does that matter? The police never got involved. I wasn't arrested or charged with anything."

"No, but one simple call to the university's public safety office brought up a detailed account of you accosting and beating a student for simply wishing you a merry Christmas."

"There was more to it than that," he said, getting defensive.

"I don't care. This whole case is built around proving to a jury that this incident with Mr. Owens was a one-time outburst. With this, it proves a pattern of violence, specifically against people celebrating Christmas. Especially in this political climate, how many jurors do you think are going to feel sympathetic for a man who is being painted as waging a one-man war on Christmas?"

"I'm not waging a war. That's ridiculous!" Tom shouted, throwing himself to his feet but quickly returning to his chair after realizing there was nowhere to go.

"Well, that's what the prosecutor is going to say, and the jury is going to eat it right up. And that's just for starters. You said that everything in your book was true, and yet here we find out that the person you refer to as Danny Chung is actually alive."

"Did you tell him?" Tom stared at me as if I had just stabbed him in the back.

"All it took was a few minutes on Google. My investigator found an article from the *OC Register* dated June of 2000 regarding a boy named Douglas Chin, who was attacked and put into a coma by a reindeer that had escaped days before from the Santa Ana Zoo. Your name is even featured in the article as shooting the animal to scare it away."

Tom chewed at his lip, like he wanted to explain, but eventually, he shook his head dismissively. "So it's all lost, just like that?"

"Let me be frank with you, Mr. Barnes. This was already going to be an uphill battle of a case. But with these new details, it's going to be damn near impossible without finding some other piece of evidence that exonerates you without a shred of doubt." Eric took a moment to calm himself down before turning to me. "Mrs. Barnes... Sarah. Please tell me you have some good news because your husband could really use it right now."

I'd come into the meeting ready to chew Tom out, but it seemed Eric had already done a fine job on his own. All the anger that had been percolating all night evaporated when I realized just how screwed Tom really was. I didn't have the heart to kick him while he was down. Even worse, there was a small part of me that thought we might actually be safer with him locked up.

"I met with Terry, Julia, and Douglas. I wish I had better news to report."

"What did you learn? Run me through your day." Eric and Tom both leaned in slightly.

Eric was hoping to catch a morsel of information that could help the case. Tom was worried about what his former friends would say about him, and for good reason.

"Okay, so first, the good news. Or at least, the best news I can give. Terry turned out to actually be quite a lovely guy. He swore like a sailor, but in terms of backing up Tom's character, he had nothing but the highest praise. He even said you were the best friend he ever had."

"But what about the details of the story?"

I wavered my head side to side as I tried to find a delicate way of describing it. "He's not going to be a ton of help there. He seems to have blocked out a lot of his childhood memories, citing heavy alcohol and drug use from an early age. I don't know if I should outright say this in front of you, but he implied pretty heavily that he would tell the jury pretty much anything we told him to, no matter how insane it is. He wants to help Tom that badly."

Eric tried to hide a frown. "Well, you're right about one thing. You probably shouldn't have disclosed his willingness to lie to me. But I like the enthusiasm, especially compared to how he's described in the book. It'll help show that Tom is capable of letting grudges go. How about Julia?"

I shook my head. "She outright told me that everything Tom said was a lie and personally blamed him for her sister's death. She said if any of us tried to contact her again, she'd do her best to make our lives a living hell."

Between the two men, I'm not sure who seemed more disheartened. Eric jotted down some notes on his legal pad.

"I'll need a more detailed recounting of that conversation later, as it sounds like we can almost guarantee the prosecution will bring her up on the stand if this goes to trial. How about the last one." He double-checked his notes for his real name. "Douglas Chin?"

"He's practically catatonic, living on life support at his parents' house."

Tom's face fell as I spoke. He seemed genuinely remorseful.

"I tried to talk to him about what happened, but he sort of had a meltdown, and I was quickly asked to leave by his father."

It was an understatement to say that the mood in the room felt grim.

"All right, so just to review what we have here...Tom attempted to kill a man by arson out of fear for his daughter's safety. Despite the unseemly appearances of their friendship, both Mr. Owens and your daughter, Emma, mutually claim nothing inappropriate ever took place, outside of her hiding the fact that she was spending time with him. None of Tom's childhood friends can corroborate any part of the story presented in the book he had us enter into evidence, and we now know he has a history of violence against Christmas itself. This shows two of the three major markers for adolescent psychopathy in that he admitted to willfully attacking birds and a reindeer in his book and admits to feeling out of control in the face of what he believed to be a divine or demonic force."

"But I never pooped my pants, so at least we've got that," Tom said with a listless smile. "That was the third marker, right?"

No one laughed.

"What about Carl Owens? Did you find any background on him?" Tom asked.

Eric nodded. "Angus did some digging. Carl was born and raised in Provo, Utah, in a Mormon community. He lived there until his twenties, when he moved to San Diego. From there, he's lived what appears to be a quiet life, until three years ago when he opened up his Christmas House program to help terminal kids in the community."

"But what about the exchange we had in his living room?" Tom said. "He not only saw me with the canister...He goaded me to do it. Are you sure we can't do anything with that?"

"Again, he swears that no conversation between you two ever took place. It would be your word against his, and after the litany of untruths you seem to be embroiled in, it's my belief that this story would actively work against your case."

For a moment, I considered corroborating Tom's story. Carl had indeed admitted to me that they'd spoken. In the end, I held my tongue, afraid I'd get chewed out by both my husband and the lawyer if I admitted to meeting with the victim.

"Look, I'm going to be straight with you. I would highly suggest, at this junction, that we start looking into a plea deal. I can't make any promises, but I still think we could knock it down to arson, with a five- or seven-year sentence."

Tom sat silently and chewed his lip. I waited for him to say something, anything, but the longer he sat, the more uncomfortable the room became.

"I can meet with the prosecutor and see what they offer before you make a decision."

Tom gave a vacant nod. "But if I don't take the plea, we go to trial, spend $150,000, and then I go to jail for seven to life, right? I'm getting locked up either way."

Eric's eyes softened, and he placed a hand on Tom's shoulder. "It's not over yet, but I think you should prepare for those possibilities."

Tom shook his head, closed his eyes, and squeezed a sigh through his nose. "Fine. Is there anything else?"

Eric flipped through a few more pages. "We're still looking into any woman in the early 2000s in the city of Orange who claimed to be Mrs. Claus, but so far, we've come up with nothing. Angus will keep digging on that." He scanned through a few more documents. "The toxicology report came back on the burned ornaments. As we already knew, they did come back as a positive match to the lighter fluid found in your backpack."

One last gleam of hope lit up in Tom's eyes. "Wait. The ornaments. What if we could match the ornaments to the ones in the book?"

With a grimace, Eric scanned the document. "The descriptions you give of the ornaments in the book are fairly specific. I suppose we could have a look. If there were enough that matched, perhaps we could use it in some way. Though to be perfectly honest with you it feels like grasping at straws—"

"Where are they now?" Tom said, his whole body getting animated with excitement.

"They're all in evidence lockup," Eric said. "About two dozen pieces were bagged and tagged from fire damage, along with a tree."

"Are you allowed to...I don't know...check them out...or something? Look at them in person?"

"I can put in a request, then inspect them within the facility, yes. I'll admit, it's a long shot."

"I don't care. We have to take any chance we can get, right? If we don't, then..." A shiver ran through his body.

I reached out and grabbed him by the arm. "Then what?" I asked.

He looked at me with more fear in his eyes than I'd ever seen before. "Then I go away, and Mrs. Claus comes to kill you and Emma."

EXHIBIT 1I: AN EXCERPT FROM EVERYTHING IS TEMPORARY, BY TOM BARNES

Tim, Larry, Julia, and Stephanie spent the rest of the afternoon booby-trapping the house, not just against Mrs. Claus, but against a potential army of toys. Danny was the one exception.

Once he was properly bandaged and given some Vicodin Julia found in her mother's medicine cabinet, he was carried upstairs to the twins' bedroom. They propped him up against the window with his Daisy air rifle on his lap for him to act as lookout. Aside from that room, every other window in the house was nailed shut, followed by a pair of wooden boards covering the window in an "X" pattern to stop Mrs. Claus from bursting through the glass, like she had in Larry's trailer.

Initially, the team had thought they could be creative enough to come up with dozens of unique traps to rig throughout the house. As it turned out, planning and executing complicated booby traps was a lot harder—and more time-consuming—than they could have ever realized. Most of their innovations were made up of boards with nails pounded through them, hidden around the entry points of the house. Buckets of glue were hung above each doorway so, even if a dozen Candy Stripers or Humble Hummel's were to cross through a threshold, they would be trapped en masse by the sticky substance.

As the sun raced behind the mountains, they had to start abandoning plans and, lacking better ideas, stole some of the traps from *Home Alone*. They'd added a few twists to try and fool Mrs. Claus, like attaching four paint cans to the banister above the staircase instead of the two from the film. They'd also rigged several blowtorches throughout the house after seeing how effective fire had been before. The tricky thing with those was how to position them in a way that didn't end up trapping five pre-teens inside of a burning building.

The one big advantage they had over Kevin McCallister was that, in the movie, he had to activate each trap himself. With the help of a larger group of kids, they could position themselves in different areas of the house. No matter where Mrs. Claus decided to enter, there would be someone at the ready.

Additionally, each kid was armed with a weapon if it came to it. Larry gave Tim his nail-embedded bat in favor of a nail gun he'd picked up at the hardware store. Julia and Stephanie disassembled their ice skates, placing the blades along the edges of their field hockey sticks, and they both wore soccer cleats in case they needed to stomp any Candy Stripers into smithereens.

At a certain point, they had to stop tying tripwires across the hallways and get into their designated positions. The boys took the downstairs entrances, with Tim hiding behind the front door and Larry guarding the sliding glass door in the living room, leading to the backyard. Julia hid in the downstairs guest bathroom, with a tub of water balloons filled with lighter fluid, and Stephanie was on staircase paint can duty. If Danny saw anyone—or anything—approach from the backyard, he would fire a warning shot to raise the alarm.

Then, they waited.

Ten minutes went by, twenty, an hour. Pulse-pounding anxiety turned surprisingly quickly into boredom. When Tim's watch beeped, signaling the nine o'clock hour, he decided to do a check-in with the rest of the group. He called out to each of his companions, and one by one, they replied with no news to report.

All except for Danny.

When he heard nothing, Tim ventured from his post to call down the hall to Stephanie, asking her to check on him. A moment later, he heard Stephanie shout something, but her words were swallowed by the echoes of the spacious house. Tim tiptoed carefully, stepping over tripwires and into the hallway to ask Stephanie for her report again. He watched as she ventured down the stairs, stopping just before the landing, where a string connected to a blowtorch meant to work in conjunction with Julia's lighter-fluid balloons.

"He's fine. Just sitting in bed where he's supposed to be," Stephanie said.

Tim's jaw fell open when a paint can dropped without warning from the banister, swinging in full force into the back of Stephanie's head. Her small body was hurled forward from the momentum, and as she landed face-first into the tile floor, her feet caught on the string that was supposed to trigger the blowtorch. Instead, the torch itself got dislodged from its position and fell uselessly to the floor.

A door in the hallway opened, and Julia stepped out with a pair of balloons in her hands. She saw a pool of blood spreading around her twin sister's head and screamed. The balloons fell to the floor with pop-splats.

"Stephanie!" she cried, running to her sister. "Stephanie, are you okay?" She shook her sister, but the girl didn't react. "Help me flip her over!" Julia called to Tim, who rushed over to help.

They had to work together to flip the limp girl over onto her back. Tim already had a terrible feeling in his gut, and by the time they had rolled her over, things looked even worse than he had imagined.

"She's not breathing!" Julia cried, running her fingers across a blood-soaked neck, searching for a pulse.

Tim didn't know much about medicine, but it didn't take a doctor to tell him what happened. Stephanie's mouth lay gaped open, most of her teeth were caved in, and her nose had crumpled entirely into her face. Her eyes were open and unmoving, and more blood continued to spread across the floor.

Tim didn't know what to say, how to tell Julia her sister was dead. He looked up at the banister overhead, and his eyes went wide. A small Santa Claus Hummel peered down at him from above. Even through its white mittens, the figurine raised a hand and gave Tim the finger, along with a malicious grin.

"Julia, we have to move." He grabbed the girl and tried to pull her away from her other half, but she wouldn't let go.

"No!" she screamed through a face full of tears.

Tim glanced back up, and Santa was gone.

"Julia, we have to go now!" He dropped the spiked bat, pulling Julia with all his might into the bathroom moments before another paint can came soaring down the staircase, just missing Julia by inches.

"What's going on over there?" Larry called, abandoning his post and entering the hallway. "Oh fuck, what happened to her?" he said, just as the first crack of Danny's gun popped from the bedroom upstairs.

"Bad guys incoming!" a muffled voice shouted through the upstairs bedroom door, quickly followed by another pop.

Then came the crash.

From the sound of it, the entire sliding glass backdoor shattered. Everything was happening all at once. Tim's heart pounded as all their plans disappeared in a second. Larry ran back out into the living room, then fired off a series of nails from his gun.

"Shit, there's too many of them!" he shouted.

"Julia, we need you right now," Tim said. "I know this is hard, but we have to fight, or we're all going to die."

"I can't." Julia ripped herself away from Tim's arms.

"I'm sorry, but you have to. Mrs. Claus is here. We don't have time to fall apart right now."

"My sister is dead!" she screamed. "Don't you see! She's dead!"

"If we don't do something now, we're all gonna be dead!" Tim's voice came out far less sympathetic than he anticipated.

"A little help?" Larry called again from the living room. He fired his nail gun several more times but was countered by a series of smaller pops in return. "Ow, fuck!"

"Keep this door closed," Tim said, then left Julia behind and rushed out of the bathroom to meet up with Larry.

The scene was pure chaos. The door had indeed been shattered, and even though the glue bucket trap had seemed to work as intended, the figures it had rooted in place were a platoon of nutcrackers, each holding onto a little rifle that fired tiny bullets at Larry. Each shot made no more than a pin-prick against his skin, but there were at least a dozen toys unloading their little rifles at him. It didn't help that Larry turned out to be a lousy shot with the nail gun, hitting one nutcracker for maybe every seven shots he fired.

"Give me my bat!" he demanded, once the nail gun ran out of ammo.

Tim hurried back into the hallway to collect the bat, along with the field hockey stick from Stephanie's corpse. In his hurry, he almost slipped and fell on the mixture of blood and lighter fluid that had consumed a significant portion of the hallway. Once he had the stick in hand, he slipped along the floor, trying to make it back to Larry, and, in an instant, saw his brief life flash before his eyes as another paint can dropped from above, just barely missing him.

Tim wondered how the house had been breached without their noticing. He hurried back to toss Larry the bat, but the answer quickly became apparent. A cluster of Candy Stripers suddenly dropped onto Tim from above. Their tips had been sharpened into needles, and they stabbed at his shoulders and throat as he smacked them off. Tim looked up, realizing they were dropping from the slats in the ceiling's air vents.

He was so stupid. They'd nailed off all the windows but had forgotten completely about the air conditioner, storm drains, and whatever other tiny holes a two-inch figure could squeeze through.

Once he had thrown some of the Candy Stripers onto the ground, Tim swung the bladed hockey stick at them, sending them cracking into the wall. Behind him, Larry cried out in pain. Stripers were pouring down from the ceiling by the dozen. Once on the floor, they coiled themselves up like little springs, then launched themselves at Larry, impaling their pointed tips into his legs. Tim worked his hardest to smack them away before any others could strike, while Larry focused on the never-ending procession of nutcrackers and

Hummel figurines marching over the shattered bodies of their fallen companions.

The pile of broken toys was large enough now that the glue had no effect on them. They simply marched over the shards of their former ranks, and they just kept coming.

Upstairs, the steady snapping of the air rifle came to an abrupt halt, and that's when the smell hit him.

Fresh baked cookies.

"Cover me!" Tim commanded, hurdling himself over the marching toys and running out into the backyard.

He made it onto the porch just in time to see a trail of deep scrapes running up the stucco facade of the house and the tip of a massive green tail slithering through the single open window.

"It's Mrs. Claus. She's inside!" Tim yelled, sprinting back into the house, across the living room, and down the hall.

"What do I do?" Larry asked, continuing his unending assault against the toys.

"Leave them! If we take out Mrs. Claus, maybe we can stop them all!"

It was easier said than done. The moment he turned to join Tim, Larry got pelted by another round of gunfire from a fresh brigade of nutcrackers, and more candy cane snakes cascaded down from the ceiling, overwhelming him.

Larry was going to have to take care of himself. There was no time.

Tim ran down the hall, leaping over the massive red stain on the floor as he connected with the stairs. There was one more paint can, and he knew it was coming. He swung the hockey stick upwards in anticipation, and for once, luck was on his side. The paint can came swinging, just as he expected, but the ice skates blade connected with the rope before it could reach him, and the can smashed into the stairs, exploding white paint everywhere as it tumbled down. When he reached the top, he took one look at the Hummel smirking at him from the banister.

"Fuck you, Santa Claus." Tim swung the stick and shattered the Hummel into a million pieces.

Tim threw the door open to the twins' room and was horrified to find himself standing before a familiar scene. Danny's hands and legs were tied to the posts of the bed by Candy Stripers, and the beast that once was Mrs. Claus straddled him. This time, the room was fully lit, and Tim finally got a look at her true form.

Her massive snake tail gave way to a human-like torso, with bony hips and pale mounds that insinuated breasts. She wasn't fully covered in green scales. Parts of her body were fleshy, like they had once belonged to a human. Long strings of white hair hung in greasy clumps from the back of her head. Her face was an almost perfect combination of something serpentine and female.

Her eyes floated on either side of her head, careful to avoid going too high; there was a ceiling fan running at full speed, and she had to hunch over to ensure she didn't get herself caught up in the blades. Just as Stephanie had explained, instead of a nose, she had a series of holes just above her mouth, which he assumed acted as some sort of heat sensor.

The pair of snakes coming out from her eye sockets had already traveled deeply down Danny's gullet. His eyes were pure white, fully rolled back in his head, and his body twitched. He made no attempts to fight back, and the rifle lay uselessly on the ground.

Tim raised his stick, hoping to catch her off guard as she fed. But before he could take even a single step, her eyes darted over to him, and she reared back, pulling the eye-snakes out of Danny's mouth.

"You're too late, Little Elf. Your friend is dead."

"Why are you doing this?" Tim begged.

"I didn't do this. I did everything I could to protect you from yourself. But you had to show your little friends the turtle doves. You needed to save the little girl. Do you have any idea how long I've lived? How many souls I've claimed? I was prepared to offer you a gift, an opportunity at true power, and this is how you repay me?"

"You kill children!"

The beast shook its head. "I save sick children from a slow and torturous death. Compared to what they would endure, I'm a Christmas angel. I only had to kill your friends because you forced them to threaten my very existence."

"What about Janice? She didn't get sick until after I started seeing you."

The serpent-woman flashed her razor-sharp teeth at Tim in something resembling a wicked smile. "That one was a special gift for you, Little Elf. You have no idea the power you could have had. I thought you'd understand. I thought you'd be grateful."

"You were wrong. I would never hurt anyone, not like this."

Her grin widened, and her forked tongue licked her lips. "One day, you will."

Tim had heard enough. He charged at the snake, aiming the blade of his stick right at her throat. She moved so quickly, he might as well have been a snail picking a fight with a jaguar. In one motion, she knocked the stick out of his hand, then wrapped her massive fingers around his torso. He tried to curse and spit and cry, but she had him gripped so tightly, he could barely even breathe.

His eyes became transfixed on the gaping open mouths of the snakes coming out of her eye sockets. The rhythmic green and red pulsing in their mouths made him dizzy, almost as if he were in a dream.

"Even now, after I've finished off your friends, I will choose to spare you, as we go on a journey together toward immortality. Once I mark my chosen, you're mine forever. I think I'll turn you into—"

Her words were cut off as another voice interrupted her. "Put him down, you bitch." Larry held the bat over one shoulder and a handful of nails in between each knuckle of his other fist.

Mrs. Claus laughed, and with a lightning-fast strike, she ripped the bat away from Larry and tossed it out the window. "Larry Enholm. You've been a very naughty boy this year. Nothing but coal for you."

With her other hand, she picked him up by the torso. He punched into her arm with his makeshift spiked knuckles, but she didn't seem to loosen her grip as small streams of black blood ran down her forearm.

"I was wondering when you would show up. I had hoped to give Tim the gift of watching me bite the head off of his tormentor, once and for all." Without facing away from Larry, her hovering eyes turned to Tim. "Believe me, Little Elf, one day, you'll treasure this memory."

With her eyes still focused on Tim, she slowly brought Larry toward her gaping mouth. Her jaw opened so wide, it had to make several pops and clicks, unhinging itself to make room.

Larry shouted something, slowly bringing Tim back from the hypnotic state the snakes had produced with their twinkling lights. Finally, the words sunk in, and Tim knew what was about to happen.

Larry had said, "Rebel training."

It took every ounce of will for Tim to shut his eyes and turn his head away as Larry chucked the handful of nails into the ceiling fan. Unlike in school, when he would toss push-pins randomly in the air, this time, he knew exactly where he wanted to throw them. The nails hit the whirring blades of the fan, which fired like a machine gun at Mrs. Claus's face. She screamed in pain as a nail pierced straight through one of her hovering eyeballs and impaled it into the wall with a sickening splat.

The next thing Tim knew, he was on the ground, gasping for breath. Larry was next to him, doing the same. Mrs. Claus recoiled, and the snakes coming from her eyes hissed and screeched, making a sound unlike anything Tim had ever heard before. He groped around on the floor and found the hockey stick, then swung it upward with all his might. It sliced through something, though he didn't know what it was until he saw one of the small snake's heads fall to the carpet in front of him, its glowing mouth pumping out black liquid. It then went dark.

All at once, the smell of cookies disappeared, replaced by the unfathomably acrid smell of urine, like a thousand dogs pissing on a rug at the same time. It was like someone poured a gallon of vinegar down his nose, and it made Tim gag. He forced himself to look up at the beast, who screamed in torment. She had felt true pain for the first time in possibly centuries.

Mrs. Claus turned, sucking her remaining snake back into her head. Her last floating eye popped back in.

"Don't let her get away!" Tim coughed, but by the time he'd gotten the words out, it was too late.

She'd leapt from the window, just as she had in Larry's trailer. Tim forced himself to his feet and watched her slither off into the canyon below. In the backyard, the encroaching army of toys froze in place, then toppled lifelessly to the ground.

18

SARAH

Tom remained silent for the rest of the lawyer's meeting and didn't open his mouth again until the moment we got in the car.

"You went to visit him," he said. It wasn't a question, but a statement of fact.

For a moment, I considered playing dumb or confused. *Visited who?* I wanted to say. But I could tell from the tone of his voice that he had me dead to rights.

"How did you know?" I asked.

I'd started the car and was driving back home. Even still, I could feel Tom staring intensely at me from my periphery.

"The smell. When you came back from your trip to the 'grocery store,' he'd left his scent all over you."

Guilt bubbled up inside my stomach, for betraying the one thing he'd begged me not to do. It explained why he had acted so sullen after we'd had what I thought was a very productive and healthy conversation.

"How could you be so stupid?"

"I wasn't trying to go behind your back. I just wanted to get a straight answer for myself."

"Don't you realize he could have done anything to you in there? You could have been killed."

"He was perfectly friendly to me. If I thought at any point I was in danger, I would have gotten out of there." I tried to reassure him, but it only served to set him off further.

"And how would you have expected to do that? I know you don't believe in what I wrote in the book, but I'm telling you, if he had wanted to end you right then and there, it wouldn't have taken much. And that's not even factoring in the damage you could have done to the case by interacting with the so-called victim!" He was shouting now.

For fifteen years, I could have counted on one hand the number of times he'd raised his voice. In the last week, I'd heard him yell more than in all our lives together combined.

"Tom..." I glanced from the road over to him to make my point clear. "I'm trying as hard as I can to be supportive here. Especially after meeting with Julia—which, by the way, raises a whole series of other concerns. I don't even want to touch on why she hates you so much, or why we look so eerily similar. You want to talk weird? Marrying a woman who looks like your pre-teen crush is pretty fucking weird to me."

Tom shrunk back in his seat, clearly uncomfortable.

"Oh, you don't want to talk about that? Then how about we back up a bit. I went to see Carl because I was looking to see if I could get him to share anything that the police couldn't. And guess what? He did tell me that you two had talked."

"Really?" Tom's eyes lit up with hope. "Why didn't you tell this to Eric? This helps my case!"

"Because he said the reason he lied was to protect you so he couldn't identify you in a lineup. He was doing you a favor."

"A favor?" He spat the word out like it had tasted rotten in his mouth. Before he had a chance to speak again, his phone started to jingle in his pocket. "Huh, well, that was fast," he said, looking at his phone. He answered the call, putting it on speaker.

"Hey, Eric, did we forget something at the office?"

"Tom? I'm not sure how to say this," Eric said with trepidation.

"What is it?"

"I just called in to the evidence lockup to prepare the materials you wanted, and when they went to go check on it, they said it was all gone."

"I don't understand." Tom glanced over to me with a combination of excitement and worry. "What do you mean, gone?"

"I mean, all evidence is labeled and stored in boxes, and when the clerk went to check on it, the box for your case was overturned, and all the contents were missing. Even the half-burned Christmas tree that was too large and had to be leaned against a wall."

I felt a tingle in the back of my head as Eric spoke, and my breath seized up in my chest.

Tom stuttered out a few half words, trying to wrap his head around the situation. "Aren't there cameras in the building? Can't they see who took them?"

"Well, that's actually the other weird thing. All the footage has been covered up by these flashing red and green lights. They can't find anyone entering or leaving the building."

I pulled up to a stop light. Tom and I exchanged a look that chilled me to my core. Then his phone started to buzz again.

"Hey, Eric, can I call you right back? I'm getting a call from Emma's school." He pressed a button on his phone. "Hello, this is Tom Barnes."

"Mr. Barnes, this is Jeannie Shrieve from the administration office at Friars Middle School."

"What's wrong? Is Emma in trouble again?"

Now it was someone else's turn to stutter their way through a conversation. "Emma didn't show up for homeroom this morning. I was calling to remind you that you're supposed to call ahead in the event that—"

"She's not there?" Tom spoke in an urgent and commanding tone.

"Well, no."

"Excuse me, I have to go."

We both shared a look of terror with each other. In the last two minutes, all the skepticism I had about Tom faded away, replaced by a deep and mind-aching fear as I considered, for the first time, that everything he had said might actually be true.

"Call my parents," I said, reaching into my pocket and handing Tom the phone.

Something else came tumbling out of my pocket, but before I could check to discover what it was, I was prompted into action by the sound of horns honking behind me. The light was green, and I stomped my foot on the gas to get back home as soon as possible.

My mother answered on the third ring. "Miss us so soon?" she said in a jovial tone that only served to twist the pit of fear in my stomach.

"Did you drop off Emma at school today?" I asked as Tom held up the phone.

"You know how your daughter is. Emma made us stop two blocks away so she wouldn't be seen getting driven by a couple of old fogies. Is everything all right?"

I made a quick glance over to Tom. His eyes were as wide as I've ever seen them, and he was emphatically nodding and mouthing the word *yes*.

"Yeah," I said, trying to force myself to sound calm. "I think she's ditched is all. I bet she's back at home."

"Do you want us to turn around?" Mom asked.

With just as much enthusiasm, Tom shook his head, mouthing the words *not safe*.

"Nah, I'm sure it's all fine. Thanks again for coming down to take care of her. We're just pulling up to the house now. Drive safe."

Tom hung up on Mom before she could finish her sentence. "This is what I've been warning you about this whole time. Don't you see now?"

I didn't know what to think. I turned into our driveway and began to ease my foot off the gas, when a lightning bolt of pain shot through my foot, forcing it to stomp on the accelerator.

"Sarah, what are you—" Tom's words cut off when the car smashed through the front wall of his studio.

I attempted to pull my leg away from the gas pedal, but the harder I tried, the faster the wheels skidded against the asphalt. The steaming front of the car ground into the building. I looked down at my foot and felt another shockwave of fear and pain strike me.

A red and white striped snake was embedded through the center of my foot. It wrapped itself around the gas pedal, holding it in place as blood ran down my ankle.

I was in no position to reach forward, so I threw the gear shift into park and flipped the car keys off. Only then did the small serpent relent. It pulled itself out of my foot, redoubling my pain, and I realized I was staring at the pointed end of a candy cane. It was the candy cane Mr. Owens had given me from his house.

All at once, it hit me.

I hadn't grabbed it by accident when visiting Douggie's house. It had slithered into my pocket on its own accord because *it was alive.*

I stared at it in frozen shock. It formed itself into a coil, then it launched itself like a spring-loaded rocket straight for my face. The best I could do was flinch my head backward and squeeze my eyes shut in preparation for it to drive itself into my brain. But the pain never came.

"Sarah!" Tom shouted, shaking me back into the moment. He had somehow caught the thing mid-flight. It writhed in his hand, desperately trying to squeeze its way through and stab me in the face.

More blood ran like a fountain down into my lap, and at first, I thought it was the remnant of my blood from it stabbing my foot. Then I realized Tom hadn't caught it at all. He had simply put his open palm out to stop its journey, and it had impaled his hand in the same way it had my foot. He grimaced in pain and used his other hand to keep the candy cane from escaping.

Not just a candy cane—a Candy Striper. That's what Douggie saw when I visited him. That's what had terrified him to the point of wetting himself. He was trying to tell me the whole time.

It's all real. It's all fucking real.

"Get out of the car!" Tom shouted.

I pulled the handle on my door, but it wouldn't budge. The entire driver's side of the car was pinned to the wall of Tom's half-collapsed studio. Overhead, there was a creaking sound, like the whole building was threatening to fall at any second.

"The door's stuck!" My voice came out high and squeaky, mirroring the panic I felt inside.

Tom tried his side. It took a few shoves, but he managed to get the passenger door open. He tumbled to the ground, ripped the Candy Striper from his hand with a grunt, then stomped on it when it hit the floor until it was nothing but sugary dust. Tom then reached back into the car for me with his good hand. "Come on!"

I grabbed onto him and let him pull me across the console and passenger side, only moments before the studio's roof collapsed onto the hood of the car, crushing everything inside. If I had been only a few seconds slower, I would be dead by now.

I dropped to my knees to catch my breath, my ears ringing. It was almost as if the world had turned into a slide show. I could only make out little details here and there inside the ruined detached garage that once served as an art studio. It was hardly recognizable from the room I'd known only a week ago.

It wasn't just the damage either.

The room had been cleared of all paintings and canvases, replaced by piles of junk that had been assembled into contraptions, the purpose of which I couldn't guess.

Tom wasted no time collecting handfuls of jury-rigged devices made out of wood, tape, and nails. There was a long black rifle case with the word "Daisy" printed in white. Only, it was stuffed with something rectangular that barely fit inside—clearly not a rifle. To further prove that point, sitting next to it was the BB gun that had presumably came with it—the logo covered with white painter's tape. Tom had scribbled the words "Red Ryder" in black sharpie across the stock. He slung both of these over his shoulder, then ran over to the roll of painter's tape on the wall. With a pinch of his thumb, he wrapped his bleeding hand in tape, gritting his teeth until he was satisfied with the length, and ripped his makeshift bandage from the roll.

"Come on. We have to find Emma."

As the ringing in my ears subsided, I heard a booming voice come from inside the main house.

"Ho! Ho! Ho! And what's your name, little boy?" It sounded like Santa Claus, and I knew exactly which version. *A Christmas Story* was playing in the living room at full volume, and Santa was just about to tell Ralphie that he'd shoot his eye out, right before kicking him down a slide.

Tom threw open the door, making it no more than two steps inside before he came to a screeching halt. I followed, then immediately regretted it.

In the center of our living room was a charred Christmas tree standing nearly seven feet tall. Half its limbs were black, and despite the fact it lacked any source of power, its string lights made up a disturbing visage. It had two red-bulbed eyes and a pair of lit strings that blinked on and off as if to match a pair of lips. It spoke in a growling, guttural voice.

"Little Elf, how you've grown."

Tom snarled at the tree. "Evergreen. Where's my daughter?"

"Oh," the tree said with a sense of malicious glee, "I'm quite sure you'll see her again, when the time is right. Presently, I believe you have more immediate concerns."

A line of string lights shot out from the base of the tree, like a twinkling whip. It wrapped itself around Tom's legs, then yanked, pulling him to the ground and sending his weapons flying from his shoulders. Tom fought against it, clawing at the carpeted floor of our house, but he was helpless against the thing dragging him across the room. A second tendril of string lights came from near the top of the tree and wrapped itself around Tom's neck. It pulled him up to his feet and held him against the burnt branches.

"Mrs. Claus says I'm to keep you alive. She wants you to watch."

Watch what? I wondered.

The answer came quickly.

From deep within Evergreen's branches, a flock of small ceramic turtle doves came bursting forth, flying straight at me. They pecked at my face, trying to stab me in the eyes and neck. I was able to swat some of them down, but there were too many. They grabbed me by the scalp and ripped chunks out of my hair.

Death by a thousand cuts. Several of them dive-bombed the backs of my legs, knocking me to my knees.

Tom was trying to tell me something, but between the assault of the turtle doves, the blaring TV, and the deep throaty laugh of the sentient tree, I couldn't make out any of his words except for: "I love you."

It was hard to see through the incessant attempts from the ceramic birds to peck out my eyes, but I wanted to get one last good look at my husband before one of the creatures inevitably nicked an artery and I bled out in front of the man who'd sacrificed everything to save me.

But something was off.

Tom's face didn't match his words. A moment ago, he had been saying his goodbyes, and now...he was smiling.

"Turn away," a woman's voice called out from behind me.

Tom leaned as far to the side as possible. I felt a blast of heat next to my face as a huge ball of fire swept across the room and blasted Evergreen on his unburnt side.

The tree screamed, and bulbs on his strings exploded into sparks. Its branches caught fire, and just like that, Tom was free from its tendrils, stumbling forward and dropping to the ground. Another blast of fire hit Evergreen directly. Only this time, instead of a small burst, it was hit by a sustained flame.

The woman who had called out stepped forward into my view. It was Julia, holding an aerosol can of deodorant with a Zippo lighter duct-taped to it. I heard more footsteps behind me, much heavier, then a series of smacking sounds as ceramic turtle doves smashed to the floor and crashed into the walls.

When the pecking assault finally let up, I turned to see Terry standing over me, holding a tennis racket that looked like it was built for the apocalypse. The strings had been replaced with barbed wire, and the entire rim of the racket had nails tied around it, like a spiked axe.

Terry reached his gigantic hand down to me. "You all right, Sarah?"

I took his hand in mine, then winced in pain as I tried to stand, remembering the hole that had been gouged into my right foot.

"Honestly, I don't have a fucking clue."

19

SARAH

Once the tree's death wail had concluded and the last of his string lights were snuffed out, Tom hurried into the kitchen to fetch the extinguisher before the whole house burned down. As soon as I was able, I limped upstairs to try and find our daughter.

Her room was empty.

I ventured down the rest of the hall. So was ours.

"She's not here," I told Tom, hurrying back toward the living room.

"Don't worry. We're going to find her," Tom replied. "She won't hurt her unless she knows I'm watching."

"What are you two doing here?" I asked, not wanting to look a gift horse in the mouth, but also perplexed as to why they had come down when they did.

"You have Terry to thank for that." Julia invited me to sit down and cleaned my wounds with a first aid kit.

"I finally read that book you wrote," Terry said to Tom. "Jesus fucking Christ, was I an asshole back then."

"I think you've more than made up for it," Tom said.

"So, you remember what happened?" I asked.

"Not totally. Some parts I've re-lived in dreams over the years, but I'd convinced myself that all the shit with the magic and monsters had been some sort of hallucination. Maybe a false memory from all the drugs. Reading the book made me realize that the nightmares were all true."

"What about you, Julia? You told me Tom was a liar and that he was dangerous."

Julia's eyes hardened and went dark, her brow hunching down. Her lips became nothing but a line across her face. "After that night when we were twelve, I told everyone who would listen what happened. They put me into a psychiatric facility, then my parents sent me off to boarding school. Everyone blamed me for Stephanie's death, but I wasn't ready to face the truth. I was the one who froze that night. I could have helped save Douggie. I could have stopped Lamia once and for all. I was on fire duty, but instead, I hid in the bathroom and just waited for it to all be over. I hated myself for that, and...I don't know...I couldn't handle it. All the doctors and therapists told me that the whole story was some sort of rationalization of guilt, that Tom was some sort of lunatic. At some point, I made a choice to believe them. It made it easier to make Tom the scapegoat for all my problems rather than accept my own failure. And then when you ambushed me out of nowhere like that, my defense mechanisms kicked in, and I couldn't help but regurgitate the story I'd been fed so many times over the years."

She wiped her eye, though whether it was from a tear or a falling ash I couldn't tell.

"I'm sorry, Tom. I'm sorry I spent my whole life villainizing you for trying to do the right thing. And Sarah, I'm sorry for making you feel like you were going crazy. I don't know that there's a way to get through all of this without letting yourself go a little nuts.

"I wish I could say I had a change of heart on my own, but after seeing you, I went to a bar, got drunk for the first time in over a decade, and that's when Terry called me. I re-read the book too. It was true."

"How did you find us?" I asked.

"I'm the CEO of a major corporation," Julia said confidently. "It wasn't hard."

"We let her get away last time," Terry said. "But what were we supposed to do against an ageless demon-thing? We were kids." He then pulled a revolver from his back waistband. "This time, we're gonna take this bitch down, once and for all."

I looked over to my husband and felt like the worst human in the world. Everything he'd done in the past week really had been to protect us. He was right all along, and I doubted him every step of the way. I didn't know I still had room in me for tears, until I felt them run down my cheeks. "Tom, I'm so sorry I didn't believe you."

He shrugged and gave me a half smile, as if I was apologizing for spilling a carton of milk. "It's all right, Sarah. I wouldn't believe me either. To be honest, I'd hoped we'd never get to the point where you *would* have to believe me. I'd prayed that we'd seen the last of Mrs. Claus. But you know what I always say: everything is temporary."

"No." I shook my head. "This time, we kill her for good."

"So where do we go first?" Terry asked. "Last time, we just sat around waiting for her to come to us. Looks like it's our turn to bring the fight to her."

Tom forced himself to his feet, clearly exhausted but trying to build up a second wind. "First, we have to go to the Christmas House. I doubt she's there, but who knows. Maybe we'll find a clue. I've been working in my studio over the last few days to build some new supplies that I think you'll get a kick out of."

"We already found some of them." Terry spun the tennis racquet in his hand. "You've come a long way since *Home Alone*."

Tom made his way out the side door and stared for a moment at the partially collapsed studio, just in time to watch the rest of it crumble in on itself. "Well shit," he said and couldn't help but start to laugh. "I guess everything *is* temporary after all."

He approached the rubble that used to be his workspace and carefully dug through. Tom managed to pull out a machete with a metal coil running along the edge, attached to a battery pack at the handle, a pair of soccer cleats lined along the entire outside with razor blades, and a duffel bag filled with several more cans of body spray, lighters attached.

"At least it's better than nothing," he said. Tom started to make his way back to us, but then his eye caught one last thing hidden under the pile of rubble. He reached down carefully, lifting a few wooden beams out of the way to make sure he could retrieve this last object undamaged.

The now-finished canvas of our daughter, painted as a tiger standing in a field of sunflowers.

In the sky above was a second tiger made of clouds, watching over her. We brought it inside and hung it up on our living room wall. Finally, he reached down onto the floor and retrieved the BB gun and black rifle case.

"What's in the bag?" Terry asked.

"A failsafe," he replied.

"I'm guessing that's your only mode of transportation?" Julia pointed to my wrecked car as we collected our gear on the front porch.

"It's fine. We'll use my truck." Terry motioned toward a huge black pickup parked out front.

We loaded up the flatbed with our arsenal, and Terry threw a tarp over it to make sure we didn't all get arrested this time. After we piled into the truck, Terry drove us around the edge of Balboa Park. We made the short journey from North Park to Hillcrest, where the new Christmas House stood.

As we pulled up, my heart climbed up into my throat. All the outside decorations were gone. The sign was missing, and the candy-striped pole had been replaced with one made of gray steel.

"She's taken it all down," I said.

"Must be getting ready to move on again," Tom noted. "We don't have much time."

It took a minute to make sure there were no neighbors or dog-walkers on the street. We unloaded from the car, and each grabbed a weapon of choice from the back of the truck. Everyone seemed to have their roles down and knew exactly what to do. I felt like a fifth wheel, having never been through this before.

Even if I had found a weapon I'd felt comfortable using, my anxiety had me shaking like a leaf. Tom had the foresight to attach belt clips to the makeshift flamethrowers, which Julia snapped all around the perimeter of her pantsuit. Terry stuck with the racket and his gun, and Tom replaced his shoes with the cleats, then slung the faux Red Ryder and rifle case over his shoulders. That left the machete to me.

"See this battery pack tied here?" Tom said, instructing me on how to use it. "Once you turn it on, the wire that runs along the blade will get super-heated. Make sure you only hold it by the handle."

We ignored the front door, opting for the side gate. It was locked, but after several quick strikes with the butt of Terry's gun, the lock popped off, and we were in. While the backyard still looked like a beautiful garden, all the string lights were gone, and the giant nutcracker I'd seen before was missing. Tom kicked out a pane in the glass back door, then reached in and unlocked it. The smell of cookies still hung lightly in the house, and as soon as we entered, Terry and Julia shared a look of disgusted determination.

Just as we suspected, the entire house was bare.

While Tom, Terry, and I searched the house for any clues of Emma or Mr. Owens/Mrs. Claus/Lamia, Julia made her way around the backyard.

"Bad news," she said, coming back into the house. "There's no canyon connected to the house, like when we were kids. No simple cave nearby to hide. Who knows where they are."

"Why would she be in a cave?" I asked.

"Remember the story of Lamia?" Julia said. "In the myths, she always lived inside of a cave. It was where she lured children to eat them. The house is just where she works. Maybe, if we're lucky, old habits die hard."

Tom and I looked at each other, both getting the same idea.

Balboa Park was more than just a park—it was a huge collection of museums, tourist attractions, and a theater. The thing was, the park itself was surrounded by a massive canyon running around the entirety of the park. It was so deep that in order to enter Balboa Park, you had to cross a bridge that stood nearly 200 feet in the air. The canyon was large enough, it could take all day just to make one lap around it. And after all that, the canyon was home to several hiking trails. It was a fairly high traffic area, with no hidden caves where a creature like Mrs. Claus could easily hide. Still, we had no other ideas, and it was our best bet.

We crammed ourselves back into Terry's car, and Tom guided him to one of the trail entryways that saw less traffic.

"We can't just wander around down there in the daylight." I checked my phone. It was only two in the afternoon. "If we get spotted with all this gear, someone's bound to call 911."

"But Sarah, it's a huge area. Every hour we sit here is another hour—"

"I know. I don't like waiting either. But we can't save her if we're all in jail."

I hadn't meant to admonish Tom by reminding him of his case, but I could see his heart sink in response to my comment. I was just as anxious to find our daughter too, but we had to be smart about it.

"What if we just do some light recon now, sans weapons, and try to mark some potential places she could be hiding? That way, when the sun does set, we'll have a plan of attack."

Tom shook his head. "Remember, she can make herself look like anyone. If she spots me or Sarah, she'll know we're onto her."

"Fine," Julia said. "You two stay here, while Terry and I pretend to be hikers. Then at sunset, we all come back with our weapons, ready to go."

Tom and I nodded. "All right."

EXHIBIT 1J: THE EPILOGUE FROM EVERYTHING IS TEMPORARY, BY TOM BARNES

The sun beat down on the boardwalk to Venice beach. Tourists bustled along the path next to the sand, and a man wearing nothing but a pink speedo and rollerblades cruised by with a boombox on his shoulder. A row of stores advertised smoke shops, souvenirs, and hot dogs for sale, while buskers lined the edge between the paved board-walk and the beach. A guitarist sang "Wonderwall," bead artists made jewelry, a caricature artist drew people with giant heads and tiny bodies...

And in the midst of all this hustle, Tim stood in front of a blank canvas, waiting for a curious client to wander by. He'd graduated art school on a scholarship, then promptly been dumped into the real world without any guidance or prospects. But he did have one artistic skill that set him out above his peers. It was a technique he'd prac-ticed in high school and college, a sort of party trick that never failed to entertain.

While he wasn't the most inspired artist in the world—and far from the most talented—he had a knack for taking suggestions from one or several participants and painting them quickly into something that looked as though it had taken hours. Beyond that, his real trick was taking directions that seemed to stand wildly at odds and finding a way to weave them together into something cohesive.

Next to his canvas, he had a large sign on cardboard reading: "Suggest *anything*."

"Paint a shark attack!" a guy in a tank-top shouted.

By the time Tim had finished the basic form of the shark attacking a swimmer, the guy's girlfriend said, "But make them fall in love!"

With just a few strokes, he turned the blood from a swimmer into marinara sauce and the swimmer's body into a messy line of spaghetti that ran over to a woman on a sailboat. They were both sucking on the same noodle, a la *Lady and the Tramp*.

"Make it a time-traveling shark!" a kid on a skateboard shouted as he zoomed past.

In the ocean, he worked on a plesiosaurus, along with a sunken blue police box from *Doctor Who*. Once he felt he had taken enough suggestions, Tim would finish the piece off with a few embellishments—a shining sun, some rippling waves, a reef of coral—and then he would scribble all of the suggestions onto a piece of paper that he would sign and slap a price on. When one canvas was done, he would set it aside, ready for sale, and start on a new one.

The money wasn't great. Hell, the money wasn't even good, but he managed to scrape by in a small apartment with a couple of roommates that were his only friends. He'd dated a girl in college, thought she could be the one, but it hadn't worked out, and that had been the end of his dating career.

"Tim Barnett." A bald man in a crisp black suit and sunglasses approached Tim directly from a nearby alley. Unlike the thousands of people meandering by, looking for a meal, trinket, or someone to sell them some weed on the down-low, this man seemed to have sought out Tim specifically. "My name's Ralph Acey. I own a gallery in Marina Del Rey. I've seen your work before. It's quite unique."

"Thank you," Tim said, humbled and a little surprised an actual gallery owner would have taken notice of his work.

"I'm planning an upcoming show called *Art in Motion*. It's a celebration of a number of local artists whose journey of creation is just as important as the final products themselves. I feel your work seems to fit the prompt quite nicely, and I was wondering if you would be interested in being a part of my show."

Tim was floored at the invitation. "Absolutely," he said, on instinct.

Ralph grinned, flashing his teeth in a way that made him look like the shark in the painting Tim had just completed. "Of course, I'll need to see you in action first, to make sure your style is appropriate for my show."

"That's not a problem." Tim tried his best to hide a goofy grin.

"Good. A man of your talent deserves to have his craft celebrated. If you make it in, you'll be paid far more than"—he checked the price of the shark-spaghetti painting—"twenty dollars a piece. Many of our works go for thousands. Of course, as the owner and dealer, I get a fee. Ten percent of each painting sold."

Deep within the recesses of Tim's brain, a tiny voice began to grow. *Acey said ten percent.* The familiar words were quickly drowned out by the prospect of making thousands of dollars in one night, instead of maybe a hundred dollars a day.

Ralph pulled a card from his pocket with an address. "Meet me here...let's say...six o'clock, and we'll do a test run. If you do well, you could have a very bright future ahead of you."

The rest of the day dragged on, and Tim couldn't wait for his big chance. In order to make it to the address in time, he'd need to pack up and get on his bicycle no later than four thirty. When he pulled up to the address, at first he thought he had made some sort of mistake. The building had no signage in front. It was a commercial space with display windows, but there was nothing inside but dusty walls. He knocked on the door.

Nearly a minute passed, and he was just starting to feel the sting of a cruel prank when there was the sound of locks turning on the other side. Mr. Acey stood in the doorway, still in his suit and shades, and invited him in.

The studio space was small, but there were several different corners where Tim imagined an artist could perform their craft and plenty of wall space upon which to hang his work when finished.

"Please, set your things up, and we will begin."

Tim did as he was instructed, and Ralph Acey pulled up a metal chair, facing him.

"You ready?"

Tim nodded.

"Paint me a home. From the inside. A living room."

Tim started with the basic outline of the inside of a home.

"Let's have a cabinet on the left side of the wall. With glass display shelves."

"Anything you would like on the shelves?" Tim asked, using broad strokes to build the foundation of the cabinet.

"Probably. I don't know yet. We need something to go on the right. A side table, perhaps with a glass jar filled with pencils."

Once again, Tim did as he was instructed. As he was halfway through drawing the pencils coming out of the jar, Acey spoke up once again.

"Actually, instead of pencils, let's make them candy canes. Add a bit of color."

Something twisted inside Tim's stomach. He was given at least a hundred suggestions a day, but he had two hard rules when accepting ideas. No nudity and no Christmas. Still, the idea of the money over-ruled his creed, and he splashed white paint over the yellow pencils, then added some diagonal red stripes.

"I think we need a bit of greenery. What about a house plant in the center?"

Tim painted a box. Coming from it, he started to work with some greens, building up a philodendron sprouting upward.

"No, I think that plant is too small. How about a tree? I know. Let's make it a Christmas tree, to go with the candy canes. And some gifts around the base."

The knot in Tim's stomach moved, gripping him by the lungs, and his discomfort grew. He quickly sketched a Douglas fir, dabbing little spots of color in lines across the tree.

"No, no. Not like that. Let's give the tree some personality. Make the lights seem like they're eyes and, beneath them, a mouth made of lights.

Acey said ten percent. Those familiar words ran through him again, and suddenly, it hit him. It was a line from *Home Alone*, a movie he hadn't seen since he was a kid. The gallery owner's name, Ralph Acey, was a combination of two characters from his favorite childhood movies: Ralphie Parker from *A Christmas Story,* and *Acey* from *Angels With Filthy Souls,* the movie Kevin McCallister watches in *Home Alone.*

All at once, the memories of his childhood flooded back into him. His knees went weak, and he nearly collapsed.

"Mrs. Claus," Tim said, and he felt a shiver run through his whole being.

"If that's what you wish to call me, Little Elf. I'm glad you haven't forgotten about me."

Tim reached into his paint kit and pulled out a box cutter.

"Oh, come now, Little Elf," Acey said, his voice rising and straining as it turned into the voice of the elderly woman from Tim's youth. "None of that. You're in no danger here. You've long outgrown the age in which your soul would be tasty. It would be like chewing on old jerky. Tough and stringy. I don't want that."

"Then what *do* you want with me?" Tim asked, still holding the blade out.

Acey pulled his sunglasses off, revealing one eye that was completely white. "I just wanted to check in on you, that's all. You may think you're finished with me, but I'm not finished with you. I do have to applaud your efforts, though. It's been many lifetimes since someone's hurt me like you did. Keep painting. Draw me the Humble Hummels."

Tim's breath heaved in his chest. He was terrified to move.

"Come on, Little Elf. Just because I don't plan to kill you doesn't mean I can't hurt you." From the bottom of Acey's pant leg, several Candy Stripers slithered down to the ground, then circled Tim's feet. Acey whirled his finger above his head, and Tim discovered a line of nutcrackers all standing at the top of the gallery walls, rifles pointed straight at him.

Tim resumed painting, but his rendition of the Humble Hummels was twisted and cruel. They had glowing eyes, and some of them looked impish, or even downright demonic.

"Why are you doing this? Why now?" Tim asked.

"Because when you were a young boy, I went out on a limb for you. You were lonely, and I'm not ashamed to admit, so was I. I tried to help you. If you had just been a good boy and stuck with me, I could have turned you into something powerful and strong. I chose you for companionship. And then you turned around and hurt me. I just wanted to drop by to let you know that one day, I will return the favor."

"Why not just get it over with now?" Tim said, his voice cracking in fear.

"Because you have nothing to lose right now. One day, you will love something more than anything you ever imagined possible. And when that day comes, I'll be there." Acey's grin stretched further than any human Tim had ever seen. He flashed a row of sharp pointed teeth, and a forked tongue of at least eight inches ran itself across his slippery lips. "And oh, Little Elf, how I'm going to cherish hurting you."

20

SARAH

"I think we found it," Julia said when they finally climbed back into Terry's truck. "It's not a cave. There's too many hikers and homeless people down there for anyone to just wander into. But there is a door to an electrical room—possibly a whole maintenance tunnel that runs beneath the park."

"And what makes you think Mrs. Claus is there?" I asked.

"Because it smells like cookies, and there's a broken padlock on the ground."

Tom let out a deep sigh. He looked out the window at the streaks of purple punctuating a quickly fading orange sky.

"You ready to finish this?" Terry asked.

Tom sat in silence. I grabbed his hand and gave it a squeeze, then felt him squeeze back.

"Let's go get our daughter."

When he turned to me, his face looked as if he hadn't rested in years. In some ways, I didn't think he had.

We loaded up on our weapons, then followed Terry and Julia down into the canyon.

"Spare a dollar?" A craggy voice nearly made me jump out of my skin.

I spun around, ready to swing the machete, but Tom wrapped a hand around my chest to stop me. It was just a vagrant camping out in some bushes under a tree.

"Jesus, never mind." He backed off and trudged deeper into the canopy of the canyon.

Pretty soon, the unmistakable smell of cookies caught my nose, and my arms began to shake. A sudden chill ran through my veins.

"I smell it too," Tom said, clueing in on what I was feeling without me having to say a word.

Through all the pain in my foot, all the terror of losing our daughter, all the fear of confronting an impossible creature I'd only read about in a book, there was one thing that held me strong. I knew, in this moment—and in all moments to come—that no matter what happened, I would never doubt Tom again. His love, his strength, and his fierce drive to protect his family made me feel closer to him than I ever had before.

Together, we reached a metal door with a yellow electrical hazard sign partially obscured by vines hanging loosely on top.

Terry placed a hand on the handle, but Tom stopped him.

"Wait."

Tom unzipped a small pocket in the black rifle case and pulled out a handful of green glowsticks. One by one, he gave them a crack, then shook them until they each emitted an eerie fluorescent glow.

"We have no idea how dark it will be in there, so we need to be ready for anything." Tom pulled out his fake Red Ryder, slipped a handful of pellets into the stock, then began pumping the lever at least fifteen times until it took all the strength he had to snap it back into place.

Terry had his pistol out and used the tennis racket to brace his firing hand. Julia pulled one of the body spray cans from her belt and flicked the Zippo lighter so a small flame burned in front of the nozzle. Finally, Tom got on his knees and unzipped the case. The reveal of what was inside felt a little anticlimactic, mostly because I still didn't really know what I was looking at.

It was a long homemade wooden box, about ten inches in diameter and maybe four feet long. A string came out of one end that he tied to a single orange glowstick.

"If things go south, grab this and pull," he said, setting the box on the floor across the frame of the metal doorway. "Everyone ready?" he whispered.

We all nodded, though I had never felt more nervous in my life. He silently counted to three, then Terry threw the door open. Tom lobbed the handful of green glow sticks inside.

Beyond the door was what looked almost like a bunker made entirely out of concrete. Electrical machinery lined the walls, giving off little blips of reds and greens, reminding me of the horrific tree that had strangled Tom in our home. It was hard to tell how far the space continued past a sharp left turn at the far side of the room, but when I saw what sat against the wall, I didn't care.

Tied up in a line of dead string lights sat our daughter, Emma. She was propped up in the corner, below a black and yellow striped electrical box, and my heart nearly beat out of my ribcage when I saw her chest rising and falling heavily in the dark. Her face was bruised, like she'd been beaten. Blood ran from her nose and lips, and one of her eyes was nearly swollen shut.

I ran to her, no longer feeling the pain in my foot or worry about the monster. I just wanted to grab my daughter and get her out of here.

"Mom!" she cried as I rushed toward her.

"Wait!" Tom whisper-shouted, but it was too late.

There was nothing that was going to stop me from saving my little girl.

"Are you okay, habibeh?"

She nodded. "I was so scared. Mr. Owens came, and he beat me up and carried me down here."

I flicked on the switch to the heated wire on my machete and began to saw through a knot in the string lights.

"I don't get it," Terry said. "Where is she?" He ventured further into the room and peered around the corner leading deeper into a maintenance tunnel.

Then the shot rang out, so loud in the concrete room that it was nearly deafening. I looked over.

Terry stood there in shock, facing the life-sized nutcracker standing just around the corner, its rifle pointed directly at him. Terry staggered backward a few steps, then fell to his knees.

"Watch out!" Emma cried.

The nutcracker reloaded his musket and prepared to fire again. I grabbed my daughter and pulled her closer to the center of the room as another bullet fired, chipping a large chunk of concrete from the wall below the panels.

Terry dropped the tennis racket, then started to cough. Something wet sprayed from his mouth as he did. He panted and growled, using what little energy he had left to raise his pistol and fire six rounds directly into the nutcracker. The giant doll exploded into splinters of wood, finally toppling over at the same time as Tom's old friend.

"Terry!" Julia shouted, running to his aid. She stopped short as a much smaller shot rang out, forcing her to clutch at her arm.

All around the room, tiny nutcrackers climbed up from behind the electrical boxes, encircling us from overhead.

Julia saw them and started blowing controlled blasts of her torch at the little wooden figurines. It didn't take much for them to catch fire, but there were so many of them that she took several more hits before they all lit up the room like a dozen torches. When one of her flamethrowers ran out of juice, she dropped it to the floor and pulled another from her belt. Nothing was going to stop her from burning all those little bastards into ash.

I did my best to stay focused on Emma, finally cutting through the knot in her string lights. Another burst of flame passed by my head when Julia found a brigade taking aim behind me. The fire might have saved my life from the nutcrackers, but it also did so much more. It finally gave me a clear look at Emma's face. Her cheek was swollen to the point where it nearly covered her eye, and if I hadn't had such a clear illumination from the torch, I never would have noticed.

Emma's swollen cheek obscured the fact that her right eye was almost pure white.

I didn't even think to try and hide my reaction. I was so taken aback that I must have immediately given myself away. Emma's look of terror shifted into one of glee.

"What's the matter, Mom? See something you don't like?"

I stumbled backward, dropping my machete in pure terror as the little impostor slipped her way out of her bindings. Her face twisted and stretched, scales pushing their way out from her pale cheeks. It was hard to see her face change color in the green light of the glow sticks, but within a matter of seconds, I found myself staring at a grotesque creature Tom's book had been barely able to describe. She doubled, maybe tripled in size, tearing away all of Emma's clothes as she took on her serpent form. The snake-beast was clearly feminine, but it was not my daughter.

"Don't run away, Mommy. I need you," the beast said, still stealing my daughter's voice.

A hand made up of impossibly long fingers wrapped around my throat and squeezed with alarming force as she lifted me up. Her eyelids opened way too wide, until the eyeballs themselves popped out of their sockets. Instead of falling to the ground, they floated inches in front of her face, and a pair of vicious-looking snakes slithered out of the dark crevices. Their mouths bobbed open and closed. The warm glow that emanated from within scrambled my head, like eggs on a frying pan. I struggled to remember what I was doing, even who I was or why I couldn't breathe. I barely noticed her other claw-tipped hand drive itself toward my gut.

The pain of her piercing my stomach brought me out of the snakes' hypnotic lightshow. I was prepared any second to feel her fingers puncture my stomach and spill my intestines out to the floor.

Instead, she only drove her nails about a half-inch into me before some force stopped her. Between her fingers and my stomach, there was a tennis racket, with my husband pushing all of his energy into holding her hand at bay. The barbed wire threading tore at her fingers, shredding the scales off them and causing dozens of micro cuts to drip black blood onto the floor.

The serpent screamed in frustration and pulled her hand away, slicing through several lines of the barbed wire in the process. Before she could mount a second attack, Tom took another swing, grinding the surface of the racket upward across her torso, descaling a prominent line across her front. Dozens of scales fell to the ground, and now there were small rivers of blood running down her midsection.

She released me, and I fell to the floor, gasping. Before she could mount an attack against Tom, Julia pressed in with her blowtorch, forcing her to make a hasty retreat around the corner, past the wrecked nutcracker, and into another room.

"Grab the machete!" Tom shouted, giving her no quarter and rushing around the bend.

I did as he said, making sure to avoid the reddening blade, picking it up by its black-taped handle. I hurried around the corner and nearly burned my husband's shoulder off when I came upon him standing completely still.

At the far end of the room sat Emma.

The real Emma.

Her mouth, hands, and feet were duct taped together, and she was surrounded by what I imagined to be the rest of the evidence that had fled from lockup. Half-melted Hummels stood guard in a semi-circle. Their faces were blackened and deformed. Their ceramic hands had been sharpened to points, while others held miniature versions of needlepointed candy canes like spears. Little carved eyes were melted halfway down their faces, and they all looked hungry for vengeance.

And of course, standing between all of them and us was the monstrous Mrs. Claus.

She hissed out a laugh, clearly having the upper hand. "Looks like you're one soldier short," she said, gesturing to Terry.

He lay face down on the floor, moaning as a pool of blood spread around him. Terry was alive but clearly in bad shape.

"I'm actually grateful you stopped me from killing your bitch wife first," she said, her floating eyes staring at Tom. "This way, you can both watch me rip your daughter apart."

"That's not going to happen," Tom said, with more confidence than I'd ever heard. He pulled the BB gun from over his shoulder and gave the lever one more pump for good measure.

Mrs. Claus snickered, her tongue dancing in front of her fangs. "And what do you think you're going to do with that?"

Tom took aim. "I'll shoot your eye out." The gun made a dinky little plink, but the resulting squishing sound as the BB pierced her one good eye caused her to shriek so loudly, it almost made Terry's earlier gunfire sound quiet in comparison.

"Kill the girl!" the snake commanded to her burnt Hummels as she darted for us.

Julia wasted no time blasting as many figurines with her torch before they began leaping onto my daughter. However, her efforts were only so effective. Once they had mounted Emma, she couldn't risk hitting our little girl with the flames.

Mrs. Claus lunged toward us, though her movement seemed erratic, not like she was targeting any one of us in particular. I swung my machete as she tried to surge past me, and my swing connected with something thick and solid. The blade, combined with the heat, carved through scales, muscle, and bone. I pushed hard, past the resistance, and something solid fell to the floor with a heavy thump, which forced the beast to screech again.

I glanced down, finding a twitching claw and forearm on the floor. Smoke rose from its charred end, and I was hit with an overwhelming stench of burnt meat and vinegar.

"Stop her!" Tom shouted, rushing to Emma's side. He ripped Hummels off our daughter, then stomped them with his bladed shoes.

As much as I wanted to help rescue Emma, I realized this was our last chance to stop this monster for good. I nodded to my husband and chased the serpent back into the main room of the bunker.

She was too fast. By the time I'd rounded the corner, Mrs. Claus's powerful tail had propelled her nearly to the door. Once she was through, there would be no chance of chasing her down.

That's when I realized what the box was that Tom had set on the floor.

I grabbed the orange glowstick with the string attached and yanked it as hard as I could. At first, an unimpressive line of little flickering flames sparkled up from the box. Then, there was a hissing sound, and a wall of fire erupted. Tom had taped nearly two dozen aerosol cans together, and pulling the string caused a chain reaction for them all to send a blaze straight upward, covering the door completely in fire.

It caught the serpent just as she reached the doorway. She reared back in a combination of fury and terror, spun around, and swiped her claw at the air. Above her head, the milky eye darted around wildly but couldn't seem to settle on anything.

She was blind.

The beast bared its teeth, and its tongue danced in front of its mouth, tasting the air in an attempt to find me.

"I can feel you, Sarah," she said.

It sent a shiver through my whole body. Even though she couldn't see me, it didn't make her any less dangerous. I tried to step as softly as I could around her left flank, hoping to get a chance to chop off her other arm, but she managed to follow my every move, using the half dozen nostril holes and flicking tongue to guide her. She darted at me again without warning, and I leapt to my side, landing hard against the concrete floor. Pain shot through me, not just from the impact, but because her claws had carved a series of streaks across my shoulder.

Even worse, she'd knocked the machete from my hand, sending it scraping across the floor.

I considered scrambling for it, possibly retreating back into the room where Tom and Julia were fighting off the melted Hummels, but as her head darted around the room, I realized she had lost me. Her head tilted to the side, and the holes just above her mouth widened and contracted as she searched for me.

I slowly moved my hand in front of my mouth to conceal my breathing as best I could. The machete had slid across the ground and was sitting maybe five feet from me. If I made a move, there was no way I could reach it in time.

I felt like a spring-loaded trap—ready to skitter as fast as I could whenever her inevitable strike came.

When she darted forward, every nerve in my body screamed for me to move, but I held fast. She had chosen the wrong target. Her claw flew at the ground next to the hot machete, causing her to grunt in frustration.

I remembered something Stephanie had said in Tom's book. She wasn't listening or sniffing for me. All those nostrils weren't there to smell out prey—they were heat sensors. She was going after the warmest thing she could find.

I brought myself up into a squat as quietly as I could and snuck in front of the wall of fire to better mask my heat signature. It seemed to work. She was flailing her arm around now, desperately trying to connect with something, anything. I counted my breaths and tightened my muscles. She made her way toward me, eventually shifting directions once the heat from the firewall seemed to overload her senses.

I was safe for now, but the aerosol cans would only last so long, and as soon as I moved, she would be on me. There was no way I could get to the machete and attack her before she could gut me or rip out my throat with her fanged maw. And if I just sat here, the firewall would run out of juice, she would finish me off anyway, then escape into the night, only to continue her cycle of torment.

On the other side of the room, Terry let out a wet, gurgling cough. In a flash, Mrs. Claus surged toward him. She dug her claw into his back and lifted him up just high enough so she could mutter into his ear.

"Terry. In case you were wondering, your sister tasted delicious."

Her mouth opened impossibly wide. I watched in horror as she bit down and ripped off half of his face. She didn't even bother to swallow, just spat a hunk of flesh and muscle as he let out his last dying gasp.

This was my only chance.

I lunged forward, using my hands and legs to propel me toward the glowing red machete. The snake spun her head around, dropping Terry's mutilated body to the ground.

It was a trap.

Her tail was coiled tightly so she could fly toward her target in a split second. I didn't bother to swing the machete, instead stayed low and threw it as high into the air as I could in the direction of the blinking junction box where she had pretended to be my Emma. Mrs. Claus fired herself with her full weight at the strongest heat source, thrusting her claw out to impale the hot moving object. She followed the machete right up to the wall of the room and dug her claws into the electric panel.

Within an instant, I was blinded as white-hot sparks exploded from the junction box. The beast screamed, trying desperately to pull herself from the power source. Without a second hand to brace her body, her nub of a forearm swung wildly, and her mouth foamed black goo. The snakes coming from her eye sockets writhed until their little heads popped.

I couldn't tell if she was stuck there for two seconds or two minutes, but by the time she fell back to the floor, the room was dark, save for the glow sticks. The wall of fire had burnt out, and the serpent twitched, smoke steaming up from every inch of her being.

And yet, somehow, she wasn't dead. Her head snapped around in jerky movements, still searching for someone to punish. "Y-You. You...can't," she muttered.

I found the machete on the ground and stood over her, ready to bring it down.

Something stopped me.

There was one lingering question that had bothered me ever since I'd found out Tom had been right all along.

"Emma's friend, Maya. Was that you? Did you make her sick?"

It took an extreme amount of effort, but I saw what I believed to be the traces of a smile stretch across her cracked, blackened mouth.

"Huh, huh." It came out as something between panting and laughing. With each passing moment, it grew stronger, louder.

I knew then she wouldn't answer. It was her one card left to play, to keep us wondering forever just how vindictive she could be.

In response, I decided to show her the same kindness. I brought the machete down, cleaving her head from her body, just like the goose at the end of the movie Tom loved so much. Steam poured out of the hole, and her head rolled across the floor.

I couldn't take my eyes off the charred body, half expecting it to come back for one final move. But this was it. I knew for sure as soon as I heard my daughter call out my name. Tom was carrying her in his arms. She was covered in several dozen tiny cuts. I ran to both of them, squeezing as tightly as I could.

"Ow!" Emma yipped as I pressed myself against her and her father.

"Habibeh, are you okay?"

Tom nodded. "We're good. She's just a bit shaken up." He looked over the charred, headless corpse of his childhood tormentor. "It's over now."

THE REAL EPILOGUE

I drove down a suburban street, past all the houses fully decorated in tinsel, string lights, and huge inflatable Santa Clauses.

"Look at that one." Emma pointed to a home that had spelled the word "NOEL" across its façade in all caps using string lights. The lawn featured a life-sized sleigh, with eight huge reindeer being guided by the big man himself.

"Yeah, they went all out," Tom said with a quiet hint of amusement.

Even as we pulled up to the courthouse, the building itself seemed drenched in the holiday spirit. Upon each of the hundred or so windows covering the front of the building sat a wreath promoting peace on earth.

We parked our car, a 1998 Toyota Camry. It was the best we could afford in the aftermath of destroying both our only car and Tom's studio. Even at that, we could barely make the initial payment. It wasn't perfect, but it would do. I'd been lucky enough to get a job at a new marketing firm. Jen had managed to land a position there before me and put in a good word. In fact, now she was *my* boss. Of course, I wasn't the creative director like I used to be, and I was once again surrounded by underachievers who made my job feel more like babysitting than managing. But it was fine. As long as I still had my family, I would do whatever they told me and do it with a smile.

"I think, next year, we should put up some Christmas decorations," Tom said, prompting a look of shock from me and Emma both.

"Are you sure you want to do that?" I asked.

Tom nodded subtly. "I think it's time. Besides, we could all use a little bit of good will toward men."

"And women," Emma said, unable to stop herself from sniping, even now.

Tom and I both laughed.

"And women. Good will toward all," he corrected himself with a smile.

"You ready?" I asked him.

"Am I allowed to say no?" His lips still held a grin, but there was sadness in his eyes. "Come on. Let's get this show on the road."

We all climbed out of the car. Eric Walsh was waiting for us by the courtroom steps.

"Good morning."

Tom shook his hand and thanked him for everything he had done.

"Don't thank me yet. We still have to hear what the judge says." Eric turned to me. "Sarah, Emma, you head to the courtroom and find a seat. Tom and I will join you when we're able."

I hugged my husband so tightly I was afraid I might crack one of his ribs, but he didn't complain. Next came Emma, who stood up on her toes to get her arms around his neck.

"I love you, Dad. I'm so sorry—"

"You have nothing to be sorry for. This was all about me. I don't want you to spend one second thinking you did anything wrong."

A tear ran down her cheek, and she sniffled back her emotions.

"You stay strong for me, okay? And take care of your mother."

Emma nodded. "I will."

"I'll see you both inside."

Once we were in the courthouse, Eric took Tom over to meet with a bailiff, while Emma and I found the courtroom and opened the doors. The pews were lined with people waiting for sentencing for their loved ones, and for a second, I was worried the room was too crowded for us to be able to find a seat where Tom could see us.

Then I saw her.

Julia had nabbed a seat in the front row, and she was saving two spots next to her. She raised her eyebrows, an invitation for us to join, and patted the seat next to her.

"Thanks for coming," I said.

"Of course. After what we've been through, it was the least I could do."

I hadn't seen her since Terry's funeral. Tom wasn't allowed to attend, as he was forbidden to leave the city, but it had been an intimate ceremony with a few guests. Julia had paid for the whole thing, along with having her people relocate his body to make it seem like he'd been attacked during a home invasion. As it turned out, being the CEO of a major company had made Julia a very powerful woman.

"How are you holding up?" I asked her.

She pursed her lips and nodded in the way I'd come to understand for myself. "I'm okay. Normally, I'd never tell anyone this, but since Tom went ahead and shared all my childhood secrets with you in his book, I watched *She's All That* last night for the first time in forever."

"How's it hold up?"

She shook her head. "I'll tell ya, if Freddie Prinze Jr. wasn't happily married with kids, I think I'd have a shot."

I couldn't help but let a small laugh escape my lips, much to the chagrin of the people surrounding us. "Does that mean you're ready to start dating again?"

Her eyebrows jumped. "I guess that depends on your definition of *again*. I know this will sound weird, but the only person I ever really dated was your husband, and we were twelve at the time."

I forced back another giggle, and next to me, Emma looked like she was about to be sick.

"I think it's finally time for me to not be the tin man anymore."

She leaned over to my daughter. "Sorry if that grosses you out. How are you doing, kid?"

Even Emma couldn't hold back a smile this time. She looked like she wanted to say something but instead just nodded. Since that night, she'd asked a bunch of questions about Julia, processing what I was sure was a cocktail of complicated emotions regarding a woman who looked incredibly similar to her own mom.

We hadn't been able to find the manuscript of Tom's book after settling back into our home. While Emma swore she hadn't taken it, I was almost positive she'd read the whole thing.

"Oh, before I forget, I have one last thing I wanted to give you." Julia reached into her suit jacket and handed me a check for more money than I could possibly accept. Before I managed to say a word, she grabbed my free hand and held it over the other, sandwiching the check between my palms. "Please take it. Lord knows I have more money than I know what to do with, and Tom's going to need a new studio when he gets home."

I felt tears well in my eyes, and the court proceeding hadn't even started yet. "Thank you," I said.

The sound of a door opening brought our attention to the front of the room. Tom and Eric then entered through a side door over by the judge's bench, and the judge called them forth.

"Your Honor, the defense and prosecution have reached a plea agreement in this case. The defendant has agreed to plead guilty to the charge of arson in exchange for a sentence of two years in prison, as outlined in the plea agreement."

Judge Merlowe looked at a file. "Mr. Barnes, do you understand the terms of this plea agreement?"

Tom nodded. "I do, Your Honor. Yes."

"Is the plea voluntary and informed? Have you discussed it with your attorney?"

"Yes. I've discussed it with my attorney and understand the consequences of pleading guilty."

The judge looked over at Jim Murphy, the prosecutor. "I must admit, Mr. Murphy, this is quite a step down from the state's original charges for attempted murder. Now you're agreeing to a plea deal of two years for arson?"

The prosecutor nodded. "Yes, Your Honor. Given the disappearance of evidence and the fact that the victim left town without warning, we felt the plea was appropriate."

Judge Merlowe turned back to Tom. "Well then, Mr. Barnes, as far as plea deals go, I have to say, it seems you've received something of a Christmas miracle."

Tom let out a small, breathy laugh. "Yes, Your Honor."

"In that case, I hereby sentence you to two years in the Richard J. Donovan Correctional Facility. You are to report immediately to begin serving your sentence, where you will be subject to the rules and regulations of the correctional facility."

The judge nodded to the bailiff, who escorted Tom out of the room. Eric followed and gestured for us to join him.

"You have two minutes," the bailiff said, stepping back and letting me hug Tom one last time.

"It's all right, Sarah. Everything's going to be fine. Remember what Eric said. I'll probably only be serving a third of the sentence. I could be home before Emma starts eighth grade."

"I know," I said, putting every ounce of willpower into keeping the flood of tears behind my eyes. "If you need anything, we'll be by to visit as much as we can, and we're always just a call away."

"I'll be home in no time," Tom said, then gave me a wry smile. "Remember, everything is temporary."

ABOUT THE AUTHOR

Jon Cohn is a writer and professional board game designer based out of San Diego, California. More than anything in this world, he desperately wants to give you free short stories, audiobooks, and games by getting you to sign up for his newsletter at www.joncohnauthor.com. He promises he won't spam you with stupid content—just announcements for new books and lots of free stuff.

As an independent writer, every single Amazon and Goodreads review helps immensely, even if it's just as simple as "I liked it." Then again, if you're intending to give this book a 1-star review that says "I didn't like it," then maybe it's time to get some of that Christmas spirit in you and not be a Grinch about it!

OTHER BOOKS BY JON COHN

The Island Mother

Slashtag

For free stories, games and the latest news on upcoming giveaways and releases, follow Jon Cohn's newsletter at www.joncohnauthor.com. You can also find Jon on Instagram, TikTok, Twitter, and Facebook @joncohnauthor.

Made in the USA
Columbia, SC
09 December 2023

28128198R00139